More Praise for

Praise for *Deafening*

"Some books just demand the adjective 'wonderful.' This is one
of them."　　　　　　　　　　　　　　　　*—The Times* (London)

"As good a book as *Crow Lake, Deafening* provides more varied
pleasures just as flawlessly. . . . Itani creates as deeply affecting
a central character in Grania O'Neill as Clarke's Miss Mary-
Mathilda or Gowdy's Louise Kirk or Mary Lawson's Kate
Morrison—and that's very good company indeed."
　　　　　　　　　　　　　　　　　　　—The Globe and Mail

"A moving and memorable first novel. . . . Frances Itani is an
artist who understands what to include and what to leave out,
when to whisper and when to shout. . . . Utterly absorbing."
　　　　　　　　　　　　　　　　　　　　　　　—Newsday

"*Deafening* is a slow and graceful read, richly textured, keenly
felt and witnessed, and at times almost unbearably moving."
　　　　　　　　　　　　　　　　　　　　—Quill & Quire

"Like other gifted writers in the best tradition of once upon a
time, Itani has the power not only to make us see and hear, but
to believe."　　　　　　　　　　　　　*—The Hamilton Spectator*

"There's not a single false gesture in Frances Itani's *Deafening*. . . .
It's a story of careful, measured emotion, bleached of all senti-
mentality. . . . There are passages here so beautiful that we can't
help straining to hear more."
　　　　　　　　　　　　　　　　—The Christian Science Monitor

Praise for *Leaning, Leaning Over Water*

"Itani's writing is consistently strong, polished and refined in the best sense of the word. Her work is reminiscent of Margaret Laurence's—Itani has a real gift for showing the world through an articulate, intelligent, curious, and observant girl's eyes."
—*The Edmonton Journal*

"This is an imagined world built accurately, with hundreds of small, sweet little realities to ground the reader. . . . This authenticity of character, of incident (which, once achieved, seems so natural, so easy) is pleasurable evidence of Itani's skill."
—*Ottawa Citizen* (critical list)

"*Leaning, Leaning Over Water* . . . [stands] on its own in the company of some of Canada's finest short story collections."
—*Quill & Quire*

"The stories reveal, slowly and with a sureness of touch, the cluttered cares of childhood, the confusion that accompanies the coming of adulthood and stolid acceptance of unavoidable sorrow."
—*London Free Press*

Poached Egg On Toast

Frances Itani

Poached Egg On Toast

STORIES

HARPER **PERENNIAL**
A Phyllis Bruce Book

HARPER ● PERENNIAL

Poached Egg On Toast
© 2004 by Itani Writes Inc.
All rights reserved.

A Phyllis Bruce Book, published
by Harper*Perennial*, an imprint of
HarperCollins Publishers Ltd

First hardcover edition: 2004
This trade paperback edition: 2005

HarperCollins books may be purchased for
educational, business, or sales promotional
use through our Special Markets Department.

HarperCollins Publishers Ltd
2 Bloor Street East, 20th Floor
Toronto, Ontario, Canada
M4W 1A8

www.harpercollins.ca

Library and Archives Canada Cataloguing
in Publication

Itani, Frances, 1942–
Poached egg on toast : short stories /
Frances Itani.

"A Phyllis Bruce Book".
ISBN-13: 978-0-00-639378-8
ISBN-10: 0-00-639378-0

I. Title.

PS8567.T35P62 2005   C813'.54
C2005-901850-X

RRD 9 8 7 6 5 4 3 2 1

Printed and bound in the United States
Set in Aldus

This one's for you, Sam.

(*This book belon's to my darlin'*)

Acknowledgements

These stories, with occasional variations, have been published and/or broadcast, as follows:

"Clayton" in *Canadian Fiction Magazine*; *Moving Off The Map: from story to fiction*; *Coming Attractions 3*; *Pack Ice* and broadcast by *CBC Anthology*. "An August Wind" in *The Fiddlehead*; *Contexts: Anthology Two*; *The Ottawa Citizen* and *Man Without Face*. "Megan" in *Queen's Quarterly* and *Pack Ice*. "Marx & Co." in *Pack Ice* and *The Penguin Anthology of Stories by Canadian Women*. "Pack Ice" in *Pack Ice*. "P'tit Village," my first published story, was published in *Queen's Quarterly*, in *A Land, A People* and in *Man Without Face*. "Truth or Lies" in *Room of One's Own*; *Truth or Lies* and in *Common Ground*. "Separation" in *The University of Windsor Review* and *Pack Ice*. "An Evening in the Café" in *The University of Windsor Review*; *The Journey Prize Anthology*; in *Truth or Lies*; and an excerpt was broadcast by *CBC State of the Arts*. "Scenes from a Pension" in *Queen's Quarterly*; *Coming Attractions 3*; *Truth or Lies* and broadcast by *CBC Anthology*. "Messages" in *Room of One's Own*. "Accident" in *Quarry* and *Symbiosis in Prose*. "Touches" in *Grain* and *Man Without Face*. "Foolery" in *Truth or Lies*. "Earthman Pointing" in

Canadian Fiction Magazine and *Man Without Face*. "Man Without Face" in *Prairie Schooner* and *Man Without Face*. "Sarajevo" in *Man Without Face*. "In the Name of Love" in *Toronto Life*. A two-page excerpt, notes for "The Thickness of One Sheet of Paper" was published in *Rikka* under the title "Black Eyes, Almond Skin." "What We Are Capable Of" was published in *The Walrus Magazine*. "Poached Egg On Toast" won the 1996 Tilden/CBC/Saturday Night Literary Award and was published in *Saturday Night* and *Emergent Voices: CBC Canadian Literary Awards Stories 1979–1999* and was broadcast by *CBC Between the Covers*. Blaine Harden's article on designer coffins in the *Washington Post* supplied background detail used in "Earthman Pointing."

Thanks again to my husband, Ted. I thank my friend and former editor Dilshad Engineer, my agent, Jackie Kaiser, at Westwood Creative Artists, and Nicole Winstanley, also at WCA. Once more, a special thanks to Phyllis Bruce, my Canadian editor and publisher, for her perceptive comments, her concrete suggestions and, against all odds, her unflagging enthusiasm for the short story.

Contents

❦

Introduction

❧

With weeping and with laughter
Still is the story told.

Lays of Ancient Rome

As a child, I loved to sit around the dinner table after a meal and listen to stories. I was surrounded by, entertained by, ambushed by stories. It was my understanding that life doled out its portions in stories. No doubt this had something to do with the fact that I have a large extended family. The more relatives one has, the more life stories one hears.

When I was four, my parents moved our family from eastern Ontario to a small village in western Quebec. Our house was located at the edge of the fast-flowing Ottawa River. After the move, we seemed to be on the catch-up end when it came to hearing family news. Celebratory events and tragedies were narrated from the lips of visitors. Mood was an important part of each telling—excitement, commiseration, mystery, surprise. Stories could be bizarre and, to a child, baffling. Despite the fact that I had four siblings, I managed to be alone a good part of the time, exploring the river's edge, watching, listening, learning. It was against this backdrop that I began to create my own stories.

Two decades later, when I started to write fiction, I was immediately attracted to the short story. I read everything I could
find in the genre. The writers I most admired were those with
the finest observational powers, the ones who trusted their
readers, who used understatement, who hinted and suggested,
and left room for the reader's imagination. I was also fortunate
enough to meet W.O. Mitchell when I was starting out, and I
was greatly encouraged by him.

I learned from non-judgmental Chekhov, with his ability to
brushstroke a single image and transfer a vivid picture to the
reader's mind. I read Heinrich Böll because he was a great storyteller. I loved the works of Virginia Woolf because of the fluidity
of her prose, the sense of illusion, the intimacy and rhythm of
emotion. I read American and Irish and New Zealand and Czech
and South American writers, and I read the literature of my own
country and knew that it was somehow about me. At the same
time, I was mothering two young children, inventing stories for
them, listening carefully to the stories they themselves were
creating.

During a time when we lived in a small German village near
Heidelberg, I was writing a letter to my sister in Canada, and
asked my seven-year-old daughter if she had a message to send.
Her voice dropped into what I recognized as *story mode*, and she
dictated: "I grow fairly easily. First I was born. Then I turned
one, then two, then three . . ." and so on, until she reached seven.

My son, at the age of eight, told me while tying his shoe-
laces—a serious moment—"You know, already I have stories to
tell my children. Just like you." It was clear that, for all of us,
story was in the blood and the bone.

The story genre is an exacting one for a writer, a genre with
no real rules. For me, each story begins because of unlikely con-
nections. I stow away images and sensory impressions and overheard fragments and somehow, out of the tumble of memory,

one thing connects with another to suggest story. The Oxford definition of *stow away* is to "place a thing where it will not cause an obstruction." It's a perfect definition, I think. Writers stow many things until one image nudges another and creates excitement. But that's only the beginning. Each story holds the mystery of its own creation.

Of the new and selected stories in this collection, "P'tit Village" is the first story I sold for publication. The others were written over the next twenty-seven years. Some of the settings are drawn from places I've lived and travelled. Some are sea stories, set on Canada's east coast, an area I've visited almost every year since my children were young. I have grouped the European stories together, as well as what I think of as the war stories.

No matter what the story, my interest is in the human condition, the perpetually amazing range of struggles and delights that make up human behaviour. I have always had an underlying preoccupation with theme, but if my characters are preoccupied it is with trying to recover their balance when life knocks them over. And my greatest wish? That I will never lose the fragile, tentative strand of hope I wake with each morning before I sit at my writing table. Every day, I tell myself, Today, today might be the day the wild horses will break in.

FRANCES ITANI
April 2004

Clayton

〰

In the morning, he heard their cries. He lay on his bed and for a long time thought of nothing, allowing the cries to wash over him like waves, soothing. And when the sun rose, silvery on the water, he stood at his window in the attic room to which he had carried a narrow spring bed. Zeta had objected to this, knowing that if he took a mattress to the attic, he would also sleep there. But he had taken it anyway, ignoring her. There was a table there, too, a lamp, and electricity. He had run an extension cord up the attic stairs—Pa's cord. He smiled as he thought of it. Morgan, the undertaker, had left an extension behind when Clayton's father died and they had needed a lamp up front by the coffin. Clayton had returned to the empty room alone after Pa was carried out and, seeing the forgotten extension on the floor, picked it up and pocketed it, no hesitation. Morgan's fee had been too high anyway. And Clayton felt a foolish affection for the cord. It had supplied Pa's last light, hadn't it?

At first, Clayton could not see their wide dark backs. But when the double blow, the high bushy blow, rose above the waterline, and when he heard them answering one to another, he felt the quick surge of joy. He knew with certainty they were humpbacks, feeding and playing in the Gulf. Frisking on their way north.

It had been seven years since he'd seen a whale, although last year he'd come close. He'd heard them through the fog. He'd even stood with raised binoculars many winter hours at the attic window, hoping to catch a glimpse of them on their return, late December, early January. They seemed to stay closer to shore on the home journey, though for what reason Clayton could only guess. Currents? Or maybe food supply. Perhaps, if this was a good year, he'd see the sperm whales, too. Old bulls that left their families every summer and headed for polar waters. These he would recognize by their forward slanting blows and their deep moaning sighs. When he was a boy, he'd learned to differentiate. His father had taught him what to look for. Just as Clayton, in turn, had taught his own children—William, Latham, and his daughter, Maureen. But he and Zeta were alone now. And there were fewer whales. Most years, he saw none at all. You could thank the ships for that, and the whalers, and the oil spills. What was the use even thinking about it?

Clayton dressed and went downstairs. He shook the fire, waking Zeta, and she entered the kitchen still fastening the tie of her maroon dressing gown. She was silent, and put bowls on the table while he filled the kettle.

"I'll be doing the road fill today," he said.

She didn't answer; she was sullen and hostile. She hated him taking the bed to the attic, but what did she do if he stayed in the house, if he did sleep in their room? She ignored him. She wanted to have him around, but didn't pay any attention when he was there. She didn't know how to please him anymore. For that matter, what did he do to please her? Nothing, that he could think of.

But despite the fleeting misgivings he had about his relations with Zeta and where they had gone wrong, after breakfast, Clayton was aware of the spring in his step when he left the house, binoculars swinging from his neck. He headed for the shed to get the tractor, and felt Zeta at his back, standing at the half-open screen, though she did not call after him. He hitched to the tractor a low wagon he and Latham had built to hold sand and gravel. Latham had his own farm now, and sons of his own. Clayton sat high on the tractor and bumped along the knotted dirt road that crossed his fields and led along the swells of land, rising, falling, to the creek bed that emptied into the pond, and even farther to the cliffs and then, to the gently sloping beach that tilted into the Gulf. It was the kind of day that made him push back his hat and look around in every direction. Clear skies, an occasional puff of cloud on the horizon, gulls soaring high, the early summer sea lapping and calm, barely a noise. He had to hush, remind himself to listen, face the slightness of the waves to watch rather than hear them as they slipped on shore.

It was at the creek bed that he began to dig for fill. The road was so full of holes, it was dangerous to have the tractor on it. He would work all week, a little each day. He began to toss sand with his shovel, listening to the spatter against the floor of the shallow wagon. He thought of how he'd always kept a mound of coarse sand at the side of the house for cleaning the bottoms of kitchen pots—especially in summer when the pots were black from the wood stove. He and Zeta and the children used to kneel at the edge of the mound, rotating pots and pans back and forth against the grating, cleansing sand, until the bottoms and part way up the sides were scratched and silvery. Clayton thought about Pa's cord again, and smiled. If that were the worst thing he had to live with, he'd have a clear conscience indeed. But being a man who still had an occasional song in his heart, there were, of course, other things.

* *

On the northwest edge of Clayton's farm, along the cliff, stood a skimpy row of unused one-room cabins. Beside those stood an abandoned barn, both doors off. He could see through to the water, in one doorway and out the next—by standing in the field above it. Inside, there were rotting timbers and tangled grass, but the roof was sound and the ladder nailed firmly to the wall. It was this ladder that Clayton climbed for the first time in fifteen years, his binoculars still on a strap about his neck. At the top, he tested, and saw that he could walk a wide beam from one end to the other, even though the attic floor had fallen through. He could perch on a cross beam and look out either way, north to the beginning expanse of ocean, and south up the slope to the house.

At the south peak, he held the binoculars to his eyes, wondering, the knowledge of Zeta at the door still in his memory. She was there, yes, but he saw William, too. William, the eldest. Darkness had fallen around him. William had forgotten to take out the ashes, bring in the coal. A bitter winter night, and William was in bed.

"Don't wake him," Zeta said. "I'll do it myself. He's only nine and he has school in the morning. Let him make a mistake."

But no, if William hadn't been made to dress and go out to the barn in the dark, he'd have forgotten again. Wouldn't he?

Zeta drew her lips together, looking helplessly at Willy's back. She held the storm door open to give the child light, though she and Clayton and William had known that the coal bin would be in blackness at the end of the yard.

Oh, Willy, do you still have nightmares about standing on the steps, falling into that pool of fluid darkness?

Clayton allowed the binoculars to fall back on his chest. William was in his thirties, thirty-six, thirty-seven; Clayton could not remember which. What had he seen? He climbed down and went back to the tractor, and drove to the south field. He inspected his fences along the boundary of the clay road, and spent the rest of the day doing repairs.

* *

In the morning, Zeta stood at the door looking out after him. He had slept in the attic again, but not restfully. There was something wrong and he did not know what it was. He drove down to the old barn, climbed the ladder and again lifted the binoculars towards the house. He was shocked when Zeta stepped suddenly into focus, pointing a pistol at his face. She aimed, but did not pull the trigger. Instead, she turned towards the poplar and aimed at it. Then, at the stoop from which she hung the clothes. Then, at the birdhouse. Smiling, she turned quickly and went back into the house.

Feeling weak and perspiring, Clayton realized that she could not have seen him. From the ground below, he could not even see the back door. What had Zeta been doing? What was it about her that had changed so startlingly since he'd left her a half hour ago, standing at the back door like a shadow of his stricken conscience? He remembered that in the glasses her lips had been moving. Singing! She must have been singing. He thought of her smile as she'd turned to go inside. A self-satisfied smile, undisturbed. And her brisk step. He had not seen her move that quickly since before Maureen had left to marry Johnny Chency from down the road. Johnny was a good ball player but not much good at anything else. Zeta had wanted to open one of the old cabins for the wedding. They had invited Reverend Orland and a few neighbours back after the ceremony. Zeta made lunch and served it on the open cabin veranda, and Maureen and Johnny stayed on and honeymooned in the cabin. No money to go anywhere else. Clayton still held some of the pain he'd felt when he'd driven down to the cabin after leaving the church and had seen what someone had strung up on the veranda post as a joke—a pair of ladies' violet-coloured panties. Probably one of Johnny's ball-playing friends. Clayton had ripped down the panties and thrown them into the back of his truck. No joke. Not for his Maureen.

Clayton climbed down and stood on the cliff before the door-less, gaping barn. His boots smothered some of the early wild strawberries at his feet. Zeta's little get-together for Maureen had been awkward, a failure. The half-dozen cars had to be driven across the fields to get there, and the occupants had stood around, cheerless in Sunday suits and ties, on the raw wood of the veranda. Maureen and Johnny posed for a camera in the long grass on the cliff, a rough surf behind them. And the veil Maureen had sewn herself lifted beautifully, in one quick swoop of wind, and blew out to sea. Seven and a half months later, their son had been named Clayton, after him.

But Zeta. What was she up to? He turned to walk back to the creek where he had left the tractor and, as he did so, his ears caught a smart cracking sound, sharp as a rifle shot. He searched the horizon for signs of whales, but could see nothing in the rolling sea. One had probably breached, or smacked its huge flukes against the water. He would not have mistaken the sound.

* *

When Clayton returned to the house for lunch, Zeta served him and sat in the rocker by the stove with her cup of tea. Hardly a word passed between them. She was so like the uncommunicative woman he had left at the door in the morning, he did not, *could not* ask about what had intervened. He had not, after all, been meant to see. She would accuse him of spying.

After lunch, he went upstairs to check the bureau drawer, where he kept his .38. It was there, but it looked as if it hadn't been touched for years. Unloaded. He replaced it in the drawer and went downstairs to have his nap on the kitchen sofa.

While he slept, he dreamed. He dreamed that he had gone to Honest Albert's—the Island Furniture Warehouse—and that Albert was trying to sell him a sofa. The colour was apple green.

"It's just what you need for your naps, Clayton. I tell you, Zeta will love it in the kitchen."

Albert kept pushing Clayton towards the end of a long, low room that was barnlike and musty. Sofas and daybeds were stacked there, and an enormous SALE sign hung from the ceiling. Beneath that, on the floor, was a black coffin filled with nickels.

"It's the hottest sale this Island has ever seen," Honest Albert said. He was laughing and wheezing, and kept pointing to the coffin.

"Put both those big hands of yours into the box, Clayton, and pull out as many nickels as you can carry."

Clayton hesitated. He took a deep breath and dug both hands deep down until he touched the bottom of the coffin. He came up dripping nickels, and emptied his hands of them onto a spotted cloth which Albert had spread out over an Arborite table. The two men counted the nickels—two hundred and thirty-three.

"Not bad, Clayton! That's more'n anybody's got yet. You did all right for yourself. Let me see a minute—that's eleven dollars and sixty-five cents off the price of the sofa. Zeta'll be some proud of you."

When Clayton drove home with the sofa in the back of the truck, Zeta was standing at the back door with the .38.

"You've been made a fool of again, Clayton," she shouted, "You're a damned fool."

She took a shot at him and missed. She took another and he ducked behind the sofa that was halfway off the truck. She filled the sofa full of bullets until the gun clicked, empty, and then she began to hum a little tune and turned to go back inside the house. Maureen and Willy and Latham were standing under the poplar, watching.

"Don't you think you've slept long enough?" Zeta said, standing over him. "I've got work to do in here."

Clayton looked down at the sofa, but it was a faded blue-grey and the only holes in it were the ones where the springs stuck through. He got up, and splashed water on his face at the kitchen sink, and went back out to the tractor.

* *

In the morning there was a cool, light drizzle, and Clayton went out in his shirt sleeves to work on the road. A cloud cover hung low over the surface of an indifferent sea; the waves were the darkest blue. Apart from Clayton and an occasional screeching gull, there wasn't another living thing in sight. He thought of Latham who had always loved every living thing. Latham, second son, released from the bondage of being eldest.

Latham and Maureen had been outdoor companions to each other throughout their childhood. Following the tracks of the dune fox, sitting silent for hours in the cove watching the great blue heron. Latham had been one to scramble around shore, overturning rocks, collecting shells and sand saucers, trapping what he could in tidal pools, examining, sometimes bringing his finds home to raise in the aquarium he kept in his room. Clayton and Zeta had never worried about Latham around the water because he had been born with a second sense for it, a fearlessness that neither of the others had. But he was easily hurt in other ways. One time, he'd caught a hermit crab that had made its home in a moon shell, and he kept it as a pet. It had been doing badly and Latham had suspected it was dying, but couldn't let it go. He'd come to the door of his parents' room in the night, holding two narrow pieces of wood he had nailed together.

"If the crab is dying," he said, "I have a cross ready. The only thing is, I love it dearly."

After it had died and been buried under the roots of the poplar, Latham came to their room in the night again, and stood by their bed. Clayton and Zeta had been making love. Clayton was angry at first, not knowing how long the child had been standing there.

"Dad," said Latham. "I'm having trouble sleeping. I hear the spirit of my crab crawling around the aquarium. It's clacking against the glass."

What could you tell a child like that? What did Latham tell his own sons?

Clayton filled three more deep-pitted ruts in the road, but his mind kept going back to the rotting barn, to Zeta and the .38. He took the binoculars from the edge of the wagon where they'd been hanging, and headed back to the spot where he'd been the day before. Crazy. He must be crazy to spy on Zeta. For it could not be called anything else. He climbed the ladder and walked the beam, admitting to himself that spying was exactly what he had come to do.

But he felt a safety, a surety, hidden away up there in the peak of the barn. For a long time he just sat, looking out into the Gulf. The clouds were breaking up and the sun flashed through linear folds of sky. As if they, too, were pleased, the whales suddenly began their songs, echoing far, far out. Clayton held his binoculars to his eyes and saw a large herd, moving and playing, keeping close. They were turning lazily, spouting through the haze. The sounds drifted past as if the whales were swimming just below him, beneath the cliff. He knew there had been a time when they would have come this close, but that would have been in his grandfather's day, when his grandfather had been a boy, scoping out the whales. Clayton had heard the stories often enough during his own boyhood.

Far off, the humpbacks called to one another with eerie repetitive cries—long, low echoing sighs and high-pitched squeals.

The herd noises rolled in as patterned bursts of sound, followed by long silences. Clayton did not focus his glasses on the house. He felt peace such as he had not experienced for a long time, and he climbed down the ladder and went back to work, trying to hold that peace around him.

* *

The next morning, Clayton managed to stay out of the barn, but when he woke from his after-lunch nap, he went directly there, climbed the south peak and raised his glasses to see if Zeta had come out of the house. He had scarcely looked at Zeta across the lunch table, so anxious had he been to get away from her to see what she would do. Now, he was startled, frightened, unprepared, as he caught sight of himself running across his own visual field, running and calling for Maureen. Yes, it was he, Clayton. Looking everywhere for Maureen, who was lost. He was at the picnic fair and the boys were with him and they were small. Clayton was younger, had dark brown hair, more of it than the hand now knew against the familiar scalp as he felt instinctively for it there.

He was running everywhere, looking for Maureen. Although the fair was held at the exhibition field in town where the local farmers shopped, Clayton saw not a single familiar face. Where could she have gone? Zeta had told the children that morning to stay with their father, not to get lost. After the pony rides and the outdoor tightrope walk, he had taken them to a new event, the pig races, which had been held in the livestock building. But the event had not been what he had expected—greased pigs and tumbling overgrown boys in overalls, slipping and sliding and laughing. No, there had been a small narrow stretch of cement floor around which metal chairs had been placed in rows, and here he had sat with the children, waiting. A truck backed in through the parting crowd and stopped at the end of the row of chairs. A man stepped out and called to some of his boys to give him a hand. They unloaded eight of the puniest, most frightened, squealing piglets that Clayton had ever set eyes on. And then, on cue, eight local girls, all contestants in the fair's Beauty Contest, came forward, awkward and shy and disgusted, but each determined, Clayton could see, to get through this initiation rite, which could lead to a year's reign over the other seven. Each girl slipped into a pair of overalls, and each pig had a leash snapped to its collar. Although the girls were supposed to hold their charges in their arms to await the starter pistol, the legs of the pigs kept shooting out from the girls' grasp, and the pigs and the pigshit were flying high. By the time the gun went off, the girls were smeared from the neck down and the pigs were criss-crossed and tangled, their leashes knotted and uncooperative. Yet, somehow, in their fright, two of the pigs managed to cry their way diagonally up the marked area of floor, prodded and pulled by their own Beauty Queens. The other six pigs ran helter skelter in all directions, and were cowering behind booths and under chairs. Two of the girls were crying. Clayton made a move to get the children away, but saw that Maureen had already run out of the building.

"Stay here!" he shouted to William and Latham. Too sternly? Their small round faces stared up at him. "Don't move until I get back."

He ran all over the grounds and found her, finally, perched in the crotch of a tree, sobbing against its bark.

"They were mean to the pigs, Daddy," she yelled, accusing him. "They were cruel to those pigs."

When Clayton got her calmed down, he carried her back to the building where his boys were standing in the doorway, looking out. He gave them each a dime and sent them across the path for a soft drink, and they wandered ahead, confused and hazy-hot.

Clayton rubbed his eyes. He had come up here like an old fool trying to spy on Zeta, and now for the life of him he did not know why he had come or what he'd expected to see.

"He who digs a pit for another will himself fall into it," was one of Zeta's favourite expressions, and now it repeated itself in his head. He had been surprised all through the years of his marriage to discover in Zeta a part of self that was unbending, that would never yield. And powerful as he sometimes thought he was, he had never been able to budge that core of Zeta.

The waves below the cliff on the other side of the barn were lashing in on a rising wind. The sky was clouding over. Clayton felt a reluctance to lift the glasses to his eyes once more, a reluctance to watch the unfolding of detail and fantasy—if indeed he had imagined what had come before. And there was fear, fear that all of his past would somehow present itself, come tumbling out. He did not want that. He allowed the binocular strap to slip from his hands, and he heard the thud on the ground below. He walked the wide beam and climbed down the ladder. Drove the tractor back up the slope and into the shed, and closed the big double doors behind him.

* *

While Zeta set the table for supper, Clayton stretched out on the kitchen sofa, his feet pointed towards the stove. He was thinking of a story he had once read to the children at bedtime. It was a Japanese story in a collection called *Animal Tales for Children Around the World*, and was called "Kachi-Kachi-Yama." He had never forgotten. The principal animal was a crafty badger that sneaked up to an old woman's farm while the old man was in the fields. The badger cut the old woman into pieces and made soup from her bones. The badger then dressed in the old woman's clothing and served the soup to the old man when he came in for his midday meal. The old man sat clicking his tongue to show how delicious was the soup, and ate bowl after bowl of—his wife.

The children had asked suspiciously, "Dad, are you changing the story?" as he'd floundered with the ending. Why did the grotesque endure? Was he a fool for imagining that if his own past would settle he might get on with his present, even look to what might be left to him of future?

Although it had not escaped his notice that scalloped potatoes, his favourite, were on the table, he pushed back his chair after eating and mumbled in Zeta's direction that he was going for a walk before it got too dark.

"The wind's coming up," she said, without looking at him. "You'd better wear your heavy jacket."

* *

In the declining light, Clayton saw the massive grey-black form as a huge silhouette, when he reached the edge of the cliff. His heart gave a jump inside his chest and he wondered for a second if he were imagining what he saw below. He took the path down to the beach, seeing and hearing the white-tipped waves as they battered the shore. As each wave broke, its curl ran along the surface of the water. The wind was softer in shelter of the cliffs.

The whale had come in head-on up the gently sloping beach. It was almost as long as the old barn, and had a huge squarish head and a great flat forehead that was scarred and glistening. Its skin was black and sleek, and Clayton knew before he stood beside it that it was a sperm. He'd heard of whales stranding, but had never seen such a thing; all his memory could supply was that they sometimes came in in large numbers. He looked up and down the beach and out into the waves, but this was the only whale to be seen. It gave a sudden shudder, and slammed its flukes against the sand. As the reverberation went through Clayton's body, he jumped three feet back, knowing it was alive. An eye, a purplish-dark eye as big as a grapefruit, opened and looked straight at Clayton. Clayton felt an immense surge of pity for the creature and was not afraid. The whale had come in to die on Clayton's land.

He did not know what to do, whether he should go to get Zeta or get help. But how could he help? It was useless to think that anyone could get this old whale back into the water. The sea had begun to ebb, and the huge body had already made a deep impression in the sand. And the whale itself seemed to be ebbing. Clayton put his hand on the side of the whale's head and wondered at the feel of it. The great eye closed, and the blowhole high up on the left released a soft moan of air. For a long time, Clayton stood with his hand on the whale. At times, it made clicking sounds. After long intervals, it released air from its lungs and snapped its blowhole shut with a soft sucking sound.

Clayton took off his plaid jacket and waded into the water in trousers and boots, the icy water numbing his legs. He soaked the jacket through and brought it back to the whale and tried to spread it along part of the whale's head and back. It was like putting a postage stamp on a boxcar but Clayton somehow felt, rather than knew, that the whale was more comfortable because of it. The narrow lower jaw had flattened into the sand, and there were small pools of water around its astonishing white mouth. The whale had begun to bleed, and the blood was trickling into these little pools. The sky was almost completely dark.

Clayton removed the jacket and soaked it in the sea again, bringing it back to the whale. Although for the rest of his life he would never know how he did it, he felt himself slipping and sliding and climbing up onto the massive rippled back. The whale made no sound. Clayton stretched his length out over the huge long back, and lay his head near the blowhole. A wide whoosh of humid warm air blew back strands of Clayton's grey hair. Clayton put his face down, and mourned.

* *

The house was in darkness when he returned. He was cold and soaked and bloody, and he stripped in the kitchen and washed there, at the sink. He rolled up his clothes and left them by the door. Tomorrow, he would phone his neighbours, and they would try to bury or burn the remains.

And if hundreds of years from now, the earth was pushed back, churned up, would anything be found? Of the whale, of him, of Zeta? Would there be no rag, no bone, no trace of themselves?

"Zeta," he called softly through the bedroom door. "Zeta, you awake?"

No answer.

"Zeta, I'm back."

"I know," she said. "You've been upset, haven't you." She lifted the covers for him and he slid into bed beside her, in the dark.

An August Wind

An August wind had lashed the coast for three days; not a single blue-and-white fishing boat had been seen on the horizon throughout that time.

A great white shark, weighing a ton, had drowned seven miles out in the cod nets four days before, and had been hauled to Covehead where its seventeen-foot length now hung by its tail from a hoist in the harbour so that people could ogle and touch, and take photographs. The wide teeth had been hacked from it, to be sold, and its mouth, gaping and slack, dragged the ground while fishermen stood, arms folded, impatient to get back to their nets, but glad of the diversion, which relieved the monotony of their idleness, their enforced obedience to the wind.

The sun had shone through three days of wind and was shining still on stray groups of swimmers up the coast, who had placed towels and blankets in shelter of the red cliffs. Close to shore, on dark sand that was lapped intermittently, a damselfly struggled on its side; its linear black body, its beaded head, had been crushed by some mishap of nature. Helen disturbed two sandpipers running side by side as she jumped through the waves, hearing Valerie's screams. At first, the wind had kept them from her. Then, had brought them in a rush, flooding her ears. There was no thought in her mind as she flung herself through shallow surf, no thought but "Valerie! Valerie!" The sandpipers waited until she passed; they stood, immobile as herons, while the lash of a small wave overturned pebbles and created new eddies, which they probed hurriedly for a meal of sandcrabs. The sandpipers scurried up the shore, away from the people now running along the beach. The birds stopped, waited, and quickened their slender curved beaks to a rhythm slightly faster than the shadows of their prey.

The old woman sat on a lawnchair at the top of the red cliff, her craggy face swept in the wind by threads of her own white hair. Long ago, in a spring-swollen pond, someone had drowned, a stone around the neck. She looked down on the scene below and saw the child floundering as she screamed, where the surf became higher, where breakers tossed her, like a rag.

* *

The sands were frantic with the activity of decay. With each large wave came other rippling, shallow waves, creating rivulets between humps of sand formed that day by sea and wind. Each movement set another in motion, causing water to trill over sandbars from three or four directions, crisscrossing, equalizing until every droplet rejoined the sea.

Up from the waves, the sand had begun to dry but it was still packed and hardened. Sand fleas, patterned like flicking doilies, created circles around upturned washed-in skates whose flat fishy moulds seemed to be made of white rubber, their long tails extended behind. Towards the dunes, the sand was loose and pale; here, large crabs had been swept by earlier waves, or by wind, or had crawled out of the ocean, or had been dropped by gulls. Now, they lay on their backs, fleshy green-white undersides exposed, their bent legs loosened or strewn helter skelter about the sand.

Helen was in deeper water now, the surf trying to pitch her back to shore. She swam, and the rhythm of her arms with each stroke cried, "Valerie! Valerie!" She had almost reached the child who, seeing her mother, began to try again; her weakened strokes brought her to Helen who pointed the child towards shore. Then, Helen gathered her strength and tried to follow.

The old woman on the cliff nodded. She turned her head and faced flat open beach, unprotected by cliffs—where a man in black swimming trunks had run and was shouting for rope, for a boat, for rescue.

* *

Wind lifted the sand and drove it to sea; lifted it in fine visible manes that tossed their slithering traces. And then, the wind turned, came down from the north and raised the breakers until they were over Helen's head by fifteen inches. The undertow began to suck at her legs, and fought with the surf for her body. Valerie had been caught up by shore waves and had finally reached safety. But the men who were halfway to Helen had to turn back. They crawled up onto the beach, exhausted by the new current that was tugging Helen out to sea. Her body was pushed towards shore by one wave, dragged out by the next. Valerie, the man in black swimming trunks helping, struggled to her feet on the beach, unaware that she had, mercifully, stepped on the thread-like neck of the damselfly. Its struggle ended, it now washed out to sea.

* *

On the beach, weed and dulse, sea lettuce and Irish moss had twisted and tangled during the three days of erratic relentless wind. Soft heaps of decay were gradually covered over, packed down. Whiskery tufts of weed clung to half-opened mussels where slipper shells had attached themselves to the hard blue curves. Limpets stuck like Oriental hats to slipper shells. Under the waves, barnacles opened and froze like yawning molars as they were swept to shore. All suffered the pounding of wind. Lashing, lifting, stinging wind.

The long grasses along the rise of the dunes bent, yielding, but did not release their grip beneath the sand. On top of the red cliffs, the soil was covered with dry stubble. In the curvatures below the edge, cliff swallows rested in chains of circular nests, watchful, waiting for early evening when they would crisscross one another's flights like swooping bats.

Thistles and hard close weeds grew then, from the top of the cliffs, grew under the chair of the old woman with the craggy face, back, back to soil which, still red, became lush and fertile. A bumblebee was thrown off course again and again in the changing wind—now from land, now from sea. The bee swerved crazily, flying low to the grass where the old woman looked down and out to the sea.

* *

The waves knocked at Helen's head until she cried out in pain, "Stop!" They knocked at her as flashing lights danced before her eyes. She thought she saw Valerie in the big yellow towel, standing with the ring of people on shore, and she said to herself, "So many, staring at me." But she closed her eyes and, when she opened them, tried to relieve the pain at the back of her head. Now, she was grateful that her vision had clouded and she could not see. She tried, though she could not, to move her neck so that she would hear the boat that would come from the side, to save her.

The waves cracked and knocked at the foot of the cliff; there was no boat that day. The old woman on the cliff could have told them that; she could see in both directions all along the coast. The nearest boats had been pulled up high in the fishing village, and the wind had tightened the knots in the ropes that held them. The wind kept the fishermen muttering, their arms folded.

Again and again, Helen's toes tipped against a sandbar; then, she lost even that in the sway. The wind rode hard on the waves. Though she could not see them coming from behind, she knew the precise moment each would roll over her head. She held the rhythm now, of dying. She tried to close her mouth and she held her breath with each wave, thinking, "Not yet, not yet you won't, not yet." And felt and heard water gurgling in her throat. "I can't hold on, but not yet," she thought. She had stopped hoping that the boat would come. The shore could not be seen because of the cloud in her eyes. She felt for the sand with her toes again, and kept her arms at her sides when she could, to keep the heaviness from her shoulders. "I am drowning," she allowed herself to say. "Valerie was turned back and if she is not wanted too, then she is safe on shore. I am drowning, and she is safe on shore." And once more, she said, "Valerie, Valerie."

* *

The old woman pointed to the ropes as the men ran up the path of the cliff. The men flung the ropes down to shore and tied them, even the clothesline that had been strung out beside the vacant barn at the end of the field. The knots jerked and held; clothespins and colourfully braided fishing ropes sailed on the waves, out and out, a child's gay purple raft bobbing at the end. The men and women made a chain—two with the raft, one at each section of line. The old woman watched the wooden clothespins dip in and out of the sea.

* *

Zebra-striped wings of seabirds wagged saucily on currents of wind. Heavy casual gulls soared, crying *pit-a-tree pit-a-tree scree scree scree*. With this last cry they dived through frothy caps of the highest waves, ducking out again as the waves furled and reached for the softness of their necks.

Helen lay on the beach and accepted the warmth of blankets and the bright yellow towel. She heard voices as men and women stooped over her. She was carried up the path to the ambulance, which had backed as far as it could down the clay road. The old woman lifted herself from the chair and began the slow walk back to her farm.

* *

In early evening, the wind shrugged and lowered its shoulder. Boats pushed off from the harbour; fishermen raised their hands to one another as their small vessels chugged out of the bay in a steady purposeful line. The nets would be inspected; perhaps, if damage was slight, an evening catch would be hauled in. The sun-rotted carcass of the great white shark was towed back to sea. Cut free from the little boat, it was torn at and ogled as it sank past its fellow creatures.

Just before sun began to set, each blade of marram grass was still; each blade gleamed in the last bright light so that together, all of the grasses covered the curves of hills and dunes, like clumps of sparkling diamonds.

Megan

∞

The sounds of the dying were comforting. Comforting to Megan because she hated fur and fuzz and flapping wings, hated the quick brush against the cheek. Every few seconds, another night insect was electrocuted by the persuasive violet light, and each death was accompanied by a sizzling snap that could be heard up and down the long veranda. Sometimes two deaths occurred simultaneously—zzap zzaaap. Inside the dining room, she listened, and folded thick linen napkins into neat piles.

Her guests—not hers, but hers all things considered—were still reading, or talking in the lounge. Beginning the bedtime conversation. The windows had been thrust up to allow any existing current of air to seep through the pores of the screens. In the morning (Megan would be last to bed but first up tomorrow), she would sweep into the peony bushes the indiscreet layer of winged bodies that she would find lying in a soft circle on the boards of the veranda. She would be pleased, self-satisfied, as she was each morning with her new array of dead. It was at moments like these, broom in hand, when she would look up to the violet light and feel that the modern world had justified itself.

In her early days, there had been sticky rolls of caramel-coloured flypaper coiled down from ceilings, hanging over open pots of gravy and over floured tables of dough. She recalled ceiling fans cutting the heat, shouts of "Shut the screen door!" You never knew in those days what you had in your rice pudding or your raisin bread. It made your stomach sick to think of it. One of the cooks—who could remember which, there had been so many—had told her that flies were high in protein, that in the poor countries long flat containers of milk were left sitting on top of mud huts so that flies could be collected for the evening meal. The milk caked and was sliced, like stiff pudding. Megan had never had the urge to travel; if she did, it would not be to the hot countries but to a place like the north of Scotland where it would be too cold for spiders, where she could relax in someone else's wicker chair and listen to the brogues and burring tongues. She would wrap herself in thick mohair blankets and tartan spreads and the cold would not penetrate. Her cheeks would be ruddy and her guests would say how healthy she looked when she retired back to the sea.

But for now she would set the last table for tomorrow's breakfast, shake the tablecloth, polish the last piece of silver. She reminded herself to listen to the zapping of the violet light, and she whispered, "Good for you," after each electrocution. She envisaged soft separate thuds on the veranda floor.

ᵡ ᵡ

How had it begun—the after-dinner group? The bedtime group, Megan called it, to herself. How had it begun? There they were, her guests, fidgeting a little, not quite settled. Things would not be exactly right until Megan sat among them. But there was work to do. She listened as she folded, her mind partly on tomorrow's breakfast, partly on the owners in Montreal to whom she would send the account book in two weeks. The season was ending. Then, it was back to her rooms in Charlottetown; back she would go.

One year, Megan returned to the lodge in winter. She'd been

there so many summers, she'd purposely stopped counting. Every year, the lodge was sealed tight the day after Labour Day and reopened at the end of May. No central heating—from the beginning it was intended only for summer use. But Megan had always wanted to know what it was like in winter. Ravished by wild seas and north winds? Her nephew had driven her from Charlottetown, where she kept her rooms year round. It had been a bleak day; they'd followed slippery roads while shadows of farm buildings fell over the rim of sea-worn land. They left the car to follow the path made by park rangers, and circled in from behind. Megan stood on a hill and looked out to sea and back to the lodge. She'd known, of course, that from the lodge the sea could be seen only from the windows upstairs. The building itself was huddled behind a nest of dunes. Outside the dining room, the small fresh-water pond was frozen. Reeds and rushes were bent, windlocked to the snow. Megan had been unaccountably saddened by this raw glimpse of the place. She returned to Charlottetown with a chill and wondered what had ever possessed her.

Someone was shouting into the telephone under the big oak stairs—one of her newcomers. A three-way conversation: wife to husband in the lounge, and back to the telephone again.

"What's the name of this island, Henry?"

"Prince something."

"Prince Charles? Philip?"

"Prince Philip! Isn't he a Duke or something? Tell them we're at Prince Philip."

"You're wrong, Henry. It's Edward. We're at Prince Edward Island, darling. All greens and browns. No, the carrots were all right, it was the string beans I couldn't manage. Oh, we drove all day. All day. Teed-jus, you know. The lodge is fine. But old. No television."

The lodge barely managed to stay alive because of the new-comers: transients, drifters looking for one or two nights' shelter. Megan gave them the same outward welcome she gave her old-timers, her guests, but the former did not have ironed sheets, a wildflower in each room, an electric heater sent up when the sea breeze rose. The lodge, though sprawling, was small enough to allow Megan to control each careful favour. She heard the click of the receiver as it was replaced; she sighed as she looked out the dining-room window to the sheltering dunes. "No matter what I do," she thought, "the curve of earth will always be there, where sea meets sky." A long shiver rippled through her body.

* *

It was half-dark inside the lounge. Papers were folded but scattered; the rose-coloured walls above the bookshelves were more faded and cracked than they appeared by day. Megan knew that inside the covers of the books a dusty scroll spelled out: *The wicked borroweth and returneth not again.* Nothing had been added to the library since the Second World War. Most of the books were old novels, novels that could satisfy on a rainy day.

Megan sat in an armchair, and Mr. Harries immediately began to talk, as if his story were addressed to her, which it was not. She had heard it before. Mr. and Mrs. Harries were sun bronzed and unloved. Though they bathed together, they fought in the tub. The bathrooms had been modernized, but the walls were paper thin. There was little Megan did not know about her old-timers, little she could not guess about her transients.

Mr. Harries had an audience of eleven: his wife, Cora; Megan; the Sackvilles, a couple in their fifties; the Petersons; two single women, middle-aged travelling companions from Montreal;

the couple from Pennsylvania who did not like the string beans; and Mr. Grenfell.

Mr. Grenfell beamed at Megan as she sat down, and he pointed to the extra green button sewn inside the edge of his Viyella shirt. Mr. Grenfell loved things like Viyella shirts and warm Scottish sweaters. In the dining room, he wore tartan ties and loose-fitting cardigans, but when Megan served steamed clams he drank the cooking water from the extra bowl instead of using it to rinse the sand from his clams. He noticed the way Megan dressed and paid her the same compliments again and again, though she wore much the same clothing from summer to summer: pastel blouses and longish skirts, discreet touches of jewellery—a pin, tiny circles of silver at her ears, a gold watch left by her grandmother on her father's side. Mr. Grenfell was from Ontario, and although he spent every summer on the Island, he never adjusted his watch from Eastern Standard Time because he liked the stability of living within range of the long dash. He had proposed to Megan one summer, but had upset them both by doing so. She had been rather vague about answering and finally mumbled, "I know too much about both of us to want to be married." Neither of them had mentioned it again.

"We had a magic act," said Mr. Harries. "Cora and I. There wasn't much doing that night. A VIP turned up from some important city—nobody was sure who he was. Cora and I were the only ones who brought costumes; the rest had to ask Megan for help, or sift through drawers of the lodge. Steak dinner that night, too—steak dinner, wasn't it, Megan?"

Megan nodded. Mr. Harries was broad shouldered and wore a T-shirt stretched across his puffed chest. He had a small, greying moustache and wavy greying hair, white shoes, and a maroon sports jacket over the T-shirt. His wife, Cora, kept looking away, towards the sea, although the sea could only be heard, not seen.

"Cora was my assistant," he went on. "I pulled a string of coloured scarves out of my sleeve, that sort of thing. Nice night. I tipped my hat to the VIP. Later, a chauffeur-driven limousine pulled up outside. The VIP bowed to us with a cigar between his teeth, and left. I think he enjoyed the magic. I was given a set once, when I was a boy. It was under the tree. A box of magic for Christmas." He fell silent. Cora tugged at her skirt.

Beyond Mr. Harries, Megan could see the shadows of four empty basket chairs on the front lawn, beneath a wind-stunted pine. Over the years she had watched the young trees on the north side become sea-dwarfed and squat. The basket chairs had been dragged—fetched—earlier that day, by Mr. Peterson and the Pennsylvania husband, whose wives had dispatched them. Megan had stood at an upstairs window and watched the men obey; they'd gone off glumly in opposing directions to serve their women, who expected but did not seem to appreciate their mates' compliance. When Megan observed patterns of marriage, she sometimes compared her lone status to that of the guests around her. She did not do badly by comparison. What did they have? Soft teeth and bulldog chins, knee patting and early bedtimes. Rituals no better than her own. That harpy, life, continued to repeat its games over and over again.

But there had been a time in Megan's life (she would not have denied this) when she thought she might like to have a man. Someone to lean over her as she sat in her chair, someone solicitous and caring who would pat her sleeve, tell her when her skirt seam was crooked, someone who might make public but not distasteful gestures of love. Mr. Grenfell did not fit this vague description; she could not think of him in this role. What she did think was that she had never been familiar with the things men and women told one another, the core around which they built relationships and marriages. She half-suspected that there was no such core. What, for instance, drew this group together now?

"We're a little faded," she thought. "Everything has changed around us, but we have remained the same." Ah yes. Everything was changing. Those who came back came because they did not know what else to do.

The elder of the two middle-aged women from Montreal shifted in her chair. A signal to the other. Newcomers, transients, they had been here only two days. They moved in and out of the group, not belonging, ebbing and flowing, though the younger, Megan could tell, knew more than she let on. Mr. Sackville, who was thin in the jaw and long in the leg, was looking up the skirt of the younger woman. His wife retaliated by pulling a stack of photographs from her purse. "Pass these around, Zee," she said, nudging him. She always called him Zee, though his name was Robert. Designed to humiliate, these were photographs of Zee in the backyard of their home, bare-paunched over the Bar-B-Q, holding up huge, disgusting pieces of rare meat. He'd been acting the fool and none of the likenesses was flattering. The single woman from Montreal, whose name was Claudine, looked them over closely and glanced back to Mr. Sackville. Megan knew that, despite the photographs, there might be a fluttering in the downstairs rooms that night. It had happened other summers. Mrs. Sackville would be red-eyed tomorrow at breakfast; the middle-aged woman would quickly leave the Island with her female companion, and the two would follow the highway through New Brunswick and Maine, returning eventually through the Eastern Townships to Montreal. Zee would become attentive to his wife and would not (for a few days) send her out with her tape recorder after lunch to walk about the grounds. Her recorder, a gift from him, was leather-encased, fastened to a shoulder strap, and had in its accompanying satchel a repertoire of language tapes, baroque music and dull political speeches. Every afternoon, because he was allergic to bees, Mr. Sackville read on a chaise longue inside the screened veranda while his wife made good use of her holiday time. Every afternoon, when she returned and snapped off the recorder, he closed his book and asked, "What have you learned today?"

"So, she'll get a few days off," Megan thought. And then, there was a beautiful moment of silence.

"Anyone go out to look at the moon tonight?" asked Mr. Grenfell, breaking it. The violet light zapped outside, as soon as he spoke. The group was now sitting in the dark; no one made a move towards a lamp switch.

"Not in those mosquitoes. Not on your life," said Mr. Peterson.

"Remember the bet you made with your wife, Harry? That summer?"

"About the repellent?" Mr. Peterson replied.

"It was the summer we tried the television—thank God we voted that out," said Mr. Sackville. Though he did not add what everyone was thinking, that ever since the television had been removed, by complaint, bedtime had again slipped back to nine o'clock.

"That was the evening you rolled up both sleeves and bared your arms to the mosquitoes at an hour when everyone else had been driven indoors," said Mr. Harries. He rolled a new cigar between his teeth and blew smoke from the corners of his bronzed mouth and nostrils, remembering.

"Sure," said Mr. Peterson. "My wife said my repellent was no good. I coated one arm and left one bare, to prove my point." He flexed his muscles for emphasis.

"And Megan had to send poultices to your room half the night," his wife added, smugly.

The recollection was as clear to Megan as if it had happened the day before. First, the pathetic scratching at her door which had revealed not Mr. Peterson, but Mr. Grenfell, in a tartan dressing gown, barefoot.

"Please, Megan," he'd begged. "Let me in tonight."

But Megan had told him to go back to bed.

Then, Mrs. Peterson, tapping softly. "I didn't want to wake you, Megan. But it's for Harry—his arm is all swollen. Do you have any baking soda downstairs?"

"I'll look after it," she said. "I'll bring a poultice to your room."

Silently, she'd descended the stairs in the dark, feeling depressed and gloomy because of Mr. Grenfell's scratchings. She was better off alone, wasn't she? She argued with herself until her hand was on the kitchen switch, and it wasn't until she reached the cupboard that she realized the presence of Mr. Sackville and one of the transients of that summer—a widow named Barbara, tall, with long bleached hair. They were on a blanket on the floor. Their clothes had been folded neatly across Megan's kitchen stool.

"What the hell, Megan, are you doing scaring a person out of his wits at this time of night?" Mr. Sackville had demanded, trying to rise from the blanket. Barbara muttered, "Christ!" through her teeth, and walked out, carrying her clothes.

"Yes, that was the summer of the television," Megan told the group. "I'm just as happy that we got rid of it."

The persuasive violet light sizzled and snapped outside on the open veranda. The sounds of the dying were comforting. Claudine and Mr. Sackville had exchanged the necessary eye arrangements and Claudine's travelling companion wore the hurt look of the eliminated on her face. It was she who moved first.

"I've had enough sea air today," she said. "Too many long hours on the beach."

The others pushed back their chairs. It was exactly nine o'clock—eight by Mr. Grenfell's watch. Mr. Grenfell beamed at Megan as if to say, "Tonight I'll break down the door. I'll come armed with two clubs and won't take no for an answer." But they were past that, they both knew.

Some day, Megan would send the account book to Montreal and she would turn her back on this lodge and on the sea. She would climb into a large sleek jet, trusting what invention had done and could do. She would wander through the sights of the civilized world. And if someone leaned over her in a café, solicitous and caring? Well, she was getting ahead of herself. She would take things as they would come.

Mr. Grenfell put a hand on her shoulder at the bottom of the oak stairs and, nodding towards Claudine who was stepping onto the landing above, he whispered, "She might be all right for him, Megan, but she doesn't have earrings like yours."

Marx & Co.

∞

"She did ask for me?"

And Wilf said, yes, could she come first thing in the morning? Jill had an eleven o'clock appointment at the hospital, and she wanted Margot, no one else, to accompany her.

The purple smudges shifted on the sea far below the slope of the field. Margot hung up the phone and stood at her kitchen window, watching the tide slide off sideways towards the Point, towards the red cliffs where she and Jill had lounged in canvas chairs, where they had run down the dunes spilling onto the beach, leaving the splay prints of mammoths behind. Jill had been her friend for twenty-two years. They had raised children side by side on these two farms. But was this surprising?—only once, years ago, had they articulated the friendship. They had been laughing, but in a serious way. Jill was healthy then, her straw-coloured hair blown out behind her in the wind.

"If ever there comes a day," Jill had said, "if ever the day comes when I need you, you'll hear my cry all the way across the ridge. You'll hear it piggy-backed on the north wind."

But it hadn't been like that. During the past four months— eleven, since the mastectomy—a distance, a formality, had grown between them. Yes, it was during the last four months that Jill had withdrawn to a place Margot was not admitted. Not Margot, not Jill's husband, Wilf, not anyone. And what astonished and troubled most was that Margot could not tell Jill how she felt about her. How she loved her and valued her and how Jill had been the best friend Margot had ever had. These things didn't matter anymore, because Jill had turned her face towards death. She became irritated, impatient, when anyone tried to talk to her about love. All the while, her face sucking in the pain. Even while she slept, while Margot or Wilf sat in a chair beside her, her mouth and eyes and chin twisted to the pain. How could anyone reach through that? What did love matter then?

Margot and Wilf held brief low-toned conversations in the kitchen doorway; there was a hushed, almost secretive air in the rooms. Death was circling the old farm. Wilf continued to look after his foxes. Margot would go back to James, to her own home, and sit quietly, and think of Jill propped against five pillows in the sickroom, Jill turned towards the window where the curtains were pulled back sharply, Jill looking out and down at a sullen ribbon of sea.

* *

Was this, then, the cry, piggy-backed on the north wind? *What is meaning? What is life?* she and Jill used to call out over the sand. Tears pouring down their cheeks as they laughed and cried their way through years when they had not had a moment to themselves. The third eye of each had always looked to the flat sand as the children below skittered sideways like the crabs they pursued, as they stamped tiny feet at waves swooshing in, sucking out. "Look, Mommy, look! See what I've made in the sand." "Look at the rope, Momma." Holding up Medusa-like tangles. For the children wanted to check, to know that their mothers were there, laughing crazily as they might be, but there, to nod, to wave, to call back, to say that things were right.

And the treasures the children heaped at their feet: moon shells that lost their sparkles of pink and green even before they had dried in the sun, hermit crabs coiled in houses too large for them, chipped razor clams and mussels, rarely a perfect specimen. Dulse and twigs and brittle sea urchins and knobbed walking sticks were heaped at the feet of the two friends, who called out, laughing, crying, *What is life?* And who agreed—bringing up the rear of the parade between the paths of corn as their children turned towards home, supper, bed; as the red dog pelted past the silhouette of the Point in its last frenzy before turning to the barn—agreed, that if only they knew the right questions to ask, if only, *then* they might learn the answers. And after the children were in bed, brimming, it seemed, with excuses to stay awake, each of the women became aware of the other in the next farm, the ridge separating the two stretches of land. Aware of children, husbands, *friend.* In those fatigued moments, those final moments before giving over the end of the day, leaning separately with every one of the senses, to the sea. To the clouds, now pink, now black, now grey and dolphin-like, heaped in a corner of the sky; to the cool salt smell on the air. For always the sea could be smelled, even in a rising storm, even in the barnyard close to the fox pens and clumps of dried manure; always, could they smell sea. Gathered that last moment of day when the fields sloped through the night down and down to the outline of cliffs, when waves lapped at the edge of the continent as on a map carved from memory—memory accreted from separate days, each one distinct and brought into brilliant relief, but altering in so slight a way as to be unremarkable, the etchings grafted onto and making up the greater whole.

* *

In the kitchen, Jill's kitchen. It had been four months since Margot's eyes had been admitted beyond the cupboard doors. Wilf spoke, again in low tones; he'd be outside, feeding the foxes. Jill wanted to have a shower, and she needed Margot's help for her dressings. The spring water was in the jug, the tea in a bowl by the stove. Wilf's hand made the gesture, the final futile gesture that summed all of life. *The tea was in the bowl.* Herbal tea. A package lay on the countertop. In the cupboard above, the door open, row upon row of bottles, labelled, were arranged by colour and size. What were these? But Wilf lowered his head. And clomped outside in his rubber boots.

What had Jill been consuming? Powders, herbs, extracts, vitamins of every shape, colour, dimension; for months, it seemed, as there were hundreds, thousands of capsules and flat discs of pills. Jill, in her purple dressing gown, was suddenly behind Margot.

"What, Jill, what have you been—?"

But some questions bear no scrutiny. There were no answers, only the noise of caps removed, bottles tipped, sorting and counting, a handful swallowed with three glasses of spring water. An entire handful. No, no answers, because this was grim business, the business of holding off death. Yet Margot's eyes had been admitted beyond the cupboard doors.

In the bathroom, after her shower, Jill watched Margot's face in the mirror as she let the towel drop from her shoulders. Wilf had already set the chair before the sink. "I haven't been to my doctor," Jill said, "since May. I broke off the appointments. I've been seeing a specialist in herbal remedies, instead." She, too, made the gesture. The tea was in the bowl. She needed Margot to apply the dressings before they drove to the hospital clinic. "The teabags," she said, "squeeze them until they're not dripping; put them directly on the cancer. You'll have to cover them with gauze, tape them. My arms are too weak."

Jill watched Margot's face as Margot inspected the chest wall, now dug out in craters, even where the one breast had been removed. Some craters were pinpoint, some as wide as two and three inches. Marching across the skin. The teabags were still warm and were set, now, into the worst of the craters. Then, layers of gauze, a piece of plastic wrap and tape. It was not easy to find an area where tape could be stuck, everything so excoriated and raw.

They cried together as Margot did the best she could with the soggy tea. Poor body, she said, over and over to herself, poor, eaten-away body.

* *

Margot pushed Jill in a wheelchair through right-angled halls, reported to the desk, sat with rows of patients in a room grown silent with disease. There was nothing, nothing to say. They waited forty minutes until a nurse called Jill's name and led them to an examining room that had three white doors. One off the waiting room, one off an internal corridor—for the doctor's entry—one at the side leading to the nurses' station.

"The Marx brothers," Jill said, between her teeth. "Marx and Company. Are you ready for *The Act*?"

The nurse scowled when she saw that Margot was staying with Jill. "I want her here," Jill said. The nurse left a gown, said they had only a few minutes before the doctor would be in. Patient was to sit on the edge of the table; gown to be open at the front.

And then, Marx & Co. *The Act*. Did it really happen the way Margot's memory etchings held it in relief? She was often to wonder as she looked out her kitchen window at a sky of raw wool, raked by a wire brush. Wondered what she had been a part of when, weeks and months later, she watched the face of the sea change from day to day and without warning. Wondered until she knew she could be certain of nothing. *What is meaning? What is life?* The door to the waiting room locked; the door to the nurses' station closed; Jill hissing, "Quick, she's gone. Get the teabags off. Hide them. He'll think I've been to a witch doctor." Margot's fingers working at the buttons of Jill's blouse, slipping it over her thin and fragile bones, tugging at the tape, whipping off the gauze, stuffing the teabags into the wastebasket, ramming the bandage, the plastic wrap, the twisted tape on top, the two of them doubled over, choking, dying with laughter. *The tea was in the bowl. What is life?* The third white door opened suddenly, admitting Dr. Paley, his intern, his medical students. Smiling when he saw their tears of laughter, or were those—?

Margot and Jill suddenly sober. Dr. Paley took Jill's hand in his, his expression unchanged as he examined her chest. Jill's eyes never leaving his face, watching for a sign, a white flag waved, a piece of rudder cast adrift. Not a single question from him about where she'd been the past four months, why she'd broken off her treatment.

"You're very sick, Jill. I'd like to admit you as an in-patient. Will you? In a day or two? Will you think it over?"

Jill having left the ship to go out into the current, clinging to the rudder, yes, but already having been swept away.

* *

Margot drove back from hospital, headed up the lane into an afternoon sky of shifting violets and blues. Jill looked straight ahead, saying, "You know the way we talked all those years, Margot? About how we'll never find the answers until we know what the questions are? It's taken a long time, but I finally know some of the answers."

"*Do* you now?"

"You know what else?"

"What?"

Jill grinned. "I'm taking them with me."

And they ended the afternoon that way. Laughing until the tears poured out of them, until Jill began to cough and went into spasm and Margot thought she'd have to pull over, but she made it to the crest of the hill where Jill's house marked the descent to the other side, down, down the sloping fields to the sea. Wilf coming out of the house when he heard the car, and when he looked at Jill and Margot and saw them laughing, he, too, smiled and followed them inside, a secret, pleased look on his face.

And Margot, her thoughts both invaded and blocked by Jill, experiencing the deepest sort of pessimism, as if the structure and bone of life were falling away. Years later, looking away from the kitchen window, from the sink, from the cupboard door, from the row of corn bowed to the yoke of the sea breeze, from the clouds, blue and whipped in the western sky, recalled herself the way she sat by the cliffs, reading in the canvas chair in the stillness of afternoon heat that held only the cries of gulls. *What is meaning? What is life?* Recalled herself and the way she looked up at gulls drifting across the sky, the act confirming the sluggish feeling of somehow having been interrupted. A recollection as inconstant as the roar of sea that moved inside the head when the north wind began to blow. Weaving itself down through the cells of the brain until it was impossible to remember whether true silence had ever existed.

Pack Ice

❡

Ah, Sea. September winds blow the head clear. "Level out, level out," her friend Jay had said, over the phone. "Go to the Island. Start something entirely new. Get back into yourself. Maybe a story will come to you there."

As if stories distilled from salt air. It was he who'd phoned two weeks earlier and said, "Now I want you to put down this phone, have a long bath, soak, relax, put on your best perfume and negligee, and when Richard comes home from work, make love to him."

She heard it for what it was. Male power. The vision, the cure-all. What else could a woman possibly need? And she'd never owned a negligee. Always slept in her bare skin; could not imagine sleeping any other way. Her nakedness pressed into Richard's nakedness, every night of her life. Almost every night. Not here, at the sea, alone. Jay had added, in his quick, high-pitched voice (Ah, here was the real conversation), "It can never be me, don't you see, Josie, it can never be me."

"You're moving too close," she'd warned Jay. But he did that. Barged in, disturbed, and then pulled away quickly, as if he'd spilled out too much. Friendship interruptus.

* *

39

Cosmos—after the Greek, *Kosmos*. Order and harmony in the universe. She saw them at the road's edge in the early morning as she walked towards shore. Bright faces with their painted disks on long stalks. Showy flowers. Show flowers. Reminded her of school fairs in the fall. Pressed dried petals. Maple leaves and oak under cellophane. Smell of scrapbook paper, labels underlined. The Catholics, the Protestants, only time of year the two schools combined. Where winning a ribbon was made to be everything. Even third place better than not winning at all. Winning, and the smell of fall, the two things brought forward thirty years. Pumpkin, apple, Indian corn, arranged with random artistry across the front of the stage. And huge bouquets of brittle red leaves.

Thirteen years ago, on this island, in a holiday cottage near these same roadside cosmos, she and Richard had sat in a tiny living room, glaring. No order and harmony then. They'd fought—not a serious ongoing argument, but a fight over which of them would stay to look after the children while the other would go to the lodge to have evening tea with the guests. Both wanted to go. Both were tired at the end of a baby-filled day. Both wanted—needed—other adults.

So neither went and, once the children were asleep, the two sat in the living room, their stony heads buried in books, each knowing that the other could not concentrate enough to read.

The adjacent cottage shared a wall with theirs, but had a separate entrance. Because she and Richard sat in frosty silence on their side of the wall, the couple who checked late into the next cottage must have thought the other was vacant. Or could not have known then that the walls might as well have been made of onionskin. Or perhaps didn't care. Because they arrived and were heard to lock the door, and immediately began to make urgent love on the chesterfield, inches away from where Richard was leaning back against the wall—which began to move in and out like a bellows. Josie was in an armchair a few feet away. If they hadn't been so angry, she and Richard might have tiptoed into the bedroom and made love, themselves.

But because they'd remained motionless at the beginning, it would have seemed rude somehow, intrusive, even obscene, to start moving about the room. So suffered, yes, suffered the panting and rolling (would two writhing bodies come bursting through the wall?) and the frantic, final moments that culminated in the woman's terrible, desperate cries (Oh God, No, No!). And then, all was silence.

Josie and Richard, who hadn't looked at each other throughout this, still could not move. Uncomfortably aware of their own anger. And would it not have been in poor taste to let the couple know they'd shared their passion with unwilling strangers?

She and Richard laughed about it later, but Josie never forgot those terrible, desperate cries. Learning and relearning the ancient lessons of love and pain. (Jay barging into her life—he didn't like it when she said barging, but there were things about her that seemed to drag him to her and drive him away. Visiting her the first time—Richard was not at home, of course—telling her, suddenly, that he loved her. Phoning later, saying, "You're so sensual, Josie. Everything about you is so sensual." And another phone call—the phone was safe, after all—"I'd like to come over there right now, and take you in my arms." That was Jay all right. Blurting it out and then later, trying to cover his tracks.) And Richard? It was impossible to let Jay or anyone know how deep a love like that could go. Wasn't love just one measure of life in the same way that life was one measure of love? *Now I want you to go and make love to Richard. I want you to have it all.*

* *

41

Her feet tramped hard into sand as she skirted the cliff, a brief moment out of the wind's roar behind a dune. Urgency fell away and she slowed her pace and then stopped when a sudden rainbow arced perfectly in a sky heaped with thick grey clouds. The sun broke through over her shoulder, invisible spray blowing into her face from the northeast. No one was on the beach. Two gulls were lifted by the wind, not having to move a wing; two sandpipers scurried like busybodies on their way to market. She clenched her teeth again when a long line of geese overtook her, the *V* shaping and reshaping in flight; and then another, and another, from behind.

She reached for her shoulder pack, curled up behind the dune, out of the wind, and had a slow, secretive cigarette. (Jay would not think she was sensual, smoking behind a dune.) Richard had lowered his head over his book and said, patiently, confidently—how could he be so sure?—"You'll be all right. The next story will come. You've been writing stories for fifteen years. You're *between* things." Her friend Betsy—but Betsy was a lawyer, not a writer—had said, "You've always been the first to say that the worst place to be is between stories." And then cackled and added her own, "Or between lovers."

* *

Josie had been on the Island only once during the winter months, late winter at that. The year before last. A three-day conference called: *What IS the Story?* And being alone at the shore now, in September, the breakers whipping high, spume flying through the air, the red cliffs silent, silenced (being eaten away steadily, from below), made her think of the March day she'd left the company of her country's writers, had taken the rented car and driven to the north shore—alone then, too.

She'd been surprised at the red silt strewn through huge

chunks of ice. But why surprised? The cliffs were sandstone, the sand naturally eroded, driven, frozen to unpredictable shapes and patterns. The vast floes of ice seemed, at the time, dirty, sad. House-sized chunks were tossed on their sides, battered against the cliffs (battering, battering at the woman. Would they come bursting, in their moment of ecstasy, through the wall?).

Now, she walked an hour along the beach; rolled up her pantlegs, waded through fresh-water rivulets which emptied into the sea but were too wide to hop across, her bare feet cold, so cold they numbed, and after that, seemed warm. Her sandals were in the pack with one apple and the cigarettes. Uncertain Vs of geese trailing, overtaking her, flying into the wind.

(Jay would never be able to tolerate the wind here. He'd phoned one day and was giving the customary report on his health: he'd taken his pills, cleared up the ear infection—for reasons unknown to him and his doctor, he was always getting ear infections—had gone to bed early, and then, had asked, "Now, am I not a good boy?" And she, "I'm not going to answer *that*." Thinking, "Is it a mother he wants? I don't need another son. Already have three of my own." Betsy, who knew Jay, had said, "He's a hopeless neurotic, Josie, for heaven's sake!" And she, "That may be. But he's my friend.") Breaching. Moving, both forward and back. The human condition. The loneliness of the race, the species. *Friendship interruptus.* Friendship in various guises. Moments that eroded, from below. The red cliffs, falling, falling, into the sea. Massive irregular pieces of rock strewn like crumbled Walls of Jericho. Eaten away. Battered (Oh God, No, No!).

But she wasn't alone, after all. She climbed around the cliff, bare feet searching out shelves of rock, and saw, in a cove, two horses in the sea. One with a rider, bareback, holding the collar with his left hand, a short thick rope in his right. Dressed in waterproof pants and jacket, rubber boots. Every few steps, he slapped the horse gently with the rope. For the horse was dragging a heavy load, harvesting Irish moss, from the sea.

A second man, in chest waders, walked into the waves with his horse, the two joined by a tether, though neither seemed to lead the other. They worked in unison; each knew what had to be done. The horse made a continuous figure eight, dragging the wide heavy scoop behind, a third man on shore upending it so quickly no pause was necessary to dump the load; the scoop landing right side up, the horse entering sideways, again and again, the cold sea that whipped its belly from below, white froth tossing at its neck, its tail dripping and bedraggled, its mane tangled and green as if slow moss had been growing growing creeping up into it through time. (Were the horses glad to go back to their stables? Were their bellies shocked by the frigid water?)

Two farm trucks rattled over the rocks, making a run for it when the waves sucked out—Josie couldn't see how they could have got down here below the cliffs. They loaded the moss between the board sides, the man on shore raking and then tossing to his right the unwanted kelp with his bare hands. And the wind: preventing speech, sound, thought. The only thing that existed was dogged motion, the rhythm of work. Horse and rider, pushing against high huge waves, entering them as if one animal had been fused from two. The sea a rusty brown because of the red sand churning. For there was no harvest without high sea. The moss a green deeper than could be imagined, suspended under the surface, washing in in in because of the contours of continent, this portion of continent that had shaped this cove.

She thought of accusations that had drifted her way. That she was guilty of probing back, back, always further back. Her friends. One layer of reality skimmed close to the ground and this she insisted on facing, examining. Richard seldom looked at it, Jay wouldn't look at it, Betsy came close. (Betsy asked her once, "Have you ever fucked in the back seat of a car?" "Front," Josie had answered. And they'd started snorting and hooting. Their husbands' eyebrows moving; the men had been deep in conversation of their own, and thought, but weren't certain, that they'd heard the fringes of this one.) Yes, she sometimes faced that line across the earth with Betsy. But she freely admitted (and this itself was contradiction) that she lived largely in the world of her imagination. For how could she be a storyteller and not dwell in the land of her own creations? No single version of her fiction was the truth. She was a liar, like all the other storytellers of the world. Learning and relearning the ancient lessons of love and pain.

* *

The lodge was five hundred metres from shore. Its windows never stopped rattling in the wind. The last two evenings, Josie had sat in the big sitting room and watched retired couples come and go. (Families with children were not around, now that school had started.) What she noticed about these couples was their *feet*. They wore sensible shoes. All those respectable, sturdy shoes astonished her. Thick soles. Thick socks. Wide thick platforms. No bare feet. No risky heels. Nothing frivolous about this crowd, no sirree bob. And when she was upstairs in her room at night, staring at her blank page, she could hear first one and then another couple pause outside her room to inspect an antique in the hall. Here, too, the walls were thin, pulsing membranes.

"Now what do you suppose this is, Mother?"

"You've got me."

"A pitchfork?"

"Don't know. Read the sign."

"A bootscraper! Well for God's sake!"

"Now what do you suppose this is, Mother?" (Did all men mate with mothers? Would Richard, in his old age, call her Mother? If he did, she would leave him.)

"You've got me. Read the sign."

"A pitchfork? No, a bootscraper."

"Well I'll be damned."

"Now what do you suppose . . . ?"

This is life!

(Her youngest son, pointing to an accident his puppy had had on the kitchen floor. "This is LIFE, Mom, this is LIFE.") Those old couples continuing on down the hall at a run in their sensible shoes, following the tilt of the lodge floor, six inches to the south and east.

* *

She pulled herself up the cliff, having stayed too long in a crouch watching the horses loop their figure eights across the wet sand and into the waves. And like an image illuminated by lightning in the dark, saw, in its entirety, a flash of what had earlier eluded her when she'd thought about her one winter trip to the Island. Another fiction? Another lie? *This* would be her story.

She had kept the rented car for the return trip, and boarded the ferry for the nine-mile crossing to the mainland. The ferry was, at that time of year, an icebreaker. Pack ice was still drifting in the Strait. Only two days earlier, another ferry had been locked in the ice for twelve hours—normally a forty-five-minute trip. She'd left the car on the lower deck, and joined the other passengers in the sealed salon above, its huge windows sloping at an angle that allowed her to lean out and over the black sea below. And in the middle of the Strait, found that she was watching with two parts of herself, one frightened, one exhilarated, as the ferry entered pack ice. Treacherous ice, which looked unyielding, but parted with a grating shudder as the vessel went over and through it, shimmying as if it, too, would break into pieces from below.

The coyote appeared so suddenly, she wondered at what she herself was watching, a grey-dusky creature crazed and running running, first in one direction, then another, beside the ferry. Always the ice parting and breaking, the animal leaping across black open space, darting, finally, in front of the monstrous vessel—which had not altered speed—sure to be hit or drowned. But no. Passengers were running across the salon, cheering the animal when it appeared, wet and freezing, on the other side. A woman's voice (the sombre, confident tones of someone not herself in danger, but who enjoys passing on news of tragedy): "Would be better for it if it *had* been hit. It'll starve slow out here on the ice." Of course, nothing would save this stranded creature, unable to go forward or back, water for miles on all sides.

Far from the mainland, far from the Island, Josie could *see* how the animal felt. Caught between. And being between was about being alone. Between lovers, between stories, between friends, between the abstract and the concrete, between moments of safety and moments of danger, between moments of love and moments of despair. Between the bottom sheet and Richard (between the dash and the upholstery). Between the mainland and the Island. Open water. Adrift. Pack Ice. Ah, Sea.

P'tit Village

∞

It is whispered, Madame Lalonde, she asked the priest and he said, "No," very firmly. What does it matter to him that babies sleep in the same attic room, that children tumble over banisters, that they run through gangways pitching gravel at old Hervé, the policeman, when he rides past on his bike?

It is whispered, Madame Lalonde . . .

"No."

"Again." Lips stretch thin and curl back over the news.

"Poor Madame. What will she do with them all? And he. He's no help to her, that good-for-nothing."

"He's tired, poor man. C'est ça."

* *

At dusk the cross on the hill is ablaze. You can see it for miles, from here, from there, from across the river. In daytime the children go to the top of the hill to look for blood, for miracles.

Madame Lalonde's is the last house on the dirt road that dwindles to grass and old tire tracks at the bottom of the hill. How that cross glows at night! The bulbs are replaced the very day they burn out. Or are peppered by the stones of

48

hooligans. At night the cross carves its perpendiculars into Madame's bedroom wall. Even from her bed, she can see it. That cross.

* *

Pitou lies on his side in the dusty road. It is dry, hot. Pitou has no energy. Get up, Pitou. Shoo. Leave him alone. What car ever comes here? Only the ice wagon, and Pitou has lots of time to move before that old nag gets here. Monsieur, he walks to rue Principale and takes the grey rickety bus to work.

* *

The children are playing in a field of goldenrod and blue thistles.

> Am stram gram
> Pic et pic et colégram
> Bour et bour et ratatam
> Am stram gram
> Pic!

Amélie wants to go out, too. Not until the margarine is done. Knead the pellets till the colour bursts like shrapnel through the yielding bag. Pound it with your tiny fist, squeeze between the fingers. The colour spreads like a waxy orange a child might choose to paint the sun. Soon, the kneading is done, the margarine is uniform, harmless, yellow. Go out now, play, Amélie. Only till nine, mind.

The siren will shrill at nine. Ah yes, the curfew. From the top of the town hall, the siren blows the children tidily off the streets. But it also injects excitement and fear into the hearts of the villagers. For if the siren wails and it is not nine o'clock, you go to your back stoop to look for smoke. There is no fire truck here. Only the bucket brigade. That, and the siren, to summon the villagers.

* *

Madame Lalonde has another mouth to feed. This one sleeps downstairs. Already, Madame and her husband have moved their own bed to the dining room. No more space upstairs. If you creep to their window at night, you can see them undressing. In the light of the cross you can see them. Madame Lalonde is tired. Her breasts hang down, always being pulled and tugged and chewed. The baby sleeps in the carriage. Amédée they call him. A good name. A hungry devil, too, she says. Monsieur Lalonde has a new job now. He wears a uniform. The children are proud; their father delivers Vachon cakes to the stores in the city. Now Monsieur revs the truck as he roars home, and Pitou has to pick himself up off the road.

* *

Amélie is outside with her small brother, Jacques. Monsieur Poirot the barber has just cut Jacques' hair. Amélie has to go with her brother to make sure Poirot knows when to stop cutting. For Poirot keeps an extra bottle on his shelf. He also trades comics with the children when he's through.

Amélie and Jacques are returning home; it is seven thirty and they are leafing hungrily through the comics. The siren startles. Already? But it is not yet nine.

A little crowd clusters at the window of Madame Lalonde. Amélie and Jacques push their way to look through the limp net of curtain. From the back, Jacques' hair looks as if Poirot has turned a porridge bowl upside down over it.

Through the dining room, through to the kitchen, they see their parents. Old Hervé is there, too. Hervé the policeman. It is his bike that lies on its side in the gravel. The younger children are spinning the back wheel, holding a cardboard to its spokes. Ra ta tah tat. There is something on the table, a baby, or a doll. A baby, yes, but this doesn't look like Amédée. This baby is blue and lies very still. Hervé bends over it, breathing into its mouth. Nothing. There is no cry. Nothing. Hervé breathes again and again. The child is fixed like a china ornament on the table. Madame Lalonde wrings her hands. It is no use. You can tell by looking at her face.

Make way! The priest has arrived. His shining black car thumps over the bumps in the road where grass has grown between old tire tracks. He stops in the puddle of gravel, an inch from Hervé's bike. His black skirts swish as he walks to the door. "Leave the window, my children," he says to the sober faces in the crowd.

Poor Madame Lalonde. The cross has not even lit up yet, for the night.

When everyone has gone, she dresses Amédée's cold limbs in the gown in which he was baptized—he and all the others. It has been passed on all the way down from Joseph, the eldest. She stops for a moment beside the still bundle. The tears stream down her cheeks. She turns her head and spits on the scrubbed kitchen floor. Priest or no priest, there will be no other.

* *

When the weather is warm, Hector, the chip man, emerges from his winter cocoon and plants his white cart squarely behind the horse in front of the post office. Tassé runs the post office from the closed-in veranda of his yellow house. The mail truck arrives from the city; Tassé sorts the letters into the silver boxes that line his veranda. The villagers come and go, up and down the steps, stopping to chat with Hector, slapping his old horse gently on the neck.

"Ah, Hector, back in business, you scoundrel. You've been

getting fat all winter. Nothing to do but draw water. Come on, you dirty dog, give me some chips, and make sure you fill up the bottom, too."

Behind the murky windows of his cart, Hector scoops thick fries, fresh from the splattering grease, into the cones of waxed brown paper. The children put their nickels on the ledge and hold their breath while Hector adds extra chips on top. As they walk away they cross their fingers, hoping the vinegar will stay in the bottom so they can suck it out when the last chip is gone.

When the mail traffic dwindles and the steps of Tassé's post office are empty again, Hector knows it is time for supper. He taps the loose reins against the horse's back, lets go, and the cart begins to wheeze up and down narrow side streets. The women run out to meet him, wiping hands on aprons as they hurry down the paths. They hold out their deep white crockery.

"Lots of mouths to feed, Hector, fill it to the brim." And dip their hands into the chips on the way back to their kitchens—after they've dipped into their apron pockets for the coins.

* *

On Saturday afternoon the beerman comes. In the houses of the village, empties are stacked and ready. The beerman makes his rounds between two and four. Across the village you can hear the empties rattle and the children call, "Beerman! Beerman! La Bière!"

Mr. Smith, too, buys beer. Quincy and Marlene have gathered the empties and have put them by the porch door. They watch the gravel road to see who will come first: beerman? iceman? milkman? The iceman arrives and carries blocks of dripping ice in his steely picks, all the way around the house, down the long gangway, through the back door. He bangs the block into the top of the icebox and pushes aside the small piece left over from yesterday, melted smooth as an ocean stone.

At the front, on the road, his horse jerks and halts, jerks and halts as the children cry, "Whoaaaa!" The children shinny up the back of the cart to the slippery boards, and vie for slender ice chips to suck. Water drips through the wagon boards, leaving a chain of damp circles on the dusty road. The iceman returns and shoos the children away. He clucks to his horse.

If it is a hot day, Mr. Smith buys buttermilk from Borden's truck for his children. There is a picture of Elsie on the side of the truck—Elsie with the dancing eyes and curly horns. In August, Quincy and Marlene will be taken across the river to the Exhibition, and there they will see, year after year, the real *Elsie the Borden Cow* in her glittering stall.

At last, the beerman arrives. Mr. Smith pays his money and then settles down on the front step with his neighbour, Ti-Jean. There they will stay the entire afternoon, arguing, waving their quart bottles, deciding once and for all who *really* won in '59. No matter who comes out ahead, Mr. Smith reminds Quincy and Marlene inside, later: "It's ours by right of conquest!" His hand sweeps in an encompassing gesture out towards the land beyond the window. Quincy and Marlene are not so sure. They have had their own skirmishes and are outnumbered, after all. Dubious victors, they have rushed into their house and looked back out through the curtains at the taunting, conquered faces.

Everything around seems to be in a state of being dismissed or constantly damned. Yet nothing goes away—only, finally, and much later, Mr. Smith and his family.

* *

Oh, how the children are bored this summer. They have cut bows and arrows from green saplings; they have fashioned whistles from reeds; they have played deadman in the cove. They have scratched hopscotch into the dirt and thrown cut glass onto the squares. What is there left to do? Visit Mon Oncle Piché on the veranda of his black wooden house!

Mon Oncle is everyone's uncle. He tilts in his wide rocker, all day, in shelter of the open veranda. He is too heavy to get up to walk around; it is enough effort to get himself into his chair each morning. His head is almost as big as his belly with its layers and layers of hard fat. His hair is cropped short to his scalp, peppered with grey. His black pants, held by suspenders, fit straight up from thigh to chin. All day he sits on the veranda and eats bread and jam.

But Mon Oncle—how he loves the children!

"Viens citte, mon p'tit chou. Come and talk to Mon Oncle."

The children tell him stories. He teases them; he knows more about them than their parents do. The children know that Mon Oncle can keep a secret. They make wishes and pop brown silky weeds against the back of his spotted hands. He tells them which leaves to smoke and where to find tender shoots of grass to suck. He knows which blossoms attract the whirr of hummingbirds' wings. He knows about crickets that sing and red-winged blackbirds in the swamp. He imitates the early morning *killdee-killdeer* until the call echoes back from the river.

The children wander off. Mon Oncle Piché sits alone and thinks of all the things he used to know. Then he turns to the propped-up tray beside his chair, and goes back to eating bread and jam.

* *

In the warmth of evening, old Hervé, the policeman, sets out on his bike just as the nine o'clock siren wails to its highest pitch and drones to summer silence again.

"Off the streets. Off! Off the streets." He tries to wave his fist at the children but it is difficult to keep his balance on the dirt roads with only a single grip on the handlebar.

"Tabernac," he mutters. The children taunt, one foot in their parents' yards, the other foot on the street. The leg of Hervé's trousers gets caught in the bicycle chain and he falls to one side, trying to extricate himself and look fierce at the same time. The silver badge is dull on his plaid shirt. The children roll on the ground, puffing out their sides in fake laughter. The fender is bent and rickety as Hervé wobbles back towards rue Principale, the only street in the village that is paved.

But on Wednesdays, when the garbage truck comes round, the children do not laugh. Hervé's two big sons rattle the pails; they toss them back and forth with importance, with ease. They spit over the wheeze of truck and the stench of refuse.

"Maudit, don't get caught after the siren tonight. Our fadder, he will get you tonight."

* *

Today, there will be a confession. In Quincy and Marlene's backyard the children congregate beneath the overturned rowboat that rests on two shaky sawhorses.

No Protestant rite can match this. Marlene preens; she and Quincy will receive instruction from Pierrette and Hercules. Hercules will be priest.

The children kneel in the grass beneath the boat. Hercules' head is hidden in the shadows somewhere above one of the wooden seats. His black eyes scrutinize the souls of these young sinners.

"Do you have anything to confess?" Sternly.

"I laughed at Hervé when he fell off his bike."

"I swore at Pitou . . . and broke a plate."

"I wore shorts on Main Street. Against the priest's will."

"More? Robbery? Violence?"

"I had a bad thought in my heart," says Pierrette. Marlene is prepared for this. You have to confess all deeds committed and uncommitted. Those in your heart count for as much as the act.

"Any DIRTY THOUGHTS?" Hercules asks this gleefully.

They shriek with laughter as he doles out the penance.

"Fifteen Hail Marys before supper." He makes the sign of the cross.

But the children are gone. Like the breeze they have scattered.

* *

Jacques is sent to Chez Henri to buy peameal bacon. It is Thursday.

"We'll have bacon and eggs tonight," says Madame Lalonde. "Back to sardines tomorrow."

Jacques skulks to the store. He tosses tiny pebbles into the air, kicks a smooth round rock from square to square in the sidewalk. It must not touch a crack.

Jacques does not want to tell Henri to put anything on the bill—that pale lined pad, each page glaring accusation as Henri's wife presses upon the carbon with her soft pencil. At the end of the day, the balance will be entered in the black ledger.

"Don't forget to tell your father to make a payment," she says.

Her plump breasts try to push sideways out of her flimsy cotton dress. Madame Henri goes to the hairdresser every week. Her hair is oiled and perfect, thousands of curls erupting from her plump head. Her skin, too, is oiled. Makeup the colour of brown eggshells lies in the creases of her neck.

When Jacques tells his father about the bill, Monsieur Lalonde growls, "What do those fatheads need my money for? They're robbing us blind, cal-ice."

Monsieur does not have to worry about the thick soft pages of the bill; it is not he, after all, who must face Madame Henri each day across the counter. No, Monsieur can afford to snub his nose at the store as he drives past each morning in his Vachon truck.

* *

Summer's end. All week the river has been a mass of bobbing timber as the logs tumble and heave towards the Eddy mills. Half a mile downriver, some of the logs pile in a defiant jam between the remnants of an old stone wall and a mossy island that is inaccessible because of rapids. Later, the men will work the rafts to free the main jams. They won't bother with the logs that drift to shore. In autumn, when the water rises, the strays will float out again.

The setting sun bursts golden beyond the trees. Water flings itself towards the roar of rapids. The sounds of night drift through the air.

AUTOMNE

All fall the villagers have been fitting stovepipes, painting them with aluminum paint, banging out the soot, putting up the oil stoves, shaking down the ashes in the coal stoves. Scuttles stand ready. The coalman backs his truck into the yards, lowers his shute and sets the coal roaring into bins that have been sectioned off in corners of toolsheds and barns.

The last logs along shore have been pushed out by the children, or have floated away as the water has risen. Mon Oncle Piché sits on his veranda eating bread and jam, waiting for the children to come and sit beside him. He is sad because soon he will have to move his rocking chair back to the kitchen by the stove, where he will sit all winter, eating, filling out the mass of his shapeless body.

School has started. The Protestants and Catholics are at it again. The boys can't wait to begin their snowball fights, and search the sky for signs of the first white flakes. For now, peashooters will do.

Mothers pull breeches and duffel coats from the attics. They trace around children's feet and cut cardboard soles to stuff into last year's galoshes, trying to make them last one more winter. They sew patchy fur collars onto coats, hiding claws, hoping to keep out the wind.

HIVER

A bluish-white covering muffles the village. Rue Principale quickly freezes and the children skate on the road at dusk. The rink boards are in place in the field and the barnboard shack with its potbelly heat is made ready. Music is pumped through a loudspeaker, which is attached to a pole at one end of the rink.

The older girls skate round and round, flicking long dark hair. They sing about jealousy, flashing their eyes. Young men skate, arms around the girls' waists. Legs are sleek and synchronized to the blaring music.

* *

The orange school bus streaks into the village to collect the Protestants. Quincy and Marlene and a handful of English are driven to the one-room school miles away in the country. The Catholics have their own school in the village—a two-storey grey stone with black fire escape clinging to the side. During the school term, the orange bus reminds the children that there are differences to be considered. The older boys from both schools, the Grade Sevens, are appallingly monstrous and rowdy. In spring and fall they throw rocks; in winter they ambush with snowballs. The French, on their way to school, have to pass the English huddled at the bus stop. Across the road there is a pond in a small open field, partly fenced. The fence can easily be pushed down into the snow.

One day the boys are having their usual morning exchanges: "I hope you freeze, English."

"Pea soup and Johnny cake, Make a Frenchman's belly ache!"

"Mange la merde."

"Yellow belly."

"If you're so brave, walk on ice, English. We dare you."

The dare cannot be disregarded. The English swarm in conference, and plump Protestant Quincy finds himself pushed out of the huddle amidst heroic cheers. He's accustomed to being teased about his weight, and good-naturedly welcomes his first chance at bravado.

But Quincy does one better than walking on ice. He gets out into the middle of the pond and starts jumping up and down, with his rolls of fat jiggling and the ice creaking and heaving. Marlene feels a nervous kind of hysteria rising. Everyone, French and English, stands giggling as the ice wobbles and cracks and bobs. And there is Quincy, not jumping now, his legs moving up and down on the ice in the slow pantomime that freezes time when something terrible is happening. Quincy's eyes are full of far-away fear; his head is just above the water line; ice chunks vibrate around him. Now the boys are on the ice on their bellies, making a non-denominational chain to pull him out. They get him out, all right. He's even laughing. His red woollen toque sticks to his ears, its wetness steaming in the frosted air.

* *

In winter, Hector's horse trots right out onto the frozen river. The crisp covering of snow holds a faint tinge of blue. Hector creates his own road with horse and sleigh—his old cart on runners. At the back, the sleigh sags under two water barrels that fit against the floorboards.

When the weather gets colder, Hector chops away at the hole in the ice, for it is into the same place each day that he lowers his buckets. Even after a storm, you can see the fine welts where the runners slip in beneath the skin of snow. Hector's horse knows just where to go, just where to nudge the sleigh into the tracks. The old horse jerks ahead, back, ahead, all the while Hector standing on the little step behind the barrels, reins in hand. The horse inches the sleigh to the edge and Hector lowers the bucket into the black current. Some days, before Hector is finished, the sun sets red and flat against the crusted river snow. The man curses, breathing rapidly. The horse stomps, snorting white clouds; frost clings to its nostrils.

If it is dark by the time the barrels are filled, Hector hangs a lantern on the front of his sleigh as he starts his rounds. Door to door, he fills pails and jugs with drinking water. The yellow light bobs crazily across the night; the villagers hear the jingle of harness bells as the horse approaches. They sigh as they reach for their buckets, and they go out to intercept the bobbing yellow light.

"That Hector, it will be midnight before we get our water next time, you'll see."

* *

In November, Mrs. Smith gives Quincy and Marlene the catalogue so that each can choose one Christmas gift. There is an entire catalogue just for toys. It takes days and weeks to agonize over the choices. Skates? Meccano? So difficult, so lovely, to choose.

Quincy and Marlene have been saving since October. Every winter, they trudge up and down the village streets showing *Sparkies Sprinkled Greeting Cards*. Every year, their customers order the same box. Madame Laviolette invites them in; they remove galoshes and mittens and pull a chair to the kitchen table. Madame is weary; she has been taking care of old Mr. Potts for years. He never gets better, but he never dies, either. Madame takes the poker and shakes down the ashes in the big stove. She brushes crumbs from the oilcloth on the table; she sits down and begins to leaf through the catalogue of novelties and cards. When she is finished, she examines the sample boxes. Cats leap from dark corners. Quincy and Marlene hold their breath. Madame pushes back her chair; she stands wearily and orders *Sparkies Economy Box* of 36 assorted greetings. No matter what time it is when Quincy and Marlene arrive, it is always dark when they leave. No one has ever ordered novelties but almost everyone needs a box of cards. For every box they sell, they get a dime.

On the second Saturday in December, Quincy and Marlene go shopping in the city. Mrs. Smith pins purses into pockets, gives last minute warnings, watches through the front room window as they cross the field to the bus stop.

The bus shakes and rattles along the old gravel road until the children think their teeth will fall out. They are deposited at the end of the line in front of E. B. Eddy, where they must take a streetcar across the river. Past the mill, past the falls, past the greasy spoons and into the centre of the city.

The first stop is Woolworth's, for lunch. They pace the food counter as carols blare and startle overhead. They remove one dollar and twenty-nine cents from each purse and scrutinize pictures of club sandwiches, french fries, hot fudge sundaes. When at last they are able to find stools side by side, they hoist themselves up and order two Christmas specials with the works: turkey, cranberries, one scoop of mashed potato, one of pale turnip, a spoonful of dressing, a scattering of peas. For dessert, a banana split. As they eat, they watch lifts shoot up and down; they hear voices from the bowels of kitchens below.

Waitresses pounce upon stainless containers of chicken salad; up come butter and chocolate syrup in silver bowls. Quincy and Marlene twirl gently on their stools, sifting and storing every sight and sound.

When the spirit of Woolworth's is inside their bellies, they swivel down and head for the displays of powder puffs, ashtrays, pickle dishes, for it is here that they will purchase their gifts.

* *

Christmas Eve, Mr. and Mrs. Smith tell Quincy and Marlene they may stay up for Midnight Carol Service. They have to take the eleven o'clock bus to town, because the Protestant church is fifteen miles from the village. They arrive early and wait in the church basement while members of the choir dress in flowing robes and four-cornered hats. The children do not like to hear the choir talking of ordinary matters. They prefer to see them dressed, gowned, and singing loftily. When the first strains of the organ are heard, the members of the choir throw out their chests and roll their eyes to the sky.

Home again, the Smiths go next door to visit Ti-Jean and his family, who have returned from Mass. Madame has baked tourtières and pigs-in-blankets, neat brown bits of pork curled inside crisp pastry. Flasks and glasses crowd the edge of the kitchen table. Everyone sings:

D'où viens-tu bergère
D'où viens-tu?

Je viens de l'étable
De m'y promener
J'ai vu un miracle
Ce soir arrivé

Soon, everyone hushes, for Madame and her daughter are going to sing *Minuit Chrétien* in their silver-toned soprano voices.

The Smiths return home, crunching over moonlit snow. The swamp at the edge of the field has frozen, and cattails are trapped along the surface ice. Peace sifts down over the village.

* *

The last event of winter is *Carnaval*. There will be dog races, songs, snow sculptures, skating prizes at the rink. Everyone must wear a costume. The mayor and the priest will judge. Pierrette and Hercules will dress up, as will Quincy and Marlene, Amélie and Jacques. Any child old enough to wear skates is included, even the ones who have to crawl on hands and knees across the fields to get there.

Pierrette's mother airs out her husband's longjohns, gets out the ragbag, begins to sew. Pierrette will be a rabbit; her trapdoor in the rear hangs down to her knees; white fluff is plastered to her leggings underneath to make a fuzzy tail.

Quincy will be Aunt Jemima; his friends call him Tante Jemeem. For a night and a day, two of the large brass curtain rings will come down from the window to adorn Quincy's vainglorious ears. Mrs. Smith smears cold cream on his cheeks and darkens his skin with oxblood shoe polish. A bolster from the armchair is stuffed inside his jacket. On top of all, a colourful blouse Aunt Minn has donated for the occasion, and a long woollen skirt that stretches to the ankles of his black skates. The final touch—a plaid bandanna from Grandma Smith's old trunk.

Everyone comes to *Carnaval*. Hervé the policeman and Poirot the barber dress up as a horse; someone plays crack-the-whip with their tail. A thin Père Noël arrives, even though it is February. He has leftover cinnamon-tasting hard candies to give away.

All the little ones receive a prize. The older children are judged. The priest favours a tramp. The mayor likes the Saint Bernard with the keg around its neck. They compromise; both the Saint Bernard and the tramp are awarded fifty cents.

The priest goes back to the church, his skirts billowing around hidden legs. Everyone comes out on the ice to sing. The men swell their chests:

> Chevaliers de la table ronde
> Allons voir si le vin est bon
> Allons voir oui, oui, oui
> Allons voir non, non, non
> Allons voir si le vin est bo-o-on

Bottles are pulled from pockets; the keg is borrowed from the Saint Bernard, filled and passed around. The villagers sing and sing, and finally everyone goes home. Monsieur Poirot and Mr. Smith walk together, arms around shoulders:

> Prendre un p'tit coup
> C'est agréable
> Prendre un p'tit coup
> C'est doux!
> Prendre un gros coup
> Ça rend l'esprit malade
> Prendre un p'tit coup
> C'est agréable
> Prendre un p'tit coup
> C'est d-o-u-x!

* *

PRINTEMPS

With spring come the storms. The villagers keep flasks of holy water handy on the shelf. Waves whip across the widest part of the river, lashing shore. Lightning splits the sky; the holy water is grabbed from the shelf, sprinkled outside and in, a little here, a little there. But not everyone is blessed. The Fourniers' house goes up in flames, nothing saved but the old wringer washer and two kitchen chairs.

Storm after storm. The holy water dwindles. Run to the church, mon fils; run, ask the priest for another bottle. Light the candles inside; say your prayers; hold your breath; listen for the siren. The tall wooden houses shudder and moan in the wind.

The sun shines. Flowers bloom. In the damp cedar woods grow trilliums, dogtooth violets, lady's slipper, petit prêcheurs. Open fields are swollen with tough stalks of blue chicory, and snapdragons that the children call butter-and-eggs.

Madame Lalonde tells the children, "No swimming until the first day of June." They whimper and coax and whimper some more, but she will not budge. It is all a façade, really, because early in May each year, Amélie and Jacques sneak away from the hill, down along the road until they come to the river. Here they slide down shale and loose rock until they are at the swollen bank. The water is crystal, numbing cold. They cross their hearts and spit, swear never to tell; then, off with the shoes and stockings. Spring water laps between the toes. Amélie holds her skirt above her knees so that no dampness will show around the hem. Goosebumps erupt on her legs and skin. Her toes cramp with pain; her ankles are white with cold. She and Jacques wade back to shore. Dry their feet in the breeze, on with shoes and socks, walk with a light step, run, *race* the last stretch that turns to gravel in front of their home.

* *

Even if it is ninety degrees on the thirty-first of May, Madame Lalonde says, No, they must wait. No swimming until the first of June.

The children scamper about in their underpants, giggling and tripping one another. They form a line on either side of her as they solemnly cross the field. Madame swishes along in thick skirts; she holds high a mound of worn towelling.

The neighbours look out the windows and watch the march. "June the first," they sigh. "There goes Madame with her brood to deposit winter lice on the riverbottom."

One by one Madame takes each little one out to the current, wading as deep as the child's knees. Dips the body, soaks the thick brown hair. Together they watch white suds swirl around the legs, bubble and streak, out on quick waves towards the main flow. The head dips again, once, twice. The hair squeaks, smooth, no tangles. The way it would if washed in the rain barrel.

Along the riverbank, white birches toss their slender, bandaged limbs.

* *

St. Jean Baptiste Day at last! Even the dogs will be fancy, wearing crimped paper collars. The children have woven gay patterns of pink and white crêpe through the spokes of their bikes. The younger ones hold their windmills on sticks and run through the wind. The bonfire will be set beneath the cross, in the field beside Madame Lalonde's. All week the villagers have been gathering sticks, dead trees, an occasional pilfered log from the bank of the river.

The priest drives a big truck, stopping before each house in the village. The older boys help with the collection and chant, "Food for the poor! Food for the poor!" Everyone gives something, even the poor. A tall young man stands in the doorway rattling the priest's money box while the woman of the house makes a choice from her pantry. A can of peas will do. The priest supervises from the cab of the truck. The big boys climb back up, hanging on to the high boards, making important noises as they rumble through the streets.

Just before dark, the procession begins. It winds its way like a tattered dragon around the dirt roads and down rue Principale. There is one float, and this is covered with tissue flowers.

The children spin and whirr their bikes as they ride beside the float and then past, and turn again to rejoin the parade. The dogs become silly, and nip daringly at ankles and fleshy limbs. There are three old cars in the procession, and one big truck. The older boys are up there again, making the same important noises. The priest joins, sleek in his new black car. When the last of the stragglers reaches Madame Lalonde's field, everyone fans out in a circle around the heap of wood and scrub.

Will the timing be precise? All is still. The cross on the hill leaps into brilliance.

The priest prepares a torch and lights dried branches and kindling. "Ahhhh!" The crowd tilts back. Soon the sky roars with fire. Flat rocks beneath the wood snap and crack in the heat—hot stone splinters across the night. The celebration becomes noisy and joyous. There is much singing. Each of the children receives a little bag of hard candy. Some of the candies are stuck together still left over from last year's Christmas party and from *Carnaval*.

* *

Third week of June, the orange bus drives away for the last time. The English shove remnants of their school year out the bus windows; the French scatter their scribblers into ditches along both sides of the road.

No more pencils
No more books
No more teachers' dirty looks

The children, French, English, Catholic, Protestant, bury their differences for the summer. Together they explore the swamp in sunlight, picking marsh marigolds brighter than buttercups. They sneak up on frogs that have eyes like peeled grapes, peering over cloven lily pads; they lie in wait for hours, scooping unsuspecting tadpoles into jam jars for backyard aquariums. When they are bored, the boys chase the girls, threatening with garter snakes that twirl from their wrists. The girls turn their backs, bend, expose the insult of white cotton bloomers.

* *

Halfway through summer, construction crews arrive to work on the dirt road, and begin to carve out a highway. Rock is blasted into the air, settles in mounds, cracked and splintered.

"There goes the Canadian Shield," says Monsieur Lalonde. "Sky high! Fhooomph!"

At the end of summer, the logs will travel the *real* highway, the river. Brimful of bobbing timber, edge to edge, every log stamped with company initials. Not that this keeps the villagers from pulling in the strays, sawing them into equal lengths, chopping them up for firewood.

At nine, the siren wails. Hervé climbs on his bike. The sun sets. A remote hand pulls a switch. On top of the hill, the cross blazes once more.

Madame Lalonde sighs. "That cross!"

Truth or Lies

❧

You women have it all ways, my Creative Writing prof says. All ways. He stares past me, out the window, at a line of rooftops ascending the hill. I've always wanted to be a woman, he says. Have children, stay home. Write sixteen hours a day.

Evie caught her finger under the bedroom door this morning. Inching across the rug on her tummy. Try to keep one step ahead of her, Hugo tells me. She could tumble down the stairs. He kisses Evie, Jason, me; goes to work.

Take children for a walk along St. Catherine Street. Two tramps run out of fruit store, bananas stuffed into their jackets. Jason and I the only ones to see. Why aren't their bananas in a paper bag, Jason wants to know.

Must finish short story before class Wednesday night. Stop to pick up Hugo's shirts at cleaners in Alexis Nihon Plaza. One man ahead of me. While waiting, I review physical characteristics of glaciers. (Also attend classes on Geomorphology Tuesday and Thursday nights.) Jason fusses in his stroller. Evie sleeps peacefully in backpack. Man ahead is not a satisfied customer. Didn't get the three-shirt special.

What's this? he asks. Expressionless woman behind counter. I only work here, she says. You have to put your complaint in writing, send it to Head Office.

I had my shirts in before 6 p.m. Friday, he shouts. I'm eligible for the three-shirt special and I'm not paying.

Woman yanks shirts back across counter. Just in time. Quick, for her, I think. I lose interest in glaciers. Want to see how this comes out. Man tries to get one leg across counter. Too fast for her. Yanks at corner of package. Shirts fly: one between man and woman, two on floor. Pulling each way. Back across counter, forth across counter. Sleeve rips off in man's hand. Man and woman red in face and puffing. Jason claps hands in stroller, stops fussing. Evie wakes in backpack, drools down my neck. Why am I shaking? I leave. I'll pick up Hugo's shirts tomorrow on way to get groceries. Take Jason to washroom for pee. Behind housewares, main store, sign taped to wall over sink: *SVP Ramassez vos cheveux.* Beneath, scribbled in English across tiles: *PLEASE! Pick up your hairs.*

Later, same evening, Hugo finds Evie on top shelf of bookcase. Neither of us knew she could climb.

* *

Creative Writing prof reads my story aloud to class. All laugh at part about dream. Clearly, he says, this is the dream of a madwoman. All agree, even me. Don't tell that I dreamed it two nights before story due, no time to think up fiction this week. Only reality knocks at my door.

Madwoman? I think, as I fall asleep late, after class. My dreams are like that all that time. Hugo turns towards me, rubs my back, puts hand between my thighs. I cross legs tightly, feign sleep. Last thought of the day: forgot to look up definition of talus slope, and didn't fold clothes. They'll be wrinkled in the dryer.

* *

Jason has mumps, I'm certain. Regular sitter won't come. Hugo at late meeting tonight; have to call agency. All reliable, all with references, say Yellow Pages.

Grandma arrives. White hair, cane. Don't worry, she says. I can cope. But do you have a copy of the *Gazette*? This isn't the paper I usually read.

Remember Yellow Pages, I tell myself as I drive off. Let finger do the walking. Evie did coo at Grandma. I settle at wheel. Remember I haven't eaten. Stop at Mister Do-Nut for cardboard container of coffee and two cocoanut specials.

* *

Missed three questions in oral quiz on landforms. During break, professor sits beside me in coffee room. What's wrong? Your work is usually prepared.

Mumps, I say, revealing all. My son, three years old. Puffy, swollen, fever, unhappy.

Professor and all students within earshot edge away. Professor mumbles, aren't there supposed to be inoculations against things like that?

Hugo still not home when I return. Grandma reading paper. Jason upstairs, puffy neck, sleeping peacefully. Evie tied to chesterfield leg, rope around one ankle. I begin to shout until I see how practical this is. Grandma has smarts. Pay double time and taxi home as it's after ten. Agency rule. Hugo walks in, yells. Why the hell is my daughter tied to the chesterfield? No sense of humour, I tell him. No use mentioning Grandma. Hugo will say, Oh, did you have class tonight? Forgot.

Last thought of the day as I turn out light: field trip to glacial lake Saturday, remember to wear old clothes; this week's short story, try not to use dream. Might be a madwoman without knowing. Is this possible?

Hugo shifts to my side of the bed. No, Hugo, no, I shout. I bump him away with one hip. It's the kids, Hugo mutters.

I feign sleep.

* *

Mother phones. You were smart to have two, she says. Not fair to have an only child. Lonesome. Spoiled. Never learn about the opposite sex until too late. With my six, she says—I drop phone on floor; receiver cracks. I'll call back, I shout from above. Unplug phone.

While stirring tapioca I hear Gzowski interviewing philosopher. Discuss existentialism in literature. Make mental note to tell Creative Writing prof. Might make up for not having story ready this week. Perhaps I'll have to use dream after all. Try to choose something not too bizarre. What about the one where I set up an intravenous on Hugo? His blood runs out, wrong way down the plastic tube. Exsanguination.

* *

Good story, everyone nods. You have such imagination, they say. I bite hard on lower lip; try not to fly out of control before coffee break. Instead, change subject to existentialism in literature. Male grad student says, Pity the rest of us don't have the luxury of sitting home all day listening to CBC.

Car in garage for repairs. Go home on subway. Large man dressed as woman sits beside me. Flimsy mauve scarf tied under chin. Holds paper shopping bag between legs. Glimpse of wigs—red, brown, curls. Large knuckles. Dirty hands. I stare in opposite direction. When I get off at my stop, have to push through large crowd on platform. Singing and bearing banners:

Montreal Praise Festival
featuring
Jesus Christ, King of Glory!

* *

Jason over the mumps. Regular sitter back. Wants a raise. Fell in love with baker who tells her she should be more aggressive, ask for better salary so they can get married.

Hugo has to take business trip west. Wants me to meet him in Vancouver. Lust in eyes when he asks me to join him. Never gives up.

What about children? Bottles of milk, cold water in diaper pail, dust balls on stairs, Evie climbing on shelves?

Your mother, he says. Call your mother. She raised six, didn't she?

I tell my writing prof I'm going west.

You women who stay home, he says. Life one big holiday.

* *

Trip? Haven't taken a trip since I was twenty-two. Flew to Bermuda. Plane caught fire, return flight. Crew mouthing silent messages—FIRE! Emergency landing. Everyone okay.

Hugo leaves three days early, kisses Evie, Jason, me. See you in Vancouver, he says. Dinner every night, good hotel, expense account. Great sex, he whispers in my ear.

Babysitter vacuums living-room table with bristle attachment today. Scratches top. Heirloom from Hugo's great-great grandfather. Mother phones. Two's nothing, she says. I raised six.

I take children to park. Push stroller through mud grooves. Wheels lock. Push harder. Smile at child in swing. Her mother grabs her out of swing chair. Glares at me. Some people, she says, as she leaves with daughter under one arm. Some people are just sick. Go around smiling at innocent people, no reason at all.

* *

Class Thursday night. Mid-term exam on climatology. Clouds and winds. Highs and lows. Field trip two weeks ago over and under barbed wire. Tore jeans. Collected rock samples. Two young students in next seat held hands on bus. If I fly west Friday morning and return Monday, won't have to miss class on ocean waves. Might even get idea for next week's story. Creative Writing prof becoming suspicious. Last night one student suggested kindly, Maybe you should choose something that really happens to people. Add a little credibility.

Trips, my mother says. We never had it so good, our day. Holds Evie on one hip, helps Jason blow kiss at window as taxi pulls away.

Meet Hamish, one of Hugo's colleagues, in air terminal. Hi, he says. What are you up to these days?

Raising kids, studying, I say. I go to school. Nights. Geomorphology and Creative Writing.

Aren't you the brainy one, he says. But I thought to do any kind of writing you needed some sort of experience in life.

Sometimes am capable of violent acts. Thankfully, Hamish flying east. I wish Bagotville or Plaster Rock on him.

Lean back in armchair. Think of Ogilvy's. Instead of Muzak, recorded canaries sing to customers. Piper marches through store aisle every night at closing. Remember then, that I haven't bought flight insurance. Go to counter. Woman jabs at packaged policy, pencil sharpened both ends. I sign above her upside-down X. She points to mail slot in wall. For beneficiary, I've written Hugo Cornell. Other permutations cross my mind.

Feel as if I might laugh aloud. No banged knees, soiled underpants, tears, the children's, my own. I *will* the mind to nothingness. This is not easy. Lists go through head: vitamin drops, emergency numbers, Mother at window, shirts still at cleaners, flight numbers, did I throw in a nightie? What can I invent for next week's story—lately have been too tired to dream.

Voices intrude from row of chairs at my back. Male voices.

74

But I'm telling you, Agnes isn't going to like it, says one. Screw Agnes, says the other.

Screw the world, I think, and wonder if I've shouted aloud. Look around. No one staring.

Attendant leads us down carpeted ramp and into flying machine where steward fiddles with dials. Plane distends with voices and luggage. I sit alone, centre aisle seat. Don't want to look down. Rear door is closed, locked, bolted.

Muzak, full force. My holiday. I begin to enjoy, try not to think of Hugo waiting in Vancouver. Exsanguination.

New stewardess appears at my left. Face and body perfect. Smooth legs, blue eyeshadow. Perfections counterbalance my flaws. She wears white plastic earrings, has platinum ponytail pinned at back of neck. Her mouth exaggerates—in two official languages—emergency procedures. She mimes demonstration. I am a lip reader, I am the public deaf. I buckle in, wait, anticipate pressure changes. Plane approaches runway, stops, reverses direction, stops again.

Rear door rumbles open. I turn to look. A couple tumbles aboard. He in early seventies, she slightly younger. Both weighted with overcoats, shopping bags, hand luggage. He approaches from my aisle; she (highly rouged, blue hairdresser curls, plump) from aisle at right. Plastic stewardess motions them to vacant seats beside me.

He is at my left elbow, out of breath. Shoves a grey overcoat into my arms and lap. Hold this. My God. Thank you. We were booked on another plane, missed by a hair. Lucky to get this one, I tell you. Points to wife. She's out of breath, he says.

It's true that he can't get in. Floppy, uncoordinated, too heavy to move easily in smart grey suit, vest, Hong Kong silk tie. I hold his coat, step into aisle to let him pass, stow coat above. He shoves through to vacant seat, looks at Mrs. You all right, Mommy?

Mommy fine. Secures herself out of reach across wide armrest. Charlie, he says, offers hand.

Evelyn, I say. Reach for book while plane thunders into position. Would like to eliminate madness from my life. Look at Charlie out of corner of my eye. Think about his life. He'd look comfortable in Bermuda shorts drooping below sun-ripe patch of red. Drinks lime rickeys, goes to bed early, lives the good life. Once wrote jingles for cereal ads, worked his way up. Gives Mommy plenty of spending money, summer cottage, one trip every winter.

I close my eyes. Plane no longer on tilt. Open book. Beckett's plays. Try to concentrate on *Krapp's Last Tape*. Below me: Mother, Evie, Jason, Hamish, two million citizens.

* *

Plastic Stew wheels bar down aisle. Charlie orders whisky. Mommy and I do not want drinks. Mommy, wearing earphones, ignores Charlie except when spoken to or prodded. Eyes closed, but manages owl-eyed quick blink as Charlie buys three miniature bottles of whisky.

Charlie finishes one bottle, breaks seal on next. Leans towards me. Stewardess should bring out wine soon, he says. Is that Capp you're reading? He's pretty funny. Used to read him all the—

No, this is Krapp. *Krapp's Last Tape.* Play by Beckett. Apology in my voice? I ruffle pages, show Charlie. Several plays. Quite good.

Charlie nods. Glances at cover through thick lenses. Not Capp? Should read Capp some time. Funny. Can see you read a lot. Must have gone to college. My girl, she went to college. We're going to visit her now. Charlie's voice drops. I'm so excited, he says. Haven't seen my grandchildren since—but just for two weeks. No more. Don't want to get in the way. They have their lives too. She married a smart fellow.

He taps Mommy. Mommy, what does Sheila's husband do?

Mommy opens one eye, looks at me, shuts eye. Spray icings, she says.

Chemicals and such, says Charlie. You think you can guess what I do? Though I'm retired now.

Can't. No.

Advertising. Bet I don't look the type. His voice lowers. I have my own tailor in Hong Kong. Had this suit made—thirty percent of what it would cost in Montreal. Every stitch by hand. Charlie shows seams of one cuff and inside lapel. Breaks seal on third bottle of whisky.

Plastic Stew takes order for wine. Courtesy airlines, with meal. This will not do. Charlie wants best. Orders two bottles of best. Best is not good, Charlie proclaims, when wine is served.

Charlie stores Mommy's wine in seat pocket ahead. Plastic Stew's voice on loudspeakers. Clear aisles, take seats while trays distributed. Charlie giggles. Need nervous pee, he says. Squeezes past, heads for the loo. Mommy comes to life, removes wine from seat pocket, snaps into purse. Owl-eye shuts.

Krapp's Last Tape becoming depressing. Charlie returns with another bottle of courtesy wine. Lady at back gave it to me, he says. Doesn't drink. Took it because it's free. All paid for in the ticket.

Charlie rummages in seat pocket. Looks for other bottle. Now where did that go? Fumbles, gives up. Magical interference. Mommy eye-signals to me, flick flick.

Go ahead and read, Charlie says. Read your Crap. He's really funny. I'm just an old fool, always bothering you. You read a lot, I can tell.

Plastic Stew brings lunch trays. Mommy leaves earphones in

77

place, begins to sort and chew. I put my book away. Look at Charlie. Prevented from further sensory experience except the visual because of one large crumb from crusty roll on Charlie's glasses. Half of one lens, the left, obstructed.

Charlie does not know crumb is there. Grins at me but does not use peripheral vision. My impulse to raise elbow, polish lens. Excuse, but there's a rather large crumb. No, might take offence. Leave it. Look directly ahead. Perhaps crumb will fall when Charlie inclines head for drink. But doesn't.

Charlie to be spared nothing. I look down and see—icing? cream cheese? something from dessert? Huge smear on Hong Kong vest and left thigh. If I tell him about icing, will also have to mention crumb. The two are linked, make me honour bound. Serviettes are large; I could erase, rub out, remove indignities. I open Krapp, stare at page. Coward, I know. Choose silence.

Charlie spies his suit. Look at me! Pushes away tray. Shoves serviette into my hand. Oh look. Clumsy I am. Take it, wipe it off, what will my daughter say? Mommy!

Mommy remains calm. Watches me scrub at Charlie's thigh.

Need water, Charlie, I say. Don't think this is going to work.

Steward passes by, collecting trays. Come back with me, he says to Charlie. I'll fix you up.

Charlie returns, clean, pressed. We lean back, relax. Crumb has fallen off. I couldn't go to my daughter like *that*, he says. Mommy, between earphones, taps fingers against armrests. I skip pages, try another play as plane descends.

* *

The hatch spews forth luggage. Moving black tongue. Safe on ground. Legs betray. The wine. Feel shaky, indefinite. Travellers fidget, impatient this side of glass wall, search for familiar faces. I see Hugo waiting at Arrivals. Hide behind tall man. Don't like to stand exposed through glass partition. Might gesture, make helpless faces at each other, grin until our lips twitch.

Charlie and Mommy have found luggage. Come to stand beside me. Charlie's belt loosened. Gap of shirt shows between vest and trousers. Shakes my hand warmly.

That your young man out there? He's been watching you. Looks like a nice person. Well, I wish you happiness in life, like Mommy and me. Eh, Mommy? Sorry you didn't get a chance to read your Capp. He's a very funny writer. There's my little girl, he says. Charlie stumbles towards glass doors, arms outstretched.

Jog beside moving belt, drag suitcase backwards and lift. Must start dreaming again. New story needed by Wednesday. Final exam coming up—clouds waves rocks slides. Hugo looks like stranger from here. Walk towards him. Resembles George Burns. When did he start wearing glasses? Leans towards me in taxi. I asked for a double, he says. He kisses me on the ear.

Separation

❦

It is one of those early November evenings when the air is warm but not hot. When light is fading, but the sky, clear behind, still has a touch of blue. Where clouds, navy-grey, are brushed like bats' wings against one corner of the sky. And an early moon sits full and white, with one sharply profiled cloud across its yawning centre.

Karla, looking straight ahead, pulls me along, her five-year-old hand firmly in mine, and forces me to merge with the late Friday bustle of this small town. We stand on the crest of the hill and look down on the river and, cool on its bank, the bunker-like shopping mall that contains every place of business in this town. Another week is over. Quick footsteps and slammed car doors signal Friday relief. Cars pull out of the parking lot and others replace them. At the mall's end, men wearing plaid shirts and woollen hats, and with six-packs of beer tucked under their arms, swing through four identical glass doors. I would like to capture the colours, woven into the moving pattern. Off to the side, students from the high school are sitting around the wall of the circular outdoor fountain that is dry, never a success in this town. Nothing fancy here; life can be, and is, lived by its bare essentials.

There are times when I love the solitude, the town sitting separate and apart from all other places. But there are other, exasperating times, when I would flee at a moment's notice. I have sifted the old argument with myself over and over again. Why stay? I wanted to be far from the interminable demands of the city. I wanted to paint, more and more. But that was before we knew that Alan would be sent away. The thought of him pierces me now. I do not know if the sensation is one of grief or love or pain. I cannot think of it at all, this separation, because if I do the year ahead will break down into separate days, and there are too many of these to consider. Nine years after my marriage to Alan, I am learning to live alone.

Karla, as if she has been excluded by my thoughts, sings one of her sudden songs. It is a song of love addressed to me, and reminds that I am not, after all, as alone as I would believe:

> Your lips are red as lipstick
> Your eyes are green as grass

She creates the words and the tune as we walk down the slope. "I'm not so good at singing," she says, abruptly considering, and stops.

"But that song went inside my heart," I tell her.

We decide to visit our friend Miss Ellis on the way home. Miss Ellis' family has lived in the town since the first United Empire Loyalists stepped from their small boats on the riverbank just below the site of the present mall. She is the last of her line and has not a single living relation. She lives on the hill in a large white wooden house, just above the river. The bridge, which can be seen from her front windows, gives the impression of being too modern for this old town. I always think, as I come over the hill and confront it anew, that it should be plucked out of the view, that it would look better painted on a new, green dollar bill.

Karla loves Miss Ellis' house with its jumble of ancient

furniture, its woodpile and its root cellar, its plants twined up and down the stairs and, of course, its attic. We both love the company of Miss Ellis.

"Everything in this house is *parched* with age," she announces, as she opens the door.

"Maybe the dinosaurs lived here," says Karla, and adds, "but now they're stinked."

"*Extinct*," I say.

Miss Ellis laughs her wonderful quick laugh, closing her lips a little. She is observant; she pauses, remembering. Although at first glance she seems small and white and frail, when one is with her, one senses strength, largeness. There is something of the artist in her, I am sure. She always describes herself as a picture, someone quickly painted into a moving canvas, someone things *happen* to. Today she tells the story of the boy who carries in her wood. Somehow, she manages to get to the bottom of people's lives and stories. But she does not ask about mine, or about Alan's; nor does she mention the government job which has taken him for a year to a country at war, a country to which Karla and I may not follow.

While she prepares tea, to be shared on her veranda, she listens attentively to Karla, who tells about a dress *reversal* held by her Kindergarten. Karla then goes into an unexpected and long-winded story about a girl in her class who says mean things about the other girls.

"Ah," says Miss Ellis, "if you can see through a person, Karla, you can like them. It's when you can't, when there are surprises, that you can be caught off guard."

Karla and I ponder this on the way home. As we turn in at our street, we meet two neighbourhood women, Helen Jordan and Audrey Brooks. Audrey says to me, "Alan is away now, isn't he, Simone? How is it for you, living alone?"

"What did she mean, Mom?" Karla asks, after I've mumbled

something incoherent and they have passed. But I cannot answer. Do I misunderstand because at this point I regard any question about Alan and me as intrusive? I do know that I have been wounded, by the encounter.

* *

All day Sunday, I stretch canvases until I think I have enough ready for what I want to do. The work is in my head, growing, murmuring. I feel, at times, that I am being taken over. I let myself move, back and forth, with the images. Karla amuses herself outside in the breeze and the sun as I work. Fall has come late this year and the leaves are past their full final colour. They seem to be having an earthward race; the ground and air are thick with them. My attention roams out and back from window to easel, where I stand looking at blank space. But Karla has caught my eye, her long black hair dangling from her tire swing where she sways upside down. I have all of this *space*. I feel excited, as if I could paint anything. I wonder suddenly whether I shall enjoy living alone this long time. A large part of me seems to desire, to stretch towards the boundless free state, the state of uncommittedness. Will there be no real impact now that Alan has gone? Almost two months have passed and little seems to have changed—except for the daily contact. Yes, the ordinary human contact with one's partner—that is missing.

As for Karla, she goes to school, comes home, hums about the house quite happily. I am not really certain what has been altered for her. And Alan? Is he sitting in a room somewhere? Reading? Lying in bed? Walking some foreign street? I have no visual background for him; there is nothing to fit him against. Nothing except descriptions in letters that arrive irregularly: details of long hours, difficult negotiations. What is any of this to me? Anger bursts like a bud, a sudden inner rupture, a surprise. What, indeed, is any of this to me?

I look out again to the yard where Karla is playing. She looks like a flash of leaves herself, in bright yellows and reds. The leaves rain past her as she deftly leaps from rope to branch and back to swing. She painstakingly twists the tire round and round, lies back and allows herself to spin until her body and the movement of the rope merge to an opaque blur. I watch her with a knowledge, a certainty that she will always be a wonder to me, a mystery of spontaneous joy and selfless happiness. Restless, I leave the blank canvas and go outside. I think about my sister Kristina and her family coming for Christmas. Karla and I both look forward to that. Kristina's family will help fill the growing spaces.

* *

The week Kristina is to arrive, Karla decides to make hats. With glue and paper and paint she creates jesters' hats, soldiers' hats, clowns' hats, hats that look as if they should be worn by Popes.

The tree is decorated; we are ready for visitors. Karla's holidays have begun and I feel the relief and joy of the break in routine, of having just the two of us in the house.

Karla tires of the hats and decides to play dress-up. I go through my closets and donate to her dress-up box, two old sundresses, one of which—a bright blue—she holds to her chest.

"Children can have breastuz too," she says, peering into the top of the dress. And then, as if she has been saving this for days, she eyes me shrewdly and says, "How does a man's sperm get inside a woman?"

I can never anticipate the questions. They seem to spring from a deep well of curiosity and, for Karla, a deeper well of hilarity. Their timing is a mystery to me. We get out her book, one she has gone through many times, and we read *How Babies Are Made*. But it holds her interest only a few minutes, and off she goes, this time to build with her set of logs.

Miss Ellis arrives, for tea. She brings a bag of knitting and we sit in the living room before the fire, where an ancient and useful rite goes on. I kneel before her, a skein of scarlet strands looped about my hands. My arms sway to Miss Ellis' rhythm as she winds the wool to a furiously growing round ball. Karla watches this magical performance. Miss Ellis sits back comfortably and begins to knit—a shrug, she says, for her shoulders. A scarlet shrug.

Karla waits and then, testing, remembering the book, says coolly to Miss Ellis, "Did you know that when a man and woman are in bed the sperm eats the egg?"

"*Meets* the egg, Karla!" I say. "It *meets* the egg!"

Karla thinks this very funny indeed.

"You seem to know all about it, don't you, Karla," says Miss Ellis.

Then she tells us she has received a Christmas card from Alan. "He seems to write happily, Simone."

Yes, he writes happily to Karla and me, too, but as much as Alan and I have tried to make contact through our letters, he is removed from the fringes of my real life. There are things that I am forgetting. I am living with the new knowledge that my life is somehow changing, almost against my will. In one of my own letters to Alan, sent at the beginning of the week, I found myself scribbling—a postscript: "Do you remember who I am, Alan? Do you remember the things I do?" I have begun to feel anger, anger mixed with sorrow at missing him, and even fear, a new fear that has crept in: that our friendship, our partnership, will somehow be damaged when we meet again.

But these are all of the things that cannot be said, and I stumble over my reply. As Miss Ellis leaves, she pauses at the door. "Isolation can be terrible if you allow it. You're vulnerable, Simone. Please take care."

At dinner, Karla is quiet; she makes few demands on me,

seems to know something that neither of us can articulate. And for the first time, she leaves Alan out of her bedtime prayer.

* *

Christmas is, in Miss Ellis' words, "A great success." She joins Karla and me, Kristina, her husband, Tim, and their two children, who have now arrived. There has been only one light snowfall and, feeling cheated, Karla and her cousins manage to scrape and heap enough of it to make a thin slide. They spend hours shrieking and laughing outside the house. Tim amuses the children and moves easily in and out of the reminiscences which now surround him on all sides. Kristina and I have five days in which to remember, and talk, and remember. And we laugh. We tell stories to Miss Ellis about our childhood, and Karla and her cousins listen, agog. Miss Ellis tells us stories of the town and its past. She seems to know about every settler who came to this area in her great-great-grandfather's time.

" 'Culture' was not a word that was used in my day," she says. "Nor was 'ethnic.' People were just people then. Things used to be more simple. Sometimes I look out my window and see young people congregating around the shopping mall, and I feel as if I don't know what's going on any more."

One late afternoon, Miss Ellis describes a ballet she had seen when she was a child. She'd been taken to Montreal by her parents, and they had visited the theatre. A touring company from Europe was performing. Her eyes are bright with the memory, and she moves her hands and arms as she talks.

"Children were *banked* along the back of the stage. Then, the smallest girl, a carnation, stepped forward and danced. How that little flower danced! After that, I always played the piece for the dance, always for those tiny feet, that little flower."

Miss Ellis rises from her chair and goes to the piano bench. Her fingers stretch and falter on the keys of my old Heintzman, but she stiffens her back, perseveres, and the tune is played. Miss Ellis' head bows forward on her chest. We sit quietly, gathering the dusk.

Kristina and I walk to the big white house with Miss Ellis, who has recovered herself. At the door, her hand on the knob, she tips back on her heels and thanks us.

"There's something of the belle about her, isn't there," says Kristina.

"She's wonderful," I reply. "A wonderful friend." But I think to myself: We've left her alone, in that big old house.

That night, I sleep fitfully. In and out of sleep, I reach across the bed for Alan. I wake to the realization that he is gone and it is then that I feel the first and deepest loneliness. There is nothing I can do.

* *

The following day, Alan phones. It is the first phone call from the other side of the world. I am not expecting the call; it is sudden; the connection is poor. Kristina hurries everyone from the room and shuts the door, leaving me in privacy. But my voice echoes back through the receiver each time I try to speak, and I think of tortuous cables moaning and tangled in the deepest parts of the sea. Because of the echoes, our words are delayed. We speak at the same time, cancelling each other out. Every few seconds, there is a beeping noise in the background. What chance do we have of saying anything meaningful?

"I tried to call Christmas Day," he says. "I couldn't get through."

This is followed by loud crackling noises.

"Are you all right?" he shouts.

And I shout back, "Perhaps I would feel better if I were indifferent."

And that is the only thing Alan seems to hear clearly. He

sounds puzzled; his voice is choked. I hear, "Indifferent? No, Simone, not indifferent." But it's too late to try to erase. We hang up, suffering. For that brief second, I recognized the temptation to punish him for leaving.

* *

Kristina and Tim prepare to go. They have already extended their visit to a week. I would like them to stay longer, but they have made the emotional switch; their thoughts are back in their own home. All of the activity here moves towards departure.

I am saddened by this and think of it only in terms of being left. Karla picks up my mood and we irritate each other.

When the car is packed, Kristina and I go for a last walk in the fresh snow along the riverbank. It might be a year before I see her again, and by then Alan will be home. But Kristina, knowing my mood, is bent on handing out sympathy, which I hate. I am angry and want no part of it. What does she know of separation? I walk beside her, bitter and silent. Our conversation ends; we have had our parting. But at the car door, Kristina says, "I never realized how weak you are, Simone. All through our childhood, I thought of you as being so strong."

I think of Miss Ellis. Vulnerable, yes, but do I have to believe this, too?

"No, Kris," I tell her. "You're wrong. It's just that, from here, I can't see the end of it. But it's my life and I'll arrange it the best way I can."

* *

Karla goes back to school; I begin to paint. I work upstairs near the south window where the sun streams in. Some days while Karla is in school, I wander outside, taking walks in the cold air, keeping my back to the west wind. I hike through the woods and watch the sun as it glazes over icy patches on the surface snow.

Cars move slowly and continuously, up and down our street. The women in them seem to travel in groups, four or five to a car. In and out of cars much of the day. What do they do? Play bridge? Coffee? I cannot imagine. When we first moved here four years ago, they came calling, clusters of them, like neglected nettles. I wanted no part of that. They know I paint; they leave me alone; we greet one another on the street, that is all.

But Miss Ellis is not like that; she is unique, alive. There is nothing of loss about her, nothing of death—only life. She tells Karla, "How wonderful is life, Karla, if you only take hold."

In the bookstore I overhear two women of the town discussing Miss Ellis.

"Poor brave thing," says one. "I wonder how she manages alone in that big place."

And the other: "She is a brave little soul, isn't she. I feel so sorry for her."

And I am angry because they dare to describe her with pity.

I recognize one of the women who describes her so; she is a tall, beautiful woman who dresses in brightly coloured two-piece ski outfits. I see her from my studio window, daily, walking around and around the block. Around and around, day in, day out.

I recall another conversation, overheard at Karla's Christmas concert. I was sitting in a row of metal chairs in the school gym, awaiting the curtain. The gym was filled to the back doors, and parents who could find no chairs stood in the doorway. Behind me, someone unknown. But I watched as another woman pushed her way along the row and leaned over my shoulder to speak to that person behind.

"Angela," she said, her voice urgent and business-like. "A

boy in our parish has crashed into a fallen tree while sliding—ruptured his spleen. He's in hospital."

"What shall I do?" said the voice behind, as if accustomed to this line of conversation.

"Could you, over at St. Mark's, pray? He's Anglican, but the parents don't go to church. I thought if we all prayed, it might work better."

"Sure," said the voice. "I'll get on it right away. I'll call the minister after the concert."

"Fine. We'll do the same at St. James."

The lights dimmed; the voices hushed. The woman made her way back out to the aisle. All of this in rapid talk they both understood—drums in the jungle. A pipeline, sleek and implicit.

* *

By March, I am at peace again. The trees surrounding the house creak in the north wind. Birches bend, laden with ice. On sunny days, the snowbanks that line the street are honeycombed with their own melting. One day I see a black spider hurrying through these empty chambers, promising spring. I think of the weeks following Christmas, how preoccupied I have been with the separation. Days when I seemed to be running on the edge of despair, sinking into it, fleeing into its face. But I have been painting steadily. I have set my own rhythm. Always, at the back of my mind, wondering what it is about Alan that is essential to me. An essence, a bond that has never been broken. I see Karla watching me sometimes, searching for something of her own.

When the ice on the river begins to break up, I walk over the hill every afternoon and sit, watching. I take a sketch pad with me; my knuckles become red and cold as I work, but the sun is strengthening. I feel it, daily.

The floes shift downstream, sometimes lazily. They slur into one another, and smaller pieces hurriedly break away through fluid paths of the darkest blue. With the sun so hot, I feel as if I am part of a spell: sitting on a large stump, knees drawn up, hearing and feeling the swish of ice as it pushes on and on. Dead trees and branches waggle back and forth, caught by underwater roots or logs. Surprising objects float past on the surface of the larger floes—a sleigh, three paint cans, a car fender. No matter how much ice jams against the bank, there is always some greater force behind, ready to dislodge or crush what has gone before. This, too, has its own rhythm. Steady, steady. It is a rhythm of destruction that will yield only to spring.

* *

A brochure arrives in the mail—an application for a two-week course at an arts centre I know, not far from here, by the sea. It would be an overnight trip by train, that is all. The instructor this year is a well-known artist from the west. She has just had a show on the west coast; I read about it in the weekend papers that are sent by mail.

"How would you like to go to the sea?" I ask Karla, when she comes in after school.

"Oh!" she says. "Remember the last time? We jumped over the waves!" She is breathless with memories.

"But it will be too cold to go into the water," I tell her. "It will be during the late part of May and the water won't be warm enough then."

"We can pick up shells, can't we?"

"Yes, we can pick up shells. We'll even take the train to get there—a bedroom on the train. Would you like that?"

In response, she runs upstairs, comes back with a shell from her old collection, and threads a long string through it. She places it around my neck and says, "You are the Queen of the Mommies!"

"It's settled then. We'll go."

I decide to book rooms on the top floor of a lodge in the little town of Sea View. The rooms face the sea; there will be light enough to work. I try to remember those upper rooms, and recall a kind of loft arrangement. Alan and I stopped to eat in the lodge dining room one summer evening, and looked around while we were there. The lodge sits on a cliff, old and silent, facing the gathering winds of the north.

"So," says Miss Ellis to Karla, when we tell her. "You're travelling far as ever a puffin flew."

"And I'm suffering," says Karla. "My mother says I have butterflies and I'm really suffering."

The evening we are to leave, there is elation in the air. I seem to be doing the same things over and over, checking and rechecking uselessly. Why can't I just go? Pick up and leave— no luggage—but no, we have to prepare.

Karla studies me for a while and says, "You told *me* not to get too excited."

We drive to the country station, fourteen miles from town, and leave the car in the station master's care. We stand in the night and wait beside the tracks, peering back in at the station office— an old swivel chair, a goose-neck lamp, a rolltop desk, a wide, black iron safe. We listen for the long warning whistle. There is a full moon, and the air has a heavy sweetness about it, a promise of early flowers and still, hot nights. I think of the day before, when Karla and I were in the car coming home from shopping. There'd been a sudden heavy downpour, which stopped as quickly as it began. We drove through a double rainbow, through the arc of it, where two rainbows met and intersected. When we were through the arc, I pulled the car over and turned back to look. Karla whispered, "It must be magic. It has to be magic."

The train shakes like an old black rattle through the night. We hear it before we see it and then, a conical white beam blinds us from high in the centre of the tracks. All other noise dims before the train. Karla gasps at its size as she is lifted aboard, and the porter shows us to our sleeping compartment.

All night, she tosses against me, waking and sleeping, wide-eyed at the whistle and the rumble beneath her head. Her excitement and happiness keep us both awake and finally we push up the blind and sit close, looking out as the ribbons of dark fall away from the track. The moon casts its glow on this Maritime landscape. Karla looks up at me, independent and fearless.

In the morning, we smell the sea. It is cooler here, a forlorn damp day. The gulls fly high, coasting on upper breezes. The short-tailed swallows are here, too, swooping and diving into the cliffs. Karla and I settle into our room and a half in the loft, and I hope for two productive and undisturbed weeks. We move in on a Thursday; classes will begin half days, Monday.

But I find that, whereas at home Karla attended school every day, here she is with me every moment. We walk and walk by the edge of the sea, waking in the early morning, out before breakfast. Sun rises like moon, cool and silver across a rippled sea. Light sifts over the sand and cliffs, colours changing moment by moment. Karla talks continuously; her chattering rivets my thoughts. Any inner peace I have is continually drained off. With Alan gone, having no one with whom to share the parental responsibility, my reserves are getting low. I hadn't thought about my emotional energy in this way before and see now that I am close to having none at all. During class days, Karla will be looked after under arrangements with the centre. I find myself longing for the week to start, longing for the company of other adults.

Several students have arrived at the lodge, and we pass them, wandering along the beach. We share some sense of vigour; I see it on their faces and feel it in myself. I am glad to be here and although I think of Alan often, it is better to be away, for a time, from our home.

On Sunday afternoon, Karla and I, in our boots, wade along the edge of the waves and watch red jellyfish babies that have drifted into the Gulf. They turn on their sides, rolling in the shallow surf like rusty wayward wheels. We are delighted as we watch them sink, puff out to the surface fully billowed, turn and wheel gracefully away. They deflate and pull ahead in one perfect quiver, like strands of gossamer. It is such a wonder to watch that I am taken by surprise when a man's voice says, "Simone. I knew it would be you. I knew when I saw the list that it couldn't be anyone else."

Karla and I are both astonished. It is Justin Kempe, an artist with whom I studied years ago in Montreal. Karla has never met him, and watches wide-eyed as we hug and laugh and both talk at once. The last time I saw Justin was at a show he gave in Toronto. It was the year Justin was married and the year before Karla was born. We had dinner together and he drove me to the airport where we waited several hours because of a delayed flight. Although we've sent notes back and forth from time to time, we haven't kept in close touch. But I am happy to see him. We've been good friends in the past, and there is much to talk about and to share. Justin is also staying at the lodge and we make plans to sit at the same table in the dining room for the two weeks. He brings me up to date on the gossip and the activities of the city, which I have not missed until now.

* *

In the morning, as I dress, I watch the surf rising under a gentle wind. I am in harmony here; everywhere I look, a rugged kind of beauty hovers on the rim of land and sea. Karla, too, is content. She begins her own classes today and will meet other children in the Daycare Room that is provided in the same building. We have a short walk along the beach to the centre each day.

Again, I work. Having painted under my own discipline for the last several years, I find that the classes demand more than I thought I could produce. There is a sense of extreme weariness at the end of each day, but the fatigue is combined with a sense of elation, exchange, of growth. I see things in my work that were not apparent to me when I was painting in isolation. Justin and I spend hours discussing technique and the work each of us is trying to do.

Sometimes, in the evenings, I sit in the big armchair by my easel and watch and listen to the sea. Karla sleeps in her own narrow bed under the sloping ceiling. There are times when I must be alone—when I feel so bombarded by the activities of the day that I cannot read or talk or meet with any of the others in the lodge. Sometimes Justin comes in and we have a glass of wine, talking softly so we won't wake Karla. And when I think of Alan now, it is like thinking of a stranger: remote, foreign, unknown.

During the second week I wake one morning to know, at the instant of waking, that the north wind has come. The surf is high, the roar continuous. Throughout the day, I feel as if voices are shouting in my head, as if a new source of energy has been created. Karla and I wrap ourselves in thick sweaters and run outside, pushed and pulled by the wind.

Later, we walk with Justin on the beach; a light rain softly pelts the hoods of our jackets. Karla begins to behave petulantly. Justin tries to tease her out of her mood, but she becomes angry and shouts at him, "You're not my father!" The three of us return under a gloomy sky.

At night, Karla wakes, crying. She calls to me and sits close, sobbing out her dream. She is looking for me, but I have hidden. She looks in the room, at the centre, in the lodge, in

Justin's room. Do I not love her? Then she sees that I have climbed into one of my paintings and am disguised. I wear large earrings and a funny hat. At first she is afraid that I do not love her, but then she thinks, "Yes, she loves me, but she doesn't want me to follow her."

I comfort Karla and she goes back to sleep, confused by her dependencies and longings—for love, for order. And how long since I have been loved, as a woman? It has been more than half a year since I have wakened each morning with the same sure knowledge: that every day of my life, I am loved. Is it so necessary, then? Will it be possible to renew my friendship with Alan when we come together again?

When I sleep, I, too, dream. Karla and I and Justin are on the beach. The sand is warm and soft and deep. We begin to dig a huge hole in which we can move about freely. The sand we remove from the hole is heaped up on the sides. Justin and I lean back against the edge while Karla plays. But then Kristina, my sister, is there—an accusing presence—and I see, clearly, that she has misunderstood my motives.

* *

At the end of the week, I leave Karla in the care of the Daycare instructor, and Justin and I spend our last free day at the sea together. We share a deep close feeling. I rebound from his every thought, his every move. Our silences fit, perfectly. Could I realign myself in a total way again? But it is impossible, really. We have both experienced the joy, the vulnerability that go with the full, the total commitment. Yet there is something between us that is in such absolute harmony, we draw closer and closer. The confusion and the elation of love are there, without the self-criticism for the behaviour. But no, we are both uncertain.

In the morning, Justin takes Karla and me to the station. And when the train comes, he holds me against him, and all of the moments we have desired together culminate under a clear sky, in a bitter sea-wind.

The train pulls away. Many things have changed; many things remain the same.

* *

Miss Ellis is delighted to have us back. She sits before the fire in our living room, still knitting her scarlet shrug. She listens as Karla tells of all the things she has learned at the sea and all the new things she can do.

Miss Ellis replies, "Oh, I was versatile, too, when I was young. But when you live as long as I have, you begin to shed your accomplishments. One by one, they fall away. But there are things you don't forget, Karla—things you live with that you never do forget." She smiles and looks down at her knitting.

* *

Just before the end of summer, the ringing of the phone wakes me from an early morning dream. There is a hush. I hear Alan's voice. He is in London, on his way home. He will be here in two days. There is little to say. Silently, I replace the receiver.

After painting steadily for a year, I am nearly ready for my own exhibition. Canvases are stacked in the hall and three deep against the walls of the spare room. Alan will be home in two days. Once more our lives will turn about. After living apart, we will have to learn to live together again. How Alan has changed, I will never ask. Much will be different; much will be the same.

An Evening in the Café

∞

She stood at the bottom of the stairs behind the half-closed door, listening to the others. She would not be seen until she stepped into the dining room. Her place seemed to have become, by habit, the table at the rear of the café and from here she watched the changing light outside in the street. This night the sky was coal blue; even the walls of the Golden Lion across the street had a bluish tinge. Perhaps snow would fall; it was chilly enough. The Germans, as she expected, were dressed in thick cardigans. The two old women wore high crocheted collars bunched around their necks. She looked about as she sat down. Heads bobbed politely. In three months, the term would be over; in two months, she would advise the university that she would be flying home. *Ruth Stephens*, she would write, *wishes to return at this time to her Canadian post in the Department of English. A replacement for the overseas branch will be needed in the fall.*

Would her replacement take the room over the butcher shop? Through the café, across the passsage, up the stairs? The owners, the Muellers, owned both butcher shop and café. The director's office had sent her there; whether or not the room had been inspected, she did not know. But if she had never before known the smell of flesh, she knew it now. How it assailed, first and always, the front of the nostrils, surprising, making her suck in a breath before she could stop herself. And the reminders of clot, bone, haunch, thigh—being hung, dripped, sawed, hacked. Cold cuts for breakfast every morning. Her stomach reeled as she came down the stairs each day, groping for Frau Mueller's strong coffee, aiming to smother the pervasion of *Fleisch*.

She tilted her chair towards the front of the café so that she would not have to watch Herr Mueller's elderly parents, *Oma* and *Opa*, at the next table. If cold cuts were served for breakfast, they were also served at the evening meal. Midday it was always the pig, the calf. It was too much to think about, all that flesh hauled in from refrigerated storage at the back of the shop. *Oma* and *Opa* were digging into their *Schmalz*, their broad knives bringing up thick portions of seasoned lard from the blue-grey pottery. Now they would be spreading it on their *Brot*. They would be sipping at their wine and spreading *Schmalz* on their *Brot*.

* *

An airmail letter is propped against the tray of cold cuts on the table. It must have arrived in the afternoon mail. Frau Mueller grins as she sets a bowl of soup before Ruth. She disapproves of Ruth excluding *Schmalz* from her diet, but she also willingly serves the soup.

"Von Ihrem Mann?"

She is pointing to the letter. Ruth's head creates an ambiguous movement, which might mean affirmation or negation. Frau Mueller may think what she likes about the letter, the husband, the man. There *had* been a man, a husband, *ein Mann*. Sometimes Ruth would like to sit opposite Frau Mueller in the quiet hours between meals when the café is empty, and deliver herself of every intimate detail of the husband, the letter, the marriage, the man. Her limited German does not permit this. It is something the landlady, however, would like to know.

Because she cannot know, she creates her own stories about Ruth—*Frau Doktor Stephens, Frau Professor Stephens*. She tells these stories to her life-long friend, Frau Mohn, who comes to the café every day during the quiet hours—the way Ruth would if she could sit with Frau Mueller and speak fluent German. Frau Mohn has a daughter, Trudi, who has had brain damage since birth. Trudi must be pushed in a special chair, and she sits, wheeled up to the table, while her mother and Frau Mueller are talking. There are days when she seems to listen, even to understand. The two old friends glance at her from time to time, saying, "Look at that. Just look at that. You'd think she knows exactly what we are saying." When attention is drawn to Trudi, she begins to make loud agitated noises and pulls at her dress and her body, as if trying to pluck something from herself. Often, she is quieted by *Oma*, who, from the butcher shop, brings a thick piece of smoked sausage which Trudi sucks and drools on. In the shopping basket that accompanies her everywhere, Frau Mohn carries several absorbent bibs large enough to fit a thirty-four-year-old, and these she changes from time to time, gently and considerately. Both Frau Mueller and Frau Mohn love Trudi deeply; she is a special child, sent to them to share through blood and friendship. What they have learned is this: one does not get through life without suffering in one way or another. Trudi is part of their suffering and their love.

* *

The letter is so far unopened. It might be from Taig. Ruth met Taig two years ago when she worked at the busiest library in Montreal. The meeting was at a book sale, a Saturday morning, a line of people stretched two city blocks and out of sight around the corner towards the hill. Taig had been searching in the basement room for copies of Old Norse books. He'd stood at Ruth's side and related, in the midst of the crowd, a legend of Lapland which he had read: *A woman walking alone on a path in the woods came face to face with a large bear. It was almost dark; no one was nearby and she knew that no help was at hand. She was frightened, but stood very still, waiting. The bear began to walk towards her. Suddenly, she knew what she had to do. She knew from the stories of her grandparents. She raised her thick skirts and showed the bear that she was a woman. She revealed herself.* That is what Taig said. "She revealed herself." *The bear stood on its hind legs, came closer, dropped down and sniffed at her. Then it turned and left the path.*

Ruth did not know why Taig told her the story or why she had stood and listened. She did know that he did not find any Norse books that day and she did go out for coffee with him after the basement room was cleared of every musty book. Later in the week, Taig invited her to a special screening of *Citizen Kane* at the Museum of Fine Arts. They sat in a room of modern art on low canvas folding stools, which Taig had thought to bring. A collapsible screen had been set up at one end of the room. After the film, Taig took Ruth to his apartment, where he made coffee and an omelette. He told her that he'd had cancer of the lung, that he'd once been a heavy smoker, that the affected lung had been removed. He had lived one year and five months without a new lesion. He told her this in a quiet undespairing voice that seemed to say she should know these things from the beginning.

* *

Much of the time, she sat in her room. There was a single window over the table where she wrote letters, and this looked down on an inner courtyard where the meat trucks drove in and out every day. The dead animals were hoisted to shoulders, the skin blanched and hairless and pressed to the close-fitting smocks of the workers. Moments after the trucks drove off, the ring of the saw began. The saw and the cleaver, buzz and hack, buzz and hack, until the sounds pervaded her innermost dreams. One day, from the centre drawer of her bureau, she pulled a cotton handkerchief that lay beneath layers of clothing. She held the handkerchief to her face and smelled raw meat that had penetrated even there.

When she was not in her room, she could be found in the Canadian library, an old war building from Hitler's time. *Literature* was in the basement, and the only tables and chairs where one could work were in a drab cement corridor. She taught two classes, one in the late afternoon, the other, one evening a week. Most of her students were Canadians who had full-time government jobs and who could not attend class at any other time. She was the only English professor on staff, but she did not really have an office. There was an administrative office, and she could go there with any problems and to pick up her pay, but she never saw other faculty members except at infrequent meetings called by the Director of Overseas Studies. The few professors were mostly young men and women who wished to spend a year or two in Europe, who travelled, who were not interested in spending time with one another. Ruth did not enjoy travelling and had not yet left the city since her arrival at the beginning of last term.

Several of her students were Americans drawn from a large overseas pool that seemed to wash over most of southwestern Germany. Occasionally, some of them stopped by the café. One day, she had tea with Mr. Berkuson, who worked as a dental assistant in the local American clinic. She spilled her tea across the table, and though Mr. Berkuson had been kind, and helped to mop it up, and ordered another from Frau Mueller, Ruth had been upset. She excused herself by telling him that she suffered from an inner ear problem. "Now why did I say that?" she asked herself. When she stood to go to her room, she became dizzy and she almost lost her balance.

* *

The letter might be from Martin. She'd been married to Martin for nineteen years, before he left her for a woman who was exactly that—nineteen—and who wore faded pink cotton skirts which hung to slim ankles. The young woman giggled at everything Martin had to say. When Ruth had been nineteen, she and Martin carried on a courtship that spanned two thousand miles while they studied at separate universities in Canada. They wrote passionate, endearing letters to each other. The relationship between them was created almost to perfection on paper. She had kept Martin's letters, and never asked if he had kept hers. But in the last year they were together, one day while in the basement, she noticed a plastic shoebag hanging from a nail near Martin's workbench. She pulled it down, and sat in a heap of laundry on the floor while she went through the contents. Every one of her letters was there, smoothed down and arranged in chronological order.

At first, she laughed when she began to read her own words, sitting there in the dirty clothes, looking on like a second self. She began to have a sense of being able to predict what was coming next, even though she had truly forgotten what she had written. It had been like meeting a reverse echo of herself. But the laughter unexpectedly turned. She began to realize the intensity of the love and dependency and loneliness she had sent through these lines. She had to force herself to continue, knowing she was experiencing loss, knowing that since that time, something deep and final had been allowed to slip away.

I have made plans to come to Europe, the letter will say. *I thought I'd visit you in that wonderful old city. I'll be travelling alone. Jennifer left some time ago.*

No more than that. Ruth would have to make of it what she could.

* *

The Golden Lion across the street attracts more customers than does Mueller's café in the evenings. The owner buys his meat from Mueller's butcher shop. One can hear laughter and song coming from the heavily timbered dining room, and these sounds drift across the street and up to Ruth's room like notes of music separating from a main overture. At times, Ruth would like to go there for her evening meal, but that would be seen as being disloyal. In any case, her meals are included in the weekly charge she pays to Frau Mueller.

If she stands at the bottom of the stairs behind the half-closed door, she can hear the others as they take their places. The two old women who wear high crocheted collars arrive together, sit together, appear to live together and do not cook meals at home. They do not speak to each other throughout the meal.

Ruth's place has become, by habit, the table at the rear of the café, and it is from here that she watches the changing light outside in the street. At the other tables are: a balding man, Herr Koch, who crosses one knee over the other and reads the papers during the meal. He wears a grey suit with baggy trousers and wide cuffs. He is, Ruth thinks, a travelling salesman. There is Herr Knopf, who has a round face and white whiskers and who is overweight. He drums his fingers on the table and hums to himself, playing, revising some inner tune. Frau Montag is thin and wispy and piles her white hair high on her head. She sits next to the window. When the butcher shop closes for the evening, *Oma* and *Opa* come through the passage and into the dining room to sit at the family table. Herr Mueller the younger and Frau Mueller, his wife, are last to sit down. He is the cook and Frau Mueller serves. His elderly parents help out only in the butcher shop, not in the café. They sleep in a room upstairs, next to Ruth, who is the only one who boards.

* *

There is a letter at Ruth's table, propped against a tray of cold cuts. It is from Canada, an air letter. Frau Mueller expresses interest in the letter as she serves Ruth's soup.

"*Von Ihrem Mann?*"

When Ruth first moved to Germany, she did not know that the word for husband was *Mann*. The translation of "my husband" would be "my man." My man. Did she have a man? She had once tried to explain to Frau Mueller, who thought this most important, about her *Mann*. There had been confusion about husband or friend, and she does not know if Frau Mueller now thinks she is married or unmarried. Perhaps, when Ruth reads this letter, she will smile to Frau Mueller and say, "*Mein Mann.*"

The letter will be from Taig. Sometimes she thinks Taig is the only person who knows her real self. The self who worked at the library in Montreal before she resigned and took the teaching position at the university. One of the reasons she resigned was because of the man she worked for, Vivien. He wore white shoes and carried an enormous bunch of keys on a spring attachment at his belt. He was forever snapping the keys in and out of this apparatus. He also walked as if his head were surrounded by a cloud of bees—that is, he was preoccupied, buzzing to himself. For these reasons and the other, main reason—that he was unapproachable—the staff, mostly women, managed on its own. It was the kind of place where Ruth and the others milled about the main desk, swarming out and into the stacks with carts of books ready to be shelved, bound, repaired, cast off.

Yes, Taig knew her real self. How, when she had free time, she would go to the biography shelves and take down certain books, turn the pages to the centre photographs and inspect the faces of the great writers—Chekhov, for instance, with his serious mouth and semi-amused wide eyes; or Virginia Woolf and the look of distraction the camera stole from her as she leaned into a doorway, holding a cigarette between her bony fingers.

Later, Ruth and Taig had gone to bed in his darkened apartment, slipping beneath the covers like shy children. She woke in the night crying out because she dreamed that Taig's remaining good lung had to be removed, too.

She and Taig had laughed about Vivien. She'd told Taig about looking at the faces of the great writers, and he had told her of Orwell writing that at fifty, everyone has the face he deserves. They laughed even harder because Taig was exactly that, fifty. They'd tried to think of all the faces they had known, and they had held each other, half laughing, half crying, for all of the reasons they would never be sure of and would never be able to say.

In the letter, Taig will have written: *Come back. I invite you to come back. We will lie together and hold each other and tell each other wonderful stories. And everything will be right again.*

* *

She had gone back, once, to Martin. It was between Sherri and Jennifer. He had invited her, and she had gone. He had moved west, by then, to Vancouver. He'd even sent the ticket, a round trip in case she changed her mind and wanted to return to Montreal. It was this detail, the return ticket, that convinced her to go. She would feel free, unbound; she would see how Martin had changed and how things had changed between them. "I know I will not stay," she told the mirror the morning she flew to the west. She did not, of course, give up her apartment.

She still does not know whether what happened was surprising or not surprising at all. She and Martin spent the next week in bed—most of the week. They got up occasionally to eat, shower, but never left his apartment. It was as if each had been starved for that part of the other and there was no satisfying that starvation. They rarely talked. He did tell her about Sherri. How he'd become exasperated with her leaving empty tuna tins about, and how she splattered the bathroom mirror. A boyfriend he did not know about came one evening to collect Sherri's belongings.

Ruth felt that she had nothing to tell. Certainly not about her work, which was not at all satisfactory at the time; and nothing of men, because that was before Taig.

On the seventh day, Ruth woke early and began to pack her suitcase. Even before she finished, Martin began to clean his apartment. He changed the sheets and wiped all traces of her from the sink; he tidied the table, brought out his office papers and scattered them across the desk in the living room. A photograph that had been prominently displayed all week had disappeared. It was taken the year they were married. Martin was seated; Ruth was standing behind him and leaning slightly forward. Her arms were draped possessively about his neck. She saw in her mind that she could easily have pulled her arms upward and choked him. But why would she have done such a thing? She did not know. She knew only that in the absence of the photograph, the scene had been made vivid and possible.

By the time Ruth placed her luggage beside the door, every trace of her was wiped clean. She was at first astonished, and then depressed, at how quickly this had been accomplished. Martin had banished her before she'd even left. And this she never did forgive.

* *

In the dining room, it always seems as if someone has said, *"Hush!"* Even *Oma* and *Opa*, after all their years together, have little to say. Frau Mueller and her husband banter back and forth; they try to bully their diners into conversation. But an unvoiced direction sifts over the room. *"Hush!"*

The only time there is real human noise, noise of contact, is during the day when Frau Mohn wheels Trudi through the door and pushes her to a table, removing anything Trudi might grab at quickly—serviettes, salt, coasters, ashtrays. Frau Mohn and Frau Mueller are swift, swifter than Trudi; they have been guarding her for thirty-four years. Nothing bad will happen to Trudi while they are alive.

Some afternoons when Frau Mohn arrives, she surprises Frau Mueller by wearing a fancy dress. Frau Mueller comes out from behind the counter; she bows and laughs delightedly. Her speech is formal.

"Guten Tag, Frau Mohn. Wie geht es Ihnen?"

Her friend bows in return and lifts Trudi's hand as if to help her bend forward in her chair. Frau Mohn giggles as she twirls in awkward heels; she picks up the hem of her dress to perform an eloquent and saucy curtsey.

The year the war ended, Frau Mueller and Frau Mohn were seventeen years old. They learned of a food called peanut butter from the American soldiers who were billeted in their side-by-side homes. One of the soldiers had been mean, ugly, had tried to put his hand up their skirts. They had finally told his officer, after weeks of hiding, of locking their doors, avoiding any room that held the man. The officer had punished the soldier, and they had been all right after that.

After the soldiers left, the two women never saw or tasted peanut butter again. They still laugh about peanut butter, how it made the teeth stick together. Now, each of them wears dentures paid for by their country's health care. And once a year, Trudi is sent to a special home while Frau Mohn has one entire week only for herself.

Frau Mueller and Frau Mohn discuss their *Frau Professor*, their roomer, for they share responsibility for the woman who had once been seen to bury her face in her handkerchief when the door of her room was ajar.

Is she married? Is she not married? Perhaps she will be getting married. She does not wear a ring. She wears no jewellery, or surprisingly little. Letters arrive. She never opens them immediately; she always takes them to her room. A letter will sit unopened on the table throughout the evening meal. Is she happy? Is she unhappy? Frau Mueller and Frau Mohn would like her to be happy. They think that she will soon be getting married. Her fiancé might be coming to meet her here in their historic city. Perhaps that is why she spilled her tea the day she was sitting with another man, the American. The American had been kind; he had put his own hands in the slop rags with Frau Mueller, after he mopped up the tea.

* *

The second time Mr. Berkuson had tea with Ruth, she admitted that she was short of money. The university paid so little; the next cheque was not due for another four days. She had a toothache, needed attention. Mr. Berkuson promised to sneak her into the American clinic. He skirted bureaucratic procedure and she had a tooth filled that same afternoon. Mr. Berkuson was an amazing man when it came to accomplishment, action. He paid for the tea and offered her twenty *Mark* to help her get through to the end of the week. She declined the money, but allowed him to pay for the tea.

* *

Frau Mueller hovers over the table as she serves *Brot*, presents the *Senf*, collects the soup bowl. Will the *Frau Professor* help herself to another serving of meat? Ruth shakes her head. She begins to stammer in German. She would like, oh she would like to talk to Frau Mueller. Frau Mueller has a motherly, tender face. She is large-boned and large-bodied, and behind this is a woman who has feelings, a woman who cares about others. Frau Mueller goes to the bar and brings a small pitcher of wine. The wine is local; it can be bought by the case directly from village distributors. The grapes have been harvested for centuries from the slopes surrounding the city.

They sit together, each drinking a glass of wine; they speak in low tones. Ruth's German improves as she sips at the wine. Frau Mueller munches on a piece of meat as she listens.

She was married, Ruth tells Frau Mueller. She *is* married. She *will be getting* married. She confuses her tenses. There is Taig. No, there is no Taig. For Taig died, his good lung having been destroyed by metastases. It is the reason she took the overseas job. Only for one year, she'd told herself. Now she would like to go home. *Heimgehen*. And the letter. She picks up the letter and shows it to Frau Mueller.

"Von Ihrem Mann?" Frau Mueller asks, wanting to help the *Frau Professor*, the *Frau Doktor*.

Ruth opens her purse, places the letter inside, closes the purse. The letter cannot be from Taig. It must be from Martin. Martin will want to come to Europe. He probably thinks he will have a free place to stay.

He must not come. *"Er soll nicht kommen!"* Ruth tells Frau Mueller. And the dreams, she wants to tell her of the dreams. How she pulls a book from the shelf, opens it to the centre pages, sees the face of Taig. How she wakes, perspiring; how she wakes holding fiercely to Taig and how his body withers until there is no one beside her.

There is a hush throughout the dining room. Ruth stands to leave. She feels dizzy, lightheaded. An inner ear problem? She does not know. She moves towards the door at the back of the café. Just before she enters the passage that leads to the stairway and the butcher shop, she turns to look behind her. There they are, the two old women in their crocheted collars; Herr Koch reading his papers; Herr Knopf drumming his fingers on the table; Frau Montag, who is thin and wispy; *Oma* and *Opa*, their hands in their laps. Everyone has finished the evening meal, but each is staring separately out through the window in the direction of the Golden Lion across the street.

The sky has changed; the night is darker. Laughter and noise can be heard, even through closed windows and doors. The light over the door shines back into the café, and Frau Mueller's diners sit, grey and golden, but mostly golden in that light. All tufts and whiskers and straight backs and stilled hands and silence.

The smell of flesh encircles Ruth when she is halfway up the stairs. She is never ready for the way it assails the front of the nostrils. She sucks a breath into the bottom of her lungs. Frau Mueller has followed her through the passageway, and looks up, sympathetically.

"*Schlafen Sie gut,*" she calls up after Ruth, because she can think of nothing else to say. "Sleep well."

"But the dreams," Ruth begins. "How can I sleep?" She switches to German. "*Die Trauben!*"

Did she say *Trauben* or *Träume*? The grapes or the dreams? Now, she is not certain. A look has crossed Frau Mueller's face, but Ruth has missed it, does not know what it means. The grapes or the dreams—what difference does it make?

Ruth continues up the stairs to her room. Frau Mueller is not certain of what she has just heard. She turns back to the café, wondering. Tomorrow, she will talk with her friend Frau Mohn, who will arrive with Trudi for the afternoon visit. Together, they will try to understand.

Scenes from a Pension

∞

Bridget is a large woman, tall, angular, even muscular. With cheekbones like hers, surely she has been called handsome at some earlier time in her life. She is one of those international people of indeterminate age who have no home, no relatives, no history. No one thinks to ask about her personal life because it is assumed that she has no such thing. It is rumoured, from time to time among the guests who come to the Pension, that she has made her way to Austria via England and Australia, having come to the mountains because jobs for English-speaking workers are so plentiful in the ski resorts and hotels. Large numbers of winter guests travel here from England or America or from pockets of expatriates in Europe that spring up from one place to another. There must be people to work at these resorts—people who can deal with English-speaking tourists and answer their multitudinous questions.

Actually, Bridget made her way here twelve years ago and New Guinea, not Australia, was her last stop. In any case, every year in late November she has come to this small Austrian village in time for the Early-Bird Ski Package, and here she has remained until the end of March. Where she spends the remaining months of the year, no one really cares. Except, perhaps, Maria and Maria's father-in-law, old Opa. They, respecting her privacy, do not ask, assuming that she takes her well-deserved

113

money (Bridget can easily do the work of three, and does) and disappears to a third-rate hotel in Southern France, or perhaps to the night kitchens of Venice, or even to the Cornish coast where she might take odd jobs until the winter season begins again. Maria has stopped asking if Bridget will be back next year; she knows that one day in late November a phone call will come from the tiny railway station, and Bridget will be there, waiting to be picked up.

This year when Bridget first returned, she saw that things had changed. For a day or two she worried that Maria might no longer need her. Maria's husband, Wolf, was killed in a hang-gliding accident during the summer, and as Maria had no forwarding address for Bridget, she'd been unable to let her know. Maria buried the handsome middle-aged man who had been her husband and Opa's son, and she and the old man, mourning together, through determination and despair, decided to carry on with winter business at the Pension. The death of Wolf did not alter the list of reservations. Maria freed a double room in the new extension built by Wolf, and moved herself to a single in the loft, nearer to Opa, in the older part of the house.

* *

Each day at six, Bridget rises, puts on a faded blue cleaning smock that hangs straight from her large-boned shoulders, and ties a handkerchief round her head, the knot showing at the front. Her hair is mostly blond, but occasional streaks of red *and* blond stick out through the kerchief. She wears black eye-makeup, applying it with an orangewood stick that was once given to her by a gypsy in a small village near the French-Spanish frontier. She knows how to hold the orangewood stick horizontally so that it disappears into the fold of her lower lids and slides out again, leaving her eyes miraculously intact.

Bridget is amused and delighted each day that she can perform this act—the gypsy taught her well—and she would be surprised if she were to recall the number of years she has stood before the mirror with this same stick in hand.

It is Saturday, changeover day. Last week's guests departed hurriedly in the early morning, and the new group is about to arrive. People will trickle in from all corners of the globe, between the hours of one and six, until every room is filled.

The German and his wife the Finn are first. Three American families follow—the Markhams, Featherbys and Dickinsons. The first two are military families who have been posted to a base in West Germany; the third, the Dickinsons, have flown from Kansas City to Munich and have reached the Tyrol in a rented car. Six children accompany these three couples. There are guests from previous years, as well. The Allenbys, for instance, an English couple in their fifties who come from the Isle of Wight. Mrs. Allenby is the kind of woman who tries to assuage her friends' sorrows by sating their stomachs. If your husband leaves you or your wife dies, you receive a pot of soup. If a parent wanders away from the old folks' home, a piece of pie. Last year, when Bridget caught her foot in a doorway, Mrs. Allenby gave her a tin of sour lemon drops.

Bridget looks over each of the groups in order of arrival. She watches them stretch stiffly after the long car journeys; she listens as they stick their noses into rooms, sniffing out shabbiness, commenting through their teeth. One thing she learned long ago: if you are a maid or kitchen help, people will talk in front of you as if you can neither see nor hear. Women are especially prone to do this. What a maid sees or thinks is discounted as if hers is not a mainstream human presence. This is a useful thing to know, though there are days when even Bridget has to ask herself if people actually see through her the way they let on they do, as they look past.

Maria does not take part in first-day greetings or room allot-
ments. She hovers behind the swinging doors of the kitchen,
leaving it to Bridget to sort out an endless list of headaches that
turn out never to be problems at all. Maria knows more English
than she allows, but claims it is insufficient to deal with the
rapid one-way flow of troubles that the guests themselves seem
determined to create.

"Do you sell beer?" will be the first question from the men as
they stumble from their cars, hitching up their trousers.
Bridget shows them to the kitchen refrigerator and initiates the
chit system, the honour system, and they write out their room
numbers at the top of each little pad.

"Do you have white toast for the children's breakfast?" the
women ask.

"How much are the tows? A guy told me this place where
you can get a deal on a week's pass for three different slopes."

"One of my bindings has snapped. Goddammit, Angela,
didn't you check these before I loaded them into the car this
morning? Where am I going to get these fixed?"

"Could we have a bigger towel, please, for the bath? There's
only a shower in the hall?"

"What time is dinner? Breakfast? Would you mind writing
out the hours? We don't want to miss any of our meals."

"You don't supply facecloths? But we didn't bring any. What
about American cigarettes—can we get those?"

Yes, it gives Bridget a headache—changeover day. A screeching headache by dinner time every Saturday night.

But it is Maria who soothes the guests in the evenings. Wearing fresh *Dirndl*, diamond knee socks and Austrian shoes with
golden buckles, she brings out her home cooking, carrying it to
each table herself. And not a guest has ever complained. Opa
and Bridget, behind the swinging door, grin and marvel at
Maria who can bring the tables to silence as she whirls through

the room with rustling skirt and steaming plate. Maria gives Opa a wink as she kicks the door shut behind her, coming into the kitchen, while Bridget, knowing that the meal is irreversibly underway, pours herself a three-finger gin and begins to clean the pots.

Opa and Maria are the only hardy survivors of two disparate families; they share a bond of toughness which holds them the more tightly as others they love have fallen away. Bridget becomes part of this during the winter months each year, a kind of third wall to the triangle. The three serve and clean, launder and cook, and fall to bed under the eaves, exhausted each night after the last guest has made unsteady progress up the stairs to bed.

x x

It is the Mighty Sabbath. As Bridget wakes, she thinks, with a wry distortion of face, that it might be as much a pain in the neck as changeover day, unless the skiers are fed and shooed out to the hills before they change their minds.

At six-twenty she taps on Opa's door until she hears the old man mumbling, reaching for his teeth. She slips downstairs to the kitchen, where she makes two large urns of strong coffee, the fragrance of which, as it drifts from first to third floor, summons the guests room by room. The aroma of coffee wakes Maria, too. Try as she might, Maria cannot manage to be first in the kitchen. Bridget and Opa think that Maria has enough to do looking after the accounts and the business; they wish her as much sleep as she can take from the long and thankless hours of the days and nights.

Before Maria comes down to the kitchen this Sunday morning, Opa and Bridget stand at the window looking out over the valley. The Pension has been built on a slope, dominated by the peak of Disappearing Mountain, which also dominates every village for thirty or forty miles in all directions. For a moment, as the two watch, the clouds that bury the face of Disappearing Mountain shift slightly in the wind; or perhaps they trick the observers into thinking they have seen the stark grey face of the old mountain that is just as quickly lost to them again, its uppermost profile invisible as before.

Opa has looked out at Disappearing Mountain since he was a child, and he knows that it reveals itself to few. Somehow, in the old man's mind, Wolf's death is linked to Disappearing Mountain, even though Wolf was killed on another peak in a nearby village to the south. Some evenings, after the dishes have been dried and put away, and when the tables have been set for morning, Opa sits in the kitchen rocker and cries. He cries for Maria who is alone, and he cries for himself because he believes that sons should bury their fathers, and not fathers their sons.

"Bridget, why you didn't wake me?" Maria asks as she hurries into the kitchen. But Bridget only grins, and hands Maria a mug of coffee.

They hear the first guests enter the dining room beyond the kitchen door—children's voices and a mother's firm direction. It is the one called Ruby, Bridget knows. Ruby Featherby. She and her husband, Brighton, had been first to dinner last night, as well. They had stationed themselves at a corner table at the head of which Ruby had placed herself. Brighton sat at her left, and the children faced the row of potted geraniums along the windowsill. From this position, Ruby took charge of the room as people drifted in. She introduced herself and Brighton over and over again (college sweethearts, she told everyone), urging people to give up their first names and their background cities, urging the group feeling, unity for the week they will share at the Pension.

Not all guests had responded in like manner. The German and his wife the Finn waved a hand in the air as if to wipe out their part in this unguarded familiarity, and chose a small table for two at the opposite side of the room where they spoke in low tones to each other and to no one else during the meal. Five of the six children protested with cries and complaints until they were given a table to themselves. This meant that Angela and Spence Markham, friends of the Featherbys, would now join Ruby and Brighton at their table. The other American couple, Harry and Shelby Dickinson, sat with their six-year-old son, Chippy, in the centre of the room. Shelby, although dressed in expensive sports clothes, looked drab and seemed to be unhappy. All of the Americans, Bridget had noticed, observing every detail from the kitchen, were in sock feet.

Now, at Sunday breakfast, on the stroke of seven, the door is pushed open and Maria, Opa and Bridget carry out baskets of rolls, pots of marmalade, coffee and eggs. The kitchen door, portent of cheer, reminder of Mother's blueberry pie, swings back and forth like the refrain of a lively tune everyone has on the tip of the tongue. Maria, watching her guests, marvels as she does every week, that several are already using first names, behaving as if they have known one another a lifetime. There are shouts between tables, laughter, challenges to be taken up later, on the slopes. The Markhams are telling everyone that they had a fight in the bedroom the night before.

"My Angela's a terror, I tell you," says Spence Markham, stroking at his jaw and with proud mockery in his voice. "Didn't you hear her take after me in our room last night?"

"But where," thinks Maria, "where are their real selves? It's as if they have all shot out from under one granny's apron." She wonders why, when they were children, they had never been taught to deal with their own pain. For if they give away their laughter so readily, must they not give away their sorrow as well?

Maria has difficulty these days keeping her own pain in

order, but she would not dream of behaving so publicly. Even the day the village men and their women came to tell her about Wolf, she kept her pain to herself.

She had been hooking a rug in her room—it was after the extension had been built—and she'd raised her head from her work to look out at Disappearing Mountain. To her surprise, the triple-peaked hulk suddenly shone forth in the sun, and was as quickly covered again in mist and cloud. She'd felt Wolf in the room. He had stood behind her in the doorway where she could not see him, and he said, "You are not to worry, Maria. You will be all right."

When the others came to her doorstep to tell her the news, she had already known what they had to say.

Bridget is refilling coffee cups, gritting her teeth as she passes the children's table, teasing the lanky Mr. Featherby.

"Don't you go and break a leg today, Mr. Featherby. With this rowdy bunch to look after."

A frown shadows Ruby Featherby's face at the mention of a broken leg. It is one of Ruby's trials that she cannot control the thoughts of disaster that hang uppermost in her mind: accidents involving Brighton and the children; burning cars from which they cannot escape; decapitations; drownings. It is an ill omen, she thinks, if anyone else comes the slightest bit close to guessing her thoughts of tragedy and horror.

The German and the Finn sit silently throughout breakfast. They are heavy, bulky people and are dressed in thick ski clothing, bracing themselves, it seems, for the day ahead.

The English couple is having problems with conversation, because Mrs. Allenby refuses to answer a question her husband thinks perfectly innocuous, even solicitous and kind.

"Did you sleep well, my dear?" is all that he has said, shaking out his table napkin. Now he keeps on at her under his breath. "Answer me, Georgie, talk to me. Never mind your silent act.

I've had enough of that. I know you can hear me. You damned well answer."

But Georgina will not; she is harbouring a grudge as she is wont to do, because the night before, when they had lain side by side, he had fallen asleep while she had been telling him her deepest and innermost feelings of regret about how her life has turned out. She has never had this conversation with him before. She'd had the whole long drive to think about her life (he had done all the driving; she had only to sit and stare out the window), and at night she chanced it, hopeful that the act of sharing her sorrows would also take them away. It was only after she cleansed herself of grief—even making up things as she went along, she'd been so caught up in her woes—that she realized, when he did not answer, that he'd been asleep throughout the most important revelation of her life. And now, at breakfast, he can't understand why she is angry.

Young Chippy Dickinson begins to raise his voice at the table, and his parents, heads lowered threateningly, try to hush him, but do not seem to know how to go about this in any practical, workable way. The two Markham children jab each other with fists, spill their orange juice, and then, breakfast is over. The tables empty; the guests run upstairs for toques and mittens, and grab their ski poles; the men huddle over coughing engines and frosted rear windows and drive out of the parking lot one after the other, heading for the ski school, where lessons begin punctually at eight thirty.

Opa stays in the kitchen to clean up while Maria and Bridget tug laundry baskets out from under the stairs. They begin the week's work, trying to create the illusion of neatness in rooms above. Rooms which, without exception, have been left in that macaronic state familiar to any of us who has spent days or weeks or months delving up to our elbows in suitcase laundry.

* *

By Friday, the guests at the Pension have been through their share of successes and mishaps. There have been individual glories on the hills, but the Pension can now account for one broken ankle (Mrs. Allenby), and one pulled tendon (Mr. Featherby). Chippy Dickinson cannot take his final ski lesson because of a slight fever; his mother, Shelby, has volunteered to stay behind so her husband can have a day to himself. Mr. Dickinson, embarrassed but cheered at finding himself detached from the usual responsibilities of family, winds several lengths of scarf about his neck and leaves in the morning, whistling.

Mr. Featherby begins to drink whisky about eleven in the morning and, by three, he is dragging his swollen leg up and down stairs looking for Bridget, who, he has learned, does not mind listening as he tags after her.

"There isn't a person who truly cares about me, Bridget," he says, sorrowfully. "Even the children side with their mother. Oh yes, they know where the power lies in this family. Truth is, my Ruby is a bitch, Bridget, in every sense of the word."

"Oh now, Mr. Featherby, you watch what you say," says Bridget, agreeing with him nonetheless. What she has seen in six days this week is enough to rot your socks and more. She doesn't wonder Mr. Featherby turns to drink whenever he can get away from his Ruby.

"She's all perfume and smiles on the outside," he says, "but behind closed doors she wields her power until she has the children and me gasping for breath. At home, she leaves notes for me everywhere: *Pick up after yourself. I asked you to clean the oven two weeks ago. When are you going to fix the lid on the mailbox? Keep your dirty socks in pairs or wash them yourself.* She puts No Smoking signs on the kitchen wall, and tapes them over the toilet roll in the bathroom. There are so many notes lying around at one time they depress even her because she's forced to read them herself."

Mr. Featherby starts down the stairs to sign out another shot of whisky. Bridget plugs in the iron and dabs at it with a finger of spit until she is satisfied with the sizzle and the smell. She pushes the iron back and forth, wondering vaguely if she should do something about Mr. Featherby. Maria is away for two days, having gone to Salzburg to visit a friend and to bring back supplies.

Mrs. Allenby is also in the Pension this day. She emerged tentatively from her room at noon, asking Bridget for a bowl of broth. No one has brought food to her, and she feels deserted and comfortless. She is still holding her grudge against Mr. Allenby and has been miffed most of the week, feeling that he is somehow responsible for her broken ankle, even though he wasn't on the same slope when she fell. Now, in a below-the-knee cast, she is confined to her room, reading and resting during the day, multiplying new grudges until the pre-dinner hour when the remaining healthy skiers return frozen-fingered to the Pension and sit together over a glass of wine or beer before dinner.

And what do the members of this group discuss as they rub at aching muscles, as they try to ignore significant and painful signs of the body's deficiencies? *Which of the duty-free airports in Europe stock Spence Markham's brand of pipe tobacco? Who are the worst drivers in the world—the French or the Turks? Do little red-haired girls really have fiery tempers? Which are the best topless beaches in France between the fourteenth of July and the twenty-eighth of August?*

Mr. Featherby returns to the landing, where Bridget is still ironing. He sets a glass of gin beside the heap of freshly folded linen, and raises his whisky to his lips.

"Come on, Bridget," he says. "We'll have one together. We'll drink to the merry day when men and women will be free to look one another in the eye and say 'Screw off,' when the going gets tough. Down the hatch, Bridget. You're a damned fine woman, and the hour for respectable drinking has descended upon the house."

"Ah," Bridget thinks, as she clinks glasses with Brighton Featherby, "why is it that the world is never just? Why does Opa rock himself to sleep in the kitchen chair every night with sorrow in his heart; why should Maria have to climb the stairs to an empty room, while Ruby Featherby makes her husband and children knuckle to her iron will?"

But Bridget has been called upon to witness her own behaviour often enough; it is not in her to pass long-term or serious judgment on others. For she knows that Brighton Featherby will in all likelihood carry out his wife's orders for the next twenty-five years, that Georgie Allenby will forgive her husband once her ankle bone mends, that Opa will suffer until the day he is laid to rest beside his son in the shadow of Disappearing Mountain, and that most other injustices of the world will never be rectified. She has known for a long time that the world does not turn the way decent men and women think it should, that evil often triumphs over purity and truth, that the power-hungry, the stupid, the self-righteous and the boring will always make themselves heard.

After the ironing is done, Bridget takes some prohibitive action. She locks the doors of the liquor cupboard against Mr. Featherby's invasion; she makes a pot of coffee, but even while she pours his cup, he sneaks up behind her and pats her on the bum. He tries to lay his head on her breast, but she sits with him at the bottom of the stairs while he drinks two cups of coffee, and she listens while he continues to talk about Ruby who, he tells her, was a nurse in her younger years—before the children.

"She was a surgical nurse, Bridget. She worked on a forty-bed ward and often came home at night telling me what it was like getting those poor souls ready to go under the knife. For years, I pictured her making rounds in the early mornings with a market basket over her arm, collecting false teeth and other prosthetic devices. *'Any glass eyes? Wooden legs? Dildos?'* I know that is probably not the way it was, but it always seemed that way to me. She's forty-two if she's a day, though she'd never admit it. But who, in this day of root canal and matched crown, would know how many teeth are her own and how many are cemented in?"

Brighton Featherby and Bridget enjoy a muffled and wicked laugh, despite the fact that Brighton's own wife is the target of the laughter. And now, Bridget thinks, even a little wistfully, if Mr. Featherby were not quite so drunk, she might consider going to bed with him. Yes, she has learned to keep worry and discontent at arm's length; they do not weaken and distract her as they once might have. She knows enough of her place in the world of survivors to act above regret, and to rise in the morning without lingering over past, present and future wounds. In other words, she can imagine herself sleeping with him, in perfectly good conscience.

* *

Mr. Dickinson is having trouble with Chippy before dinner. The six-year-old has humiliated his father in a full games room, and Bridget has come upon them in the first-floor hall. The two, father and son, are in sock feet, facing each other. Mr. Dickinson, not much taller than Chippy, leans over him, holding him by the shoulders. In an apologetic voice, he questions the child's behaviour.

Bridget thinks, for a moment, that Mr. Dickinson might be close to tears. Chippy had overturned the chess set when caught cheating, had flung the pieces at one of the Featherby children—his opponent—and had run out of the room. Cries of "He's a cheater, a cheater!" had followed him out.

"That's not sportsmanlike," Mr. Dickinson is saying in a soft voice. "Why did you do it, Chippy? Tell me why you act this way. Why did you do that in front of all those people?"

Bridget finds herself slipping between them, something she would never have done had she not finished a second three-finger gin. She feels sorry for Mr. Dickinson who is so meek himself, he cannot control his son.

"Never you mind about what the others think, Mr. Dickinson," she says. "Chippy has been cooped up here all day not feeling very well. I'll go in after dinner and pick up the chess pieces. You'll help me, won't you, Chippy?"

But Chippy is sullen and will not answer. Bridget, watching the father's face, says again, "Never mind now, Mr. Dickinson. There'll always be something to humble us, no matter who we are. A small item like this won't shake the world down around us."

But father and son stand staring at each other, heads bent, when Bridget leaves them. Mr. Dickinson needs an explanation.

In the absence of Maria, Bridget and Opa serve dinner. Bridget has removed her topknot; she has slipped on a gypsy skirt and black sweater, and has twirled the orangewood stick between her eyelids. The atmosphere in the dining room has changed tonight, perhaps because of Maria's absence, or Mr. Featherby's drinking, Mrs. Allenby's all-day grudge, or Shelby Dickinson's confinement in her room with feverish Chippy. Cheeks wear a pale edge where there should be a natural outdoor glow. Conversation develops as a series of hysterical lurches. It is the eve of departure, after all. Mr. Featherby enters the dining room with eyes blazing, feet tripping, his face at once defiance and challenge—a rare combination, given his marital rank. And there he is, passing the cheeseplate to his wife during a lull, speaking in a loud, sweet voice. "Have a little tightener, Ruby?"

The evening closes on a scene in the dining room. The Finn and German have eaten excessively and sign a chit for two *Underbergs*, which they take to their room in hopes that this will settle their stomachs. The Markham and Featherby children thump one another on the back as they scatter out of the room without a backward glance. Shelby and Harry Dickinson go to bed early, Shelby in meek and unexpressed frustration, Harry in guilt over having so enjoyed himself alone today, on the slopes. Chippy does not pick up the chess pieces, which now lie forgotten in the games room and can be seen in the firelight beneath the table and behind the legs of chairs. Mrs. Allenby has glared at Mr. Allenby throughout the meal, and resolves that her husband will pay for this, *this* being her broken spirit as well as her ankle. She looks forward to the long drive back to the Dover-Calais ferry, during which he will be captive at the wheel and will not dare to *not* listen to what she is now preparing to say. Angela and Spence Markham, in sock feet, have gone upstairs to pack.

Opa dries and puts away the dishes. Because Maria is still in Salzburg, he takes a half-full bottle of brandy from the liquor shelf, tucks it inside his shirt and climbs the back stairs to his room, where he will partake of a furtive and harmless binge. Before he rinses the toothbrush cup into which he will pour the brandy, he stands looking out at Disappearing Mountain and sheds the evening tears for his son.

But what of Ruby Featherby, Brighton and Bridget, below? What are they up to?

One overhead light illuminates a corner table in the dining room. These three unlikely companions are sitting, each with a glass in hand. And they are laughing, three parallel laughs.

Brighton laughs without purpose, because he is caught in that no man's land between drunkenness and sobriety, wantonness and fidelity, deliverance and bondage.

His wife's laughter is not so undirected. No fool she, Ruby is as capable as the next woman of sniffing out a challenge to the observance of marital rites which take place between the sheets and according to the self-proclaimed laws of matrimony. This is one area over which she will never release her grip, and though Brighton's drinking disgusts her, though she is exhausted from the slalom that carried on interminably all afternoon, though she will lie like a cool stone beneath Brighton when he climbs on top of her later in the night, she will stay by his side in the room until this person wearing the black eyeshadow removes herself to her own room. Ruby has seen through and looked past this temporary rival. She will defend her territory, despite her estimation of its present worth.

As for Bridget, she knows when trump has been pulled. She laughs because she can make things uncomfortable for a short time, and does. She laughs because, despite the obstacles, she and Mr. Featherby will carry a current between them to their separate rooms. But Bridget also knows that the most pressing problems at hand are that nineteen new guests will be arriving tomorrow between the hours of one and six, and Maria will have to be picked up at the station.

Messages

❦

Pauline was startled by the memory of Mae West swinging herself around. *"Liebling, Ich habe meine Schlüssel im Zimmer liegen gelassen."* *Darling, I've left my keys in my room.* This was hopeful—Pauline's first dream in German. The reruns on the 10-inch black-and-white were invading, but they were invading dubbed.

Pauline put her key on the ring, gathered up the garbage, and called for Maggie. Maggie had been learning about Japan at school and had borrowed Pauline's kimono to practise her *Geisha* kick. Since breakfast she'd been doing a high-speed shuffle around the dining-room circuit, her right foot making a side-stepping circle, followed by a quick below-the-knee thrust under the cloth. The extra folds of kimono, a foot longer than Maggie, were straightening out behind. Pauline would have laughed if Frau Becker hadn't been on her mind.

The past five weeks, when Frau Becker came to clean on Fridays, she'd been arriving with food. Not only had she been bringing food, she'd begun to ask for food. Last week she brought windfalls, a paper shopping bag full, bumping against the front fender of her bike. They'd been in her storeroom most of the winter and were shrivelled, almost dried. The week before that, *Torte*—Maggie called it a pie, Frau Becker's solid body shaking with laughter at the abruptness of the word—and before that, six brown eggs, the feathers of her dark hens stuck to the splotchy shells.

"*Butter,*" she'd said, the first time, to Pauline. "*Sie können mir Butter bringen.*" She'd even opened her change purse and had taken out two *Mark* seventy, and snapped it shut. She offered the coins with a quick glance into Pauline's face. "*Sie verstehen, Frau Stanton,*" she said. "*Sie verstehen.*" And yes, Pauline had understood. *German in 15 Easy Lessons* had been on her bedside table for six months and, anyway, who wouldn't have understood the word *Butter*. It was just that trading-off or even selling goods from the commissary was *Verboten*. She'd been warned by Richard's host family when she arrived. Once the villagers find out you have a NATO connection, look out. Coffee, butter, sugar—they especially want cigarettes and whisky, she'd been told. It always comes down to that, cigarettes and whisky.

But Pauline was the one who had to look directly into Frau Becker's face, the one who had to read what was behind her eyes. She pushed the hand back, and Frau Becker returned the coins to her purse. But before Frau Becker reached for the mop and chamois, she held three fingers up to Pauline, her order firmly placed: "*Drei Pfund Butter, bitte.*"

The following Friday, three packages of butter were tucked into the bicycle bag and the order given for the next week: *Schinken.* Frau Becker seemed to know that ham in the commissary that week was half the price of ham in the village store, though Pauline could not even think about how she got this information. The commissary was in the city and Frau Becker did not go to the city. She did not speak one word of English—except to say to Maggie, "Byeee-Byeee," as she left each Friday at four. The rest of the time, she muttered through her work, always muttering, as if telling herself stories. Stories related in dialect that Pauline could not or was not intended to know.

As for Pauline's German, she was not able to struggle through complicated explanations such as the reasons *why* commissary purchases were *Verboten. Es tut mir leid. Ich verstehe nicht,* she could say, as her book had taught her. *I'm sorry. I don't understand.* But Frau Becker's head, with the grey-blond bun pinned tightly behind, gave the nod each week when she placed her order: *You understand.*

* *

Pauline stood for a moment by the radio. Maggie had set the dial to short wave, trying to satisfy her longings for her own language. Pauline turned the knob, catching a German voice speaking English, a woman's voice: "Ninety-five pair-cent said they pray-fair-red blon-dis." Then it was gone. Lost in a garble of static and tongues and retorts.

Pauline left the key under the lantern for Frau Becker, helped Maggie with her jacket, and together they wheeled the outdoor garbage container to the curb. She thought of Mae West, one hand on her hip, the other holding out her bathroom waste to the garbage collector: *"Come on back, honey. I think you've forgotten my garbage this time."*

* *

Their skates were in the back of the car. The rink was located at the edge of the city, a twenty-minute drive. An indoor rink and a good thing, too, as the air was unsettled today. Pauline was becoming used to the chill, the snowless winter. Already, and this was February, the farmers were burning off the feathery growth of last year's asparagus. But something wild could be smelled—the wind, perhaps. It suspended holding-patterns of dust over long black mounds in the fields. Perhaps it was a storm, unseen, about to move down into the valley in a horizontal dark line.

Grades three and four from the International School would be skating; Pauline was a parent helper. The school would be closed in the afternoon, so she would bring Maggie back home with her and stop at the commissary on the way. *Kaffee*, this week. Three half-kilo packages. Never so much asked for that Pauline could protest, not really. Still, she imagined a pantry shelf in Frau Becker's tiny farm bulging with North American staples that Pauline herself was providing. A thought flashed through her mind, not for the first time. What if Frau Becker was selling these items to the villagers? She bit hard on her bottom lip. This was paranoia. For those few things. Richard, though—she should have told Richard. In any case, it was going to stop. She would hand over the coffee that afternoon and firmly say: *Nicht mehr. Ich kann nicht.*

Wasn't Frau Becker well paid? Hadn't Pauline agreed to the exact hourly wage Frau Becker had requested that first day when she'd propped the old bike beside the rosebushes and stood expressionless in the doorway, waiting to be hired? Hadn't Pauline been more than fair? The eyes of Frau Becker seemed to be fixed on her from the windshield, and Pauline had to blink and shake her head to keep the car from being towed into the fast lane and the lunatic speed of the *Autobahn*. She hoped Frau Becker would arrive today without food. It would make it easier to say: *Ich kann nicht.*

* *

The rink was crowded with busloads of children from international and German schools. Although the loudspeaker blared instructions to skate in one direction, three or four skaters darted against the solid oval rush, which glided like a heavy murmur. Rock music, instructions again, more music. *The rules.* Pauline never entirely felt that she knew *the rules* in this country. Blasted over loudspeakers in rinks, posted on fences at outdoor pools, welded to locker doors at indoor stadiums. It was she who barged into change rooms from the wrong side, and was chased back by custodians; she who emerged wearing boots where only bare feet were permitted; she who entered turnstiles through the *Exit*; who forgot to bring her market basket to stores that did not provide bags; who pulled out the wrong currency in lineups at the *Bäckerei*; who did not know the word *Öl* at the gas station. It was she who, with Maggie beside her, had walked across village fieldroads with a present for their landlord's new baby and, when the door was opened and they were greeted, blurted out, *"Ein Gift, fürs Baby,"* not knowing until she dug out the pocket dictionary on the way home that *Gift* was the word for poison. ("Why didn't the mother invite us in to see the baby? Why?" Maggie kept asking. "I could see its crib across the kitchen. You didn't say anything awful, did you? Did you?") The door having shut slowly, in their faces.

* *

When all of the laces were tied and mittens pulled onto small hands, Maggie and her Grade Three friends entered the stream of skaters and formed a chain on the ice. The music was fast; several older teenagers were twisting in and out at high speeds. Pauline watched from the boards and stepped down onto the ice just as the music was about to change—probably the direction, too. The instruction to change direction was shouted out at that very moment, as if Pauline had thought it through the loudspeaker. The ribbon of skaters wavered, was about to buckle, and executed a surprisingly graceful about-face.

Pauline skated the oval twice and was rounding the curve for the third time, when out of the corner of her eye she saw a tall youth go down. A speeding skater had darted close to him at the far end of the rink. The youth was bigger and taller than the hundreds of school children on the ice and, when he fell, Pauline noted four things (remembering these later, much later): how far he had to fall because of his height; that his legs had been moving awkwardly; that he was not wearing a helmet—German children did not wear helmets at the rinks, whether they were beginners or not; that he went over backwards, his head being the first part of his body to strike the ice.

When her blades brought her to the end of the rink, she bent over the boy; the small group around him made way as she kneeled beside his head. The music had switched to a waltz; the skaters carried on. But the boy—he was sixteen or seventeen—was convulsing violently, his back an arc, his legs and arms spastic, saliva oozing from the side of his mouth, his head rising and falling from the ice. And the most terrible thing. A click, a regular clicking sound was coming from some deep part of him. The children who were bunched around seemed poised in terror. Two adults circled close and went back to their skating. Pauline held the boy's head and shoulders gently in her arms until the terrible writhing and clicking—which seemed to go on for minutes—was over.

"*Bitte*, a stretcher, an ambulance!"

She was shouting. If he'd been with friends, they had disappeared. If he was with a school, no teacher arrived. The boy was unconscious, it seemed, but began to stir.

"You must not move," Pauline told him softly, knowing he could not understand but that he would stay as he was.

A man wearing a navy windbreaker, shoes, no skates, slid over from the nearest gate. He was smoking a cigarette, looked at the boy, looked at Pauline, shook his head. He called out behind him and two young men brought a stretcher onto the ice. As Pauline kept the head and neck straight, they lifted the boy and transported him to a sparsely equipped First Aid room.

"Ambulance," Pauline said again. "Please call an ambulance." The man in the windbreaker waved an arm. Yes, yes, the *Krankenwagen* was on the way.

And that was that. No one stayed. No friends inquired. Only Pauline talking softly as the boy made confused attempts to move his arms, his legs, to raise himself from the stretcher. The two were alone in the room.

Maggie's face appeared in the doorway. "Mom, is he all right? Did the boy die when he fell?"

"Oh, Maggie, I hope he's okay. He had a bad fall. Can you wait for me on the benches? I'll come for you as soon as the ambulance gets here."

But when the ambulance came, she could not make the attendants understand about the convulsion.

"A head injury. It's important. He fell." Her hands pointed to the boy's head. There was not so much as a drop of blood; there was nothing to see.

She mimed the fall. Felt with her fingers for a lump. "The doctors must be told about the convulsion."

The boy was lifted into the ambulance; faces were blank; no one spoke English. They spoke in words and tones Pauline could not decipher; they spoke as if Pauline were not there.

"Convulsion!" She did not know the word. "*Es ist wichtig!* It's important!" But there was no dictionary in her bag this day; she'd wanted to be free of extra weight at the rink. She tore a piece of paper from a gauze wrapper and wrote: *Convulsion. Lasted more than 1 minute.*

"Give this to the doctor," she said.

One of the men looked at the paper, looked at her and shoved it into his pocket.

* *

As she drove home with Maggie, Pauline could see that the fires in the asparagus fields were no longer burning. Leaves, branches, clumps of black earth were scattered wildly across the road. The streets were dry; there had been no rain. Something had happened here that had not happened in the city.

The groceries and Frau Becker's three packages of coffee were in the trunk. Pauline had bought lunch for Maggie in the city, but she herself had not been hungry. The clicking noise from the boy had gone deep inside some part of her and her head seemed to move round and round with the sound, in the way that the skaters had waltzed on and on silently after the music had stopped. She pulled into the driveway. The garbage container was back in place and Frau Becker's bike was propped beside the rosebushes. An agitated Frau Becker met them at the door. She laughed to see "Mag-gee" home early, but began to speak rapidly as if an event of the greatest importance had taken place. Her bulk filled the doorway as she waved closed fists, up the street, down the street, into the air, patterns whirling over her head, the words *Wind* and *Mall* and *Damen-binden* repeated again and again. She had an urgent story to tell, a story Pauline could not understand.

But what was the smell? The door shut behind them as they entered the house. Pauline's nostrils filled with the tight stench of something cooking, steaming. Blood, meat, some combination that had never before consumed the air of the house. Maggie pulled in close.

"*Schweine,*" Frau Becker said, and nodded with satisfaction as she saw Pauline sniff the air. Her first story merged with her second, as she led them to the kitchen stove and lifted the lid off the bucket.

"*Suppe,*" Frau Becker announced, and watched Pauline's face. She held up her index finger and slid it across her throat. "*Schweine!*" she said again through the steam, and Pauline knew then that the village pigs had been slaughtered and here was blood soup in her kitchen to prove it. *Suppe* that must have been held at arm's-length while Frau Becker steered her bike with one hand through the village streets.

But now Frau Becker had returned to her first story again, and she was lifting the net curtains in the kitchen. She made whirling patterns through the air with her fists. She wrung her hands as if to convey something personal, something tragic.

"*Damenbinden*," she said, her face now flushed and severe. She lifted her chin in an accusing way towards Pauline. "*Ihre Damenbinden, Frau Stanton.*"

And Pauline received the knowledge the way she experienced all revelation from the German language, in an explosive and penetrating rush. Used sanitary pads—*her* sanitary pads — whirling through furious winds that must have lifted them from overturned garbage, the paper that wrapped them unravelling as they flew. The image tore into her. Frau Becker running behind and beneath, catching *Damenbinden* as they fell, picking them up as the wind strewed them across orderly German lawns. Frau Becker removing silent messages from the foreigner that punctuated the street in bloody dots like static over the short wave.

Pauline paid the housekeeper, thinking, *I might laugh and laugh and laugh.* She followed her to the door and tucked three packages of coffee into the bicycle bag and nodded silently as she heard the order placed for the following week.

"*Whisky*," Frau Becker said, her eyes fixed on Pauline. For hadn't she looked after Frau Stanton's most private affairs? Had she not chased the foreigner's bloody *Damenbinden* through the streets?

"Byeee-Byeee," said Frau Becker as she lifted her large body onto her bike. Pauline stood at the door until the housekeeper turned the corner, and she choked back something that was rising inside her.

"Go to the garage, Maggie, and get the spade," she said. "Bring it round to the back garden."

Pauline returned to the kitchen and lifted the bucket from the stove. Holding the stench of *Schweine* at arm's-length, lid on, she carried the soup through the house and down to the back garden. *I'm going to laugh and laugh and laugh,* she told herself again.

But after Maggie had dug the hole, after they'd poured the blood soup, a cloud of steam lifting to their faces as hot brown liquid splashed to cold winter earth, Pauline found that she could not stop crying. She held Maggie's hand in the tightest grip and her shoulders shook and the sobs came from the deepest part of her, and she could not keep herself from crying.

Accident

In the dream, she is lying by the side of a field. It is autumn in this country. A hawk sits tensed and alert on a topmost branch. The asparagus has begun to turn, and the plants are overgrown, tall and feathery. Fields and fields of asparagus, colours like Cézanne landscapes, blends of gold and orange and green. If she focusses intently, she can see clusters of sharp red berries.

The sky is clouding over. One moment, the asparagus is tossing and shining in the sun. A moment later, all is still, dull, damp. A coldness sets in. In the slightest breath, the smell of winter.

The hawk swings up to the sky. Margo has seen the white car resting on its flattened roof before she has crawled along the dirt and stones at the edge of the road. Now, she lies on her back and watches the hawk hover high above her.

* *

There are foreign voices all around. But no. *She* is the foreigner. She is a traveller in this country. German voices. She understands some of the words that are spoken.

"*Scheisse!*" Shit! This from the doctor who cannot get the intravenous started. But why? She has always had good veins.

She hears the helicopter blades. Is she in a helicopter? She flexes her hand to make a fist; the rubber tourniquet has been knotted on her upper arm. The German doctor has a black moustache, black eyes. Is this possible?

* *

In the dream, she is swimming. At first the water is cool, but she feels no shock. If anything, she is relaxed, refreshed. She is able to dip off the edge and slip in smoothly. Someone is resting on the bank behind her—Simon? She is not certain who it is, but she knows it is someone who is able to calm her.

The river is narrow, with only the slightest current. Her arms pull back in an easy crawl. She raises one arm and sees that it is blanketed with caterpillar-like drippings from trees. She remembers the colour—a furry yarn-like yellow. This does not alarm her.

In the dream, she leaves the riverbank. Just as naturally, she finds herself dressed in something long and soft, shroud-like, but soft. Several people stand around her—friends. All of them are ushered into a theatre, and they edge along the aisle as the curtain is about to rise. Margo opens her program, a double sheet. The director of the play is unknown to her. She reads that the title of today's performance is *Pain*.

* *

Who is this, digging stones out from beneath her back? One large stone—or so it seems—is pressing into her upper spine, the very place she knows she is injured. "Can they not get the stone?" she cries, knowing at the same time that someone is already trying; someone is pawing and clawing, the way one imagines a dog to dig for a deeply buried bone. She is lifted then, by four men who keep her body unnaturally straight.

* *

In the dream, the doctor stands at the side of her bed. Her pill bottle is on the bedside table. He removes the lid, turns the container upside down. A single pill rolls out. The doctor picks it up, smiles, takes it with him as he turns to leave.

"That is for my pain!" she shouts.

He doesn't hear. The door swings behind him.

* *

The mattress has been inflated and packed tightly around her body. She cannot remember anyone doing this. The mattress conforms closely to the contours of her head and shoulders. She is lying on a bed of the finest sand. The mattress squeezes at her temples until her head aches. Simon is there, leaning over her, holding the hand that is free of the intravenous. He kneels and kisses her on the cheek. She sees that the green of his jacket is the same as that of the asparagus waving above them. His eyes hold something she has not seen there before—hesitation? fear? German voices urge him away. She is being lifted onto the stretcher and into the ambulance. Simon's voice is saying, "I thought I might lose you." This has not been easy to say. "There was a moment," he says, "when I thought I might lose you." He points to his chest where the seatbelt had held him, and he tries to smile.

Will she see him again? She does not feel fear and is not worried about seeing him or not seeing him. Voices are humming and buzzing around her. A solution drips steadily into her vein from a pouch hooked to the ceiling of the ambulance.

* *

In the dream, someone has died. In another car, another man she will never have to see. His photograph is in the newspaper. Beside the inset, a photo of two cars: the white one on its roof, the other on its side. Could *she* have crawled away from this twisted carcass? Away from the sickening crunch of metal, the sound of which she shall never now escape?

She did.

But when she translates the caption, she tries to understand why it informs that *two* have died. She peers into blurred edges of the black-and-white photo, trying to see who could be trapped in that wreckage. She knows that she had kicked and clawed at the door, over and over again, with her hands and her right foot.

* *

How is it possible to breathe?

She takes rapid shallow breaths. Someone has been sent to her ward from a department below. Someone has come to frighten her. A woman smelling of cigarettes recently smoked. A heavy-boned blond. Perhaps this woman has been chosen because she can speak English. Perhaps she has come because she wears the ability to frighten on her face. She tells Margo to sit up; she listens to Margo's breathing, front, then back. She dangles a stethoscope from her right hand, jams it into the pocket of her lab coat.

"If you do not deeper breaths take," she says, "in one day, perhaps two, you will the pneumonia have."

* *

In the dream, the dead man appears. He walks into Margo's room. In her sleep, she hears him. He is barefoot. His footsteps halt at the left side of her bed. He leans over and pushes down on her chest. She tries to lie on her right side but he pushes where it hurts the most. The ribs give and sway and crack under the weight of him. When he has hurt her enough, he turns to leave.

"Simon," she cries out. "Simon! Was he here just now? The dead man?"

But there is only the answer of silence.

* *

Sometimes Margo thinks of the German doctor, of his hands. Whenever she thinks of him, it is always of his hands. He knows the importance of touch. He pats her arm, holds an ankle, a foot; touches her back as he pulls her to a sitting position. The laying on of hands. When he leaves, she lies propped against pillows that immobilize her ribs and support her neck. She sits with her eyes open, hoping for sleep, or obliteration, knowing that neither will come.

* *

In the dream, she and Simon are visiting the catacombs of Salzburg. They must stand in line in the graveyard at the foot of Mozart's sister's tomb. In a murky drizzle, a clump of visitors waits for the guide to emerge from dank hills and secretive chapels carved from the labyrinths of the hill. Graveyard attendants are clearing tangled shrubs and bushes, but the work they are doing makes no difference to the appearance of the place. It is overcrowded with stones, weather-torn and pock-marked; old candles tipped by the wind; melted wax that has clotted; withered and tattered wreaths. Margo leaves Simon to stand in line while she wanders along the row of tombs. In a far corner of the cemetery, death is depicted on nearly every stone as either a skeleton or a partial skeleton. Sometimes it is a hooded and bony creature bearing a long- or short-handled scythe. The Grim Reaper, harvesting. This is death's job, it seems.

* *

She tries to recall the car on its roof, herself lying on her back on the road, the hawk. Is she looking death in the eye? Not at all. There is only one thought. "My chest is crushed," she says to the waving asparagus. *My chest is crushed.* Thinking nothing but that. The rest is beyond her. Out of her control.

* *

Margo is lying in the hall, waiting for someone to push her stretcher. Every bone in every part of her body, except hands and feet, has been x-rayed. Now, her lungs must be checked again. A young man stands beside the stretcher. Waiting. Smiling a bland smile. An orderly? A technician? How is she to know? She tells him she does not like the *victim position.*

"It's the one position I've never wanted or liked," she says, looking up at him.

The young man nods agreeably and points to his tongue. Is he mute? Does he not speak English? Margo is never to know.

* *

In the dream, she is walking on a beach. It is a familiar and friendly place of sky, waves and sand. She approaches an empty canvas chair, the seat of which is flapping in the wind. The chair has been set at the extreme edge of shore; water laps at its collapsible wooden frame. Each time she tries to sit, the canvas seat blows upward and turns inside out. She pushes the canvas down and tries to climb in from the side, awkwardly, because she now realizes that she is carrying an armful of papers and these represent a play. It is a play that someone has been working on for a long time. She is forced to make a choice. She lets the papers go and sits in the chair, because she has needed two hands to negotiate the flapping canvas. The play—it is a play about her life, she realizes, too late—flies out over the water, the pages scattering and bouncing towards open sea.

* *

In the accident, there is no cry. Margo turns her head and sees the car as it flies out from behind the asparagus bushes. Before it hits, she has time to think only this: *It can't be avoided.* The crunch she hears is thorough and complete. As thorough as two trains hitting head-on, seizing in an abrupt and unnatural halt. There is no vibration of metal. No wave of jagged fender. Only stillness follows. While one part of her believes that both vehicles are at rest, her eyes watch the other car as it turns in the air in spectacular revolution. Over and over, a child's toy flipped carelessly from the edge of a table. Over and over it rolls and, in slow motion, rocks gracefully on its roof.

She gropes for her seatbelt. Thinking, *My hand moves, my arm moves.*

"No!" she says.

"No!" say the other voices. "No!"

As she watches the ascent of smoke from the hood, she begins to claw, kick, batter at the door. It swings out as though there has been no connection between the desperation of her efforts and the door's sudden release.

She bends forward, and feels a sharp pain in her spine. She is short of breath. Her fingers touch her neck and come away red and wet. She lies on her back on the edge of the road, again watching the smoke; she raises herself slightly and crawls farther away. She wakes in her room and hears the sea. Hears the voices, hears the man, the dead man whose face is masked by a dull streak of light. His face is small, as if it has been scrunched. He is angry and twisted and terrible. He makes a move towards Margo. But when she stares at him with eyes wide, the back of his head blurs, and he turns and vanishes. Her heart pounds. Drums through her chest wall. She sits up.

"Simon!" she calls, and looks everywhere in the room. "Simon! Was he here just now? The dead man?"

There is no one to grab. No one to tell. There is only the answer of silence.

Touches

You know you've been led to a table in the annex, the closed-in veranda, because you are alone. It's not so bad, really. You prefer this to the dining room into which you can look back from an inner window beside your table. The outer windows allow a view of the grounds, the river, the uneven hill, a thicket beside three very old trees, the trunks of which you'd never be able to wrap your arms around.

There are two men in the annex, each at a single table in this narrow veranda; places have been discreetly set so that their backs are presented to you. You can only guess at their faces. This is fine with you. You've come here to be alone.

The dining room is half-filled—it's off-season—and from time to time you glance up from your meal to look back in through the open window. It's easy to overhear conversations because most of the occupants of the dining room are elderly, and speak in loud voices. You, who are half their age, assume that hearing is a problem.

By far the loudest of these is Bert, whose name you've been forced to learn. Bert not only has a hearing problem, he has misplaced his reading glasses. He glares across the room directly at you, as it turns out, while his wife reads aloud tonight's menu. You and everyone else in both annex and dining room must now listen to the naming of each item, followed by Bert shouting it back to his wife.

"Beef?"

"NOT BEEF."

"Sautéed veal?"

"I don't like that. You know I HATE EEL."

"Mexican shrimp?"

"Yes! That's what I'll have. PEMMICAN SHRIMP."

There is another couple at Bert's table, fellow travellers, the silent kind, suffering. Probably from Bert's behaviour. You know a suffering face when you see one. Your entire professional life so far has been spent with sufferers.

You ban this thought from your head and pull a paperback from your shoulder bag, *The Beginning of Spring,* by Penelope Fitzgerald. You like this book because it's about a hearty Russian family and the unsealing of the windows in spring. All the dreary winter, the promise of unsealing the windows is held before an assortment of rowdy characters through a complicated series of entanglements. You hope that at the end of the story, everyone, including you, will experience the thrusting open of heavy panes of glass in stifling rooms, that everyone will feel the rushing in of spring.

Bert is now roaring at his wife: "I don't see one thing funny about your joke. Not one thing!" His face contorts in anger and he glares at his wife and then at you, because he sees you looking. He leaves his table and stomps out of the dining room. You tell yourself he's an old poot, you've met plenty, that you and everyone else will probably have to listen to him all week because you all have better manners than he does.

* *

You like your second-storey room, though it's at the side of the lodge, a less-than-choice location. The water is visible only as flashes of blue through the trees. An oak presses against your window; its leaves are green and new and large, but they have a touch of red, too, as if they might deceive and turn into fall maples, instead. It's early June and you smell river. There is a weedy bank, a dock, an ancient smell you know well. It's the smell of underwater, of rock unturned, of fish and weed and riverbank, all mingled together.

You think of Louisa, who is the same age as your Zoe, seven. Louisa, of the tiny boned face and the beautiful name. You approach slowly, though you have known Louisa for months; you sit next to her in a room at the Children's Aid. Louisa's pupils dilate, ready. You watch some part of her scurry inside herself. After a few moments, after listening to your voice, she lifts your hand and holds it between her own small palms as if she is the adult and you are the child. She lets your hand drop, nods her head wisely and says, "I don't think I'll talk about *that*." She gets up from her chair and goes to the window. She seems to be humming, humming behind closed lips. When she turns, her pupils are normal again. You think, *Okay, good*. A tiny, if imperceptible, gain.

Later, you go to a place provided by the court where you meet Louisa's mother, and you have a long session with her. When you return to your office, Becky, who is also a psychologist, brings you a cup of strong tea and walks you three times around the block. You and Becky are honed to rescue each other, to recognize each other's breaking point. Becky is your closest friend. Sometimes you say to her and she to you, mocking each other, "Identified the problem yet, dearie?" And you both laugh, grimly. So many problems are spilled out over the two of you, day after day.

* *

You wonder why you've come to this lodge alone. Answers rise up easily: no holiday for over a year, caseload too heavy; space, you need space away from Alec and Zoe. You see Alec standing in the doorway at home. "I know you have to go," he says. "It's only for a week," you say. You bend forward to kiss Zoe, who stands beside Alec. She's wearing her yellow trousers and top and she looks like a buttercup and you feel like hugging her and hugging her and crying out that the world is not safe, be careful, for God's sake, take care, there's a whole world out there you know nothing about. But you kiss her and walk away calmly, even though your foot shakes over the pedal as you back the car out of the driveway. You will yourself, force yourself, to drive smoothly away.

* *

Bert shouts to his wife, but clearly he is aiming his voice at you. "That girl has been alone at her table ever since she got here!" You are a cast in Bert's eye. You, the thirty-seven-year-old girl, glance up from your book long enough to stare at Bert, eye to eye. The other three at his table murmur soothing remarks to calm his outburst.

"Why don't you invite her over," says Bert's wife, "if you're that concerned."

Through the annex window, you hear his arguments as he backs down. Sometimes people want to sit alone, not like him, he says. Nosirree, he likes company, though he can be with himself for a little while. He musters his anger and shouts in your direction, "At least I'm not anti-social!"

* *

The loons call out in the early evening and don't stop until long after dark. You listen from your second-storey window. You can hear young women in the kitchen below, the reassuring sounds of backroom life that keep the place going. Dishes are scraped, cleaned, put away. Potatoes peeled, vegetables chopped for the next day. A screen door slaps and an older woman's voice yells, "Where do you think you're going?" Next, there is the sound of a young man entering, a different sort of sound; the women's voices change. After that, a water fight. Laughter, more laughter and you find yourself smiling, upstairs in your tiny room. Amidst the laughter, the women eject the man from the kitchen.

You and Alec laugh like this sometimes. The thought presses in, the way the oak scrunches against the screen at your window.

* *

Every morning before breakfast, you walk along the river. You draw in the mixed scent of late spring and early summer. In the woods, there are birds: a woodpecker you hear every day but cannot see; baby robins, long-tailed swallows, geese straggling back towards their feeding grounds.

You hear Becky's voice. "Identified the problem yet, dearie? Would a fast walk help? A wailing wall? A hair shirt?"

A rest, you answer, inside your head. Only a rest. That's all.

When you return to the lodge, an elderly couple is sitting on one of the benches along the river path. They see you, but they're so immersed in argument, they don't care. The man shouts at his wife, who is close beside him, wrapped in her cardigan. "I want you to PROMISE me—on the Bible—that we won't FIGHT." The woman wheedles, cajoles, cannot be heard. She seems familiar with this role, does not object to the way he bullies her. He shouts again, discounting your presence, your ears. "Let me finish for Christ sake. PROMISE me we won't FIGHT!" You've not seen this couple before. They probably eat during second sitting in the dining room. You never see them again.

* *

At lunch, Bert resumes his childlike rule over the table. "What do I like?" he says. "I like onions, green onions. And radishes. I can eat radishes. But I can leave them alone, too."

He lists every vegetable he can think of, a long list that represents Bert's lifetime. It's as if what Bert's bowels can or cannot digest, past and present, is not only the loudest but the most interesting list anyone has ever heard. "I'm a fast eater, too," he says. "I've always been one to clean right up."

"This is our holiday," says Bert's wife, as if the very mention of vegetables does not belong here, at the lodge.

All of the diners at all of the other tables have run out of conversation at the same time.

* *

You think of the last holiday at the Children's Aid, the Valentine party. You and Becky are at the party with other staff members, to help, to observe, to supervise games. You marvel as you watch the girls, watch the eight-year-olds dress and act as if they're sixteen. Makeup, long flashy earrings, high heels— these are not dress-ups. The girls are spirited as they tap deliberate messages in spiked heels, as they stride across the wooden floor and make too-frequent trips to the washroom. Becky, who knows what you're thinking, comes up behind you and says, "Who *buys* these shoes? Do the kids actually wear these to school?" You're both thinking, yes, they probably do.

The girls show off; they're in competition for attention from their case-workers, from you, from Becky, from the *boys*.

Louisa is at this party. She sticks to your side most of the time. You've told Becky, a long time ago, months ago, "This child is old."

An extra is needed for a team game, and Louisa's name is called. Her head goes down bluntly. Her eyes film. An older girl—older?

she might be nine instead of seven—calls out protectively, "Leave Louisa out, her father did gross touches to her. She doesn't feel like playing yet." The others, boys and girls alike, nod, knowing what *that* means. Nothing could have stopped the remark, no one could have pulled it back. It's the language these ancient abused children live and know. When the party food is served, Louisa joins the others, laughing, reaching past shoulders and heads. Everyone is a little greedy, a little grabby. For a few minutes, over pink frosting and ice cream, you are fooled into believing that they could be a group of normal kids.

* *

Zoe comes home from her Grade Two class, walks in the back door and sets down her schoolbag. "Today we learned SEX," she announces. "The teacher read the same book we have at home. The school nurse was there, too. We learned how babies are made."

"Did you now?" you say, and grab her close for a hug.

Zoe pulls back so she can watch your face. "You know that time you and Dad made me," she says, "when he had to put his penis in you? Well, when he put it inside you, did he burst out laughing?"

You and Alec *clutch* each other in laughter over that. Behind your closed bedroom door. Later, several weeks later, Zoe tells you—again she waits until the two of you are alone—"I'm never going to let any man put his thing in *me*."

She looks really miffed at the idea.

There's no answer to that, you safely decide.

* *

Every day, you walk farther and farther from the lodge. You've met the dogs on the farms, and when you're in the woods you're not afraid of bears. A humming sort of heat has descended; a profusion of dragonflies and bees, of poison ivy, thick along the edge of the dirt road. There are strawberry plants and even honeysuckle, which you've not seen for a long time.

You are as silent as you hope to be.

You think of Alec. Now that you are away, you can't keep yourself from tallying up. You know that the two of you can live together for months, asking nothing except that each is there for the other. It's as if you truly believe that marriage, life, is that simple.

Then, some urgent need for discord rears itself, gnaws up the side of you, takes form in the shape of impatience, irritation, anger.

High tide and low.

Alec always wants to wait things out. As if time is on his side, as if you both have all the time in the world. You—you admit this to yourself—want to delve to the heart; you want to *identify the problem*. But just as quickly as it has dissolved, peace reasserts itself. Fingers reach across a desert sheet. A cold toe brushes against a bare leg. You are learning, and so is Alec. In your separate system of beliefs, you are learning to leave alone what must be left alone, that debris will always be present, waterlogged beneath the surface.

* *

Louisa says she would like to move into your house and live with you. You cannot adopt her, bring her into your circle of safety, though you would if you could. Louisa has a home, whatever it might be. Louisa's mother watched Louisa's father when he did gross touches. She was forced to; some part of Louisa doesn't know this. Now, Louisa's father is not allowed to be in or near the apartment building where Louisa and her mother live. Louisa tells you that he will be arrested if he puts a toe on the grass in front of the building. You continue to see Louisa twice a week, but that is all you can do.

* *

You enter the dining room. Bert is waiting. He sees that you are carrying a book, a different one this time. He shouts out as you cross the room to get to the annex, "What does she come here for, to READ?" You stick in Bert's craw like the bone in the wolf's throat. No one at his table can explain you. "Why don't you ask her why she comes here," says Bert's wife. But he does not. Instead, he complains loudly and bitterly throughout the meal. You ask yourself if the men of his generation were born angry.

Becky has a theory that entire generations of men have been brought up to believe it's their divine right to be listened to. She's put in her years, she says, of listening to opinionated men. Once a month, you and Becky go out for dinner after work. One night, in a Vietnamese restaurant, behind a paper screen, she tells you about her first husband, Dirk. Dirk comes home drunk one night—two thirty in the morning—and chases her out of their bed, out the back door, past the blackberry bushes and around the outside of the house, trying to have sex with her. "I know my rights!" he shouts as he chases. He is running with a hard-on, Becky says. "I know my rights!" he calls after her. It's easy to get away from him, because he's drunk. Eventually Dirk falls down on the grass and goes to sleep right there. It is not long after that, Becky says, that she leaves him.

Becky is married now to a man named William, a soft-spoken, gentle man. You wonder if William has anger in him; if so, you've never seen a sign of it. You wonder if William knows the story of Dirk shouting, "I know my rights!" It's a story that causes you and Becky to collapse in laughter whenever either of you mentions it, although you both know that the story isn't really funny.

* *

You have one more night at the lodge. You've read a book every day, and you feel as if you've walked hundreds of miles. You've sat motionless on the dock and watched small dark fish, lurking in the weeds. Every evening, from your room, you listen for the loons.

You phone Alec. You talk to him and Zoe and tell them you'll be home after lunch the next day. Alec says he's glad you're ready to come back. Zoe tells you that a new boy has joined her French class, even though it's nearly the end of the school year. The girls chase him during morning break and try to tag him. She does not, she says, because she thinks they're silly.

You hang up the receiver and think about all the parts of your life. You tell yourself that you have to believe they come together to make one life, your life. The one you live every day. You insist that this is possible, that all the parts of your life can add up to one.

* *

Special meal tonight. Most of the guests will be leaving tomorrow, end of the week. There is an air of excitement in the dining room. Bert's cheeks are flushed; he seems outraged as you enter. You are going to escape, having provided no explanation to HIM.

"Here she is!" he yells to his wife. "Why she would come to a place like this alone is beyond me." You stare eye to eye, from the annex window. Is there something you should do? Something you should say?

Bert is rising from his chair. He has finally worked himself up to some action. "I'll find out about her," he tells the others at his

156

table. He stumps across the room, stands ten paces back, opens his mouth to shout.

You touch your ears, you touch your lips. Are you deaf? Are you mute? Are you neither of these? You smile as you turn away. Your head is framed by the open window.

Foolery

∞

In memory, I hold only momentary versions of my early childhood. When I was almost five, my parents suddenly announced to my older sister Jess and me (at least, looking back, it now seems sudden) that our family would be moving to Quebec. They pronounced this Kew-bec and told us we would have to learn to speak another language. Our father's work was taking us from our own province; there was little choice—none, I realize now.

We were transplanted to a tiny rural village on the Ottawa River, far from friends and family, even remote from the village itself. Our road was a kind of half-road, a ribbon of dust and gravel that contained one other house and led past one field and ended bluntly in another. The river rushed pell-mell into rapids, its roar a constant reminder of its attraction and its danger. During spring runoff, the navy-grey water even crossed the dirt road and lapped at our very step. It was on this step that at five years of age I began to teach myself French and I sat, daily, babbling and blathering to myself in unknown syllables that poured out of me as rapidly as the current that raced past the front of the house. No one could have convinced me that I was not speaking the new language at hand. And when my mother stood at the screen one day, behind me, and asked what I was doing, I wouldn't tell for fear that she would laugh or tell my father or somehow diminish my efforts. I wholeheartedly believed that my private language had fooled my mother, and she never did say whether it had or not.

* *

Jess and I found many ways to amuse ourselves during those years in rural Quebec. We shared a bedroom, each of us with a single bed, and this made it easy for one of us to pretend to retire early, pad out the bed as if a sleeping body were within, and lie in wait beneath the opposite bed. Though we did not do this often, I remember that the feelings that went with being either on top of one's own mattress or beneath the other bed, were exactly one and the same. It made no difference whether one was the feared or the fearful. There was always the burst of adrenalin, the pounding of the pulse, the holding of the breath. If I were to frighten Jess, I'd wait until she was well settled but not asleep, and then, from beneath her bed, I'd begin the far-away sounds one can make deep in the throat only when one is lying on one's back on cold linoleum. A long silence would follow. Then, the noise again. Jess would finally say, as indifferently as she could, "I know it's you, stupid. You don't fool me." But the trick was *not to answer*. By then, both of us would be frightened, and eventually Jess would call out to me for help as if I might, in fact, be in my own bed. And from the floor I would begin to shake and then to laugh.

The ritual was the same when she lay in wait for me. Success was always dependent on the timing. One must hide when hiding was least expected—after a day that had been filled with unrelated events, for instance, so that the other could be taken by surprise.

* *

A long high-ceilinged closet had been built at one end of our bedroom. This was a narrow, open-ended passageway, and served many purposes. At our end, we hung clothes. Then, we met a chimney and an even narrower space that we could squeeze past. After that, there were clothing racks, overhead shelving and a series of floor-to-ceiling cupboards set into the far end. The tunnel, certainly twenty feet long, spilled out into the living room and, for children, was a convenient, if dark, shortcut through the middle of the house. The best feature about it was that it was so dark, one could not see into it when passing either end.

This was the space into which we dragged pillows and bedding and lay in wait for Santa Claus, or listened to *Lux Presents Hollywood*, which for years was broadcast later than our bedtime. And, on rare occasions, when our parents hosted parties, we positioned ourselves single file, lengthwise, head to toe in the passage, trying to find out what adults did and talked about when we were supposed to be asleep.

During the summer holidays while our parents were at work, Jess and I would tack long dark curtains inside either end, preparing a *Tunnel of Horrors* through which we led the neighbourhood children. We blindfolded our victims, pulled back the dark curtain, and gave them a shove into the unknown. The victims had to walk the gauntlet with arms outstretched, through and past simulated cobwebs, cold-water dousings, dishes of fabricated brains, blood, wet porridge, all to a background of nasty cries and haunting calls. They emerged at the other end, spilling out into the living room, where a waiting figure jumped out at them as the final curtain was pulled.

* *

On Hallowe'en of my tenth and Jess's twelfth year, the two of us prepared for an evening of door-to-door rounds in the village. We never tried to represent anything particular in costume; each of us dressed in leggings and jackets, and layered on top of those whatever remnants of old clothes and props we could find. That year, I wore Father's long johns, the trapdoor leering. Jess wore a full skirt, a blouse many sizes too big and a bandanna round her head. Just as we were leaving, she ran back up the steps, and Mother stuffed a bolster inside the blouse, which already bagged over Jess's jacket. As we hurried through the field and towards the centre of the village, the enormous bulge led the way as part of Jess's anterior, and this kept us giggling steadily. We did not know how serious a gesture it was until we reached the third street on our rounds, a house we were curious to investigate because we knew that a man and woman had moved there within the past few weeks, and that this would be our chance to look them over.

The door was unlocked from within, and we were beckoned inside and brought through the darkness of an enclosed back porch into a smoky kitchen. The man who had let us in had only three upper teeth. Two women and another man were at a kitchen table, where a card game was in progress. The table was strewn with ashtrays and quart beer bottles.

The man who was seated spoke loudly.

"Well," he said, as much to his three companions as to us, "let's see you do some tricks."

One of the women, perhaps his wife, left the table, gathering ashtrays to dump. We heard her say, not very convincingly, from the back of the room, "Leave them alone for Jesus sake, they're only kids."

"Come on, come on," he said, "do something, sing, or dance, something." He scraped his chair towards us and Jess and I backed away in the direction of the door. We had known as soon as we'd entered this room that there was something about his jollity that was not funny, something forced and hard-edged. He drew attention, with his laughter, to the huge bulge in Jess's blouse, and looked to the other three for backup. But they appeared uneasy and glanced at us and then away, lacking the courage to be solidly on one side or the other. The woman of the house stood near the door, an apple in each hand and, as I looked at her, I knew that she wanted us to leave. At that moment, in the astonishment of realizing that she was as much trapped as we, I heard a noise coming from Jess, beside me:

En roulant ma boule roulant.

I was surprised, and then, not. Jess had been the first to recognize that this was the only way we would get out. Our voices joined as we sang together:

En roulant ma boule roulant
En roulant ma boule.

The lines came out of our mouths like wisps intertwining with the smoke.

Only one refrain. I could tell from her eyes that Jess would sing no more, though I might have gone on and on for the sake of escape. We turned, and were permitted to move to the door, not wanting the apples the woman had pushed into our hands. Indeed, we heaved them as far as we could up the road when we did get out. But the man who had made us sing followed us through the back porch. And after I had stepped outside, he pinned Jess to the door frame with one hand and thrust his other hand past the bolster, inside the oversize blouse, and rubbed hard against her chest. The two of us stumbled down the steps. It had happened so quickly, the door now being closed and locked behind us, we were unable to voice our outrage, or even to commiserate. We ran to the end of the street, near but not allowing tears, trying to resume normalcy, trying to regain our childish selves. We held our treat bags severely and, to calm ourselves, slowed at the last house where we looked up an outside staircase that led to an upper apartment. We were halfway up and had still not spoken when a man came out onto the landing. He was carrying a black wrinkled bag.

"Someone is very ill here," he said. "Someone is dying. You shouldn't disturb the family." He spoke as if he had not noticed that we were in costume or that it was Hallowe'en.

We turned and went home, and never told our parents and never spoke of the evening again. Jess said only one thing on the way home. "If you make up your mind that it won't bother you, it never will." And though this sounded fine in theory, I knew that for weeks and even months, Jess had the same sick feeling inside her as I had, almost as if we ourselves had somehow been to blame.

* *

My memory takes me now to more recent times, a period during which I moved, with my family, to Germany and then to England, where we worked and studied for several years. During my stay in Germany, Jess and her daughter visited for one month. It was their first trip to Europe and we took short trips and long, and talked and caught up, and talked some more. I found a sudden and unexpected power, too. Throughout our formal childhood education, I had always trailed two years behind Jess, and it had seemed to me that I was always having to learn what she had already got to and assimilated before me. This must have irked me in childhood more than I'd realized, because I now took my sister about Germany introducing her (with laughter on all sides) as my mute sister.

"This is my mute sister," I would say. Of course by this time, I was fluent in my new language. Jess, as a visitor, was still struggling to interpret *jawohl* and *Ausgang*.

"Now stop," Jess said. "Stop introducing me as the mute."

But there was nothing to be done. I had become my sister's voice. She could not ask for a basket of rolls without my help.

We had decided to travel through some of the southern parts of the country and, with Jess's daughter and my own, toured a town in a mountainous area some two hundred kilometres from our village. There was a Natural History Museum in the town, and the children asked to go in to spend an hour or so looking at exhibits. We decided to stay in the area overnight, visit the museum and perhaps hike into the surrounding trails late in the afternoon.

We saw wonderful exhibits: shells and fossils, polished rocks, precious stones—even an elaborate collection of live leaf-cutting ants. But in the middle of the third floor, we were suddenly faced with the choice of continuing along the corridor, or stopping at a floor-length curtain of heavy dark material that had been hung across an otherwise unremarkable door frame. Crudely attached to the outside of the curtain was a cardboard sign, which provided information in three languages. The English message read:

The parents must have to decid if the children would be better not to see behind this curtain. The child must be wit the adult.

Of course, this meant no choice at all, and the four of us pulled back the curtain at once.

We entered a small room, perhaps four feet across and six by length. Like the long closet of our childhood home, it had a curtained entrance (or exit) on the far side. And during those few moments, while we were trying to apprehend the exhibits on the surrounding shelves, startled heads and hands of other visitors continued to thrust their way in and around the curtains from both sides. When the curtains were still, it was difficult not to have the sensation of being wrapped in the inner folds of a deep cloak, a cloak in which we stood at the centre looking up, and jars of preserved human fetuses, transfixed by their own awe and terror, stared back down.

All were a bluish colour. Each was detained by an arrested state of development, imprisoned within transparent bonds of fluid, the better to bear the interrogation of posterity. In a male fetus, the navel had developed to one side; there was only a hint of genitalia beneath an internal fold. A completely developed fetus had a cleft lip and palate, its mouth open in its watery jar; another, a rubbery-looking head that looked as if it had, at some terrible moment, collapsed in upon itself. There was a body with two heads and one torso, a third arm grown out of its middle, a single penis. And on and on, shelf after shelf, jar upon jar.

If we began to feel smothered in that room, the experience prepared us, at least in part, for the next, several days later. We had been driving for an hour on a near-empty road, dominated on all sides by thick forest. It was an unpopulated landscape of rolling hills, narrow brooks and ancient trees. As it was a hot day, we pulled off the main road when we saw a weathered *Fanta* sign, and drove into a fenced yard that contained a house and roadside stand, even a small private park, unusual in that country. Several signs were nailed to fenceposts and I translated these for Jess, telling her that there was a museum on the grounds. We needed to stretch and walk, and we purchased cold drinks from a man who came out of the house. We decided to pay the entrance fee when he told us that his exhibits had something to do with local wildlife. I was not sure of the man's dialect and instructions, but in curiosity we followed him to the museum building, converted from an old barn. The man unlocked the door; we stooped to enter and descended two shallow steps.

The room was dim, but an occasional fluorescent bulb had been hung low along rough work tables arranged end to end. And the exhibits? Each was stuffed and mounted on a log, a branch, a piece of bark; each was prepared with the taxidermist's devotion to perfection. A crow's sleek black head was smoothly attached to the body of a rabbit; an adult hedgehog had a duck's bill, its tail portion a curl of feathers. We saw a rabbit with the small horns of the *reh* deer; a stuffed pike, the pelvic and pectoral fins of which had been replaced by feet that might have belonged to a turtle; a creature that began as fox but ended as a hawk.

In the short time we were in that place, the man, the owner, the taxidermist himself, followed us about, watching our faces, commenting in a low voice which I could not comprehend. The mutterings, I thought, of someone who was used to being alone. What was certain was that he expected praise, even admiration, for work well done, for the seams that did not show.

And what thoughts would such a man have as he removed the gills of his fish and attached feathers in their place, as he stalked his quarry in woods that yielded its natural life to his alterations? Perhaps he worried over proportion, or attitude, or blending of colour. We were sorry we had entered, and we left as quickly as we could, the children as offended as Jess and I. It was as if our own childhood *Tunnel of Horrors* had somehow got out of hand. I suppose that if I had dropped in for a visit from another world, so perfect was the man's work, I might have been fooled into believing that these unnatural combinations represented the inhabitants of this place. And were there subtle differences that I, during my short time in that room, had not discerned? Could he have fooled us by exchanging the otter's paw for that of the fox? the hawk's eye for the crow's?

* *

Half a year later, after I returned to Canada, Jess was diagnosed and died within a two-month period. One day she began to drag her foot; by the end of the same week she had had brain surgery and her speech centre was partially destroyed. Between the time of her surgery (which marked the beginnings of aphasia) and her death, it seemed that she was able to speak for only a few moments. But I see now that my memory fools me, that this must have been a gradual deterioration, that events were so desperate and compressed it would have been impossible to measure and consider them.

She was able to make some sounds in her throat, gesture with an arm and hand, and communicate with facial grimaces that made much use of her mouth and eyebrows. She was able to make clear, most of the time, what she needed and wanted. On the other hand, frustration and anger were not at all difficult to read.

What I did not know was that in the last weeks of Jess's life, her physician had sent a consult to a speech therapist, asking her to assess the degree of aphasia in order to attempt to retrain Jess's speech. I was in the hospital room when the young woman arrived. She was cheerful, slick, I thought, and clinical. I did not much like clinical people then, and I resented the intrusion. Perhaps this was a reaction to her obvious good health, her enthusiasm and her youth, her confidence. She introduced herself and said how delighted she was to have Jess *and* her sister present, because there was something she would like Jess to do and it would be easier if the two of us were to do it together. Jess and I exchanged our "Oh, no" looks, and glanced back to the therapist, but our communication had not been intercepted.

The young woman first ascertained that Jess could create sounds. "What I would like you to do," she announced, "and it might seem foolish to you now, is to *sing* together. We've found that in patients with this type of problem, before single words and sentences are uttered, sometimes lines of songs will come rushing out, whole and complete, exactly as they were learned years before." She looked to the two of us. "Can you think of a song you'd like to try?"

But we could not. Not only that, we *would* not. Jess's lips closed, though she raised an eyebrow, and we laughed when we looked at each other. But each of us knew that the other would not.

The therapist egged us on. "There must be something. A childhood song? Anything will do."

And I found that, once again, I had become my sister's voice and, this time, I knew that she was glad to be out of the running. Her expression was saying, "Does she think we are fools?"

I mumbled that we'd been taken by surprise, that all I could think of were songs in another language—one or two stanzas of French songs we'd learned when we were children, living in Quebec.

"Great!" said the therapist, and waited.

But we would not.

And perhaps this time it was because we knew that singing would not help. That a French refrain would not buy us an escape.

The young woman became gloomy and said that, while we were thinking of songs, she would begin to do her testing.

She had brought with her a flat board containing a series of interchangeable cardboard backgrounds, each marked off in squares, each square containing a picture, or a number, or word. She told Jess what to do (we had rolled Jess to a sitting position in bed) and said that she must point to the correct square when a word or number or name of an object was called out.

Jess nodded that she understood. She even looked eager— whether to get out of having to sing, or because it excited her to do the test, or whether it was just to get the woman out of her room, I was never to know.

And what happened was that Jess got almost all of the tasks wrong. At first, I thought she was fooling; and then—I could not have stopped myself—I began to laugh. Surely this was my sister's sense of humour. But Jess drew her lips together and, with two fingers, she continued to point and gesture and point to the squares on the board.

And I began to experience the pounding of the pulse, the holding of the breath, the oneness of the feared and the fearful. Had I been a child again, I might have said, "I know you can do it, stupid. You can't fool me!" It was as if the therapist and I had knowledge that Jess *must* and *would* have, and I became very much afraid as I watched her arm move faster and faster to the board, pointing and pointing and pointing, but always to the wrong squares.

And what was impossible to let in was the realization that things were not what they seemed, that we had become grotesque partners near the end of one life, that we had both been fooled, I by the outer signs, Jess by the inner ones. I had to allow what my eyes were perceiving: Jess did not know that she did not know.

She became impatient with both me and the therapist. Her face betrayed self-righteousness and, then, a haughty sort of pride. And I felt as violated by that knowledge as I had been years before, while I stood helplessly by and watched the man on the step molest Jess as we tried to leave his darkened porch on Hallowe'en. We were unable to voice our outrage, or even to commiserate. The decision not to let it bother us was not ours, and we were still learning that when one pulls back the dark curtain, the fool, the madwoman, the jester might come rushing out.

Perhaps Jess saw something in my face during those moments; perhaps she died being fooled, died knowing that I had tried to protect her from her own knowledge. I do not know. I know only that it mattered very much; that never again would I be eager to examine what was behind the locked door.

Earthman Pointing

∞

Roseanne is fidgeting at the sink because she has just watched Jack walk through the patio screen, face first. The screen went with him, his right arm scrabbling to thrust it away, while his left arm propelled his body forward. Jack has had too much to drink; Roseanne has been counting. To be exact, eight beers, and now a start on the whisky. Jack wipes his chin with the back of his hand, and hums each time he walks through the kitchen—to let Roseanne think he's sober and in control. But Roseanne has been married to Jack thirty-six years, and is on to all of his tricks.

Sometimes Roseanne attempts to look back over her years with Jack and sees them not as years wasted, but as time put in. Like everyone else she knows, her time so far has been filled without her lifting a finger to help it. Years gone. Years spent. And she knows why Jack is drinking tonight—it's the Big-Little book, she's pretty certain. She and Tibbs went too far. They got together this afternoon before the others arrived for the Bar-B-Q, they started acting foolish, and they just went too far.

* *

The others, out on the patio, have finished eating. They're pretending they haven't noticed that Jack has just scrunched the armful of screen into a grey ball and dropped it off the side of the deck. The mosquitoes are sure to start invading. Roseanne crosses the room and slides the glass door so that it shuts tight, no crack. She goes back to take up position at the sink, and listens through the screen of the kitchen window to hear what's being said. Most of it, she's heard before. Still, she listens because she likes to hear how they twist and tangle the old stories to suit themselves.

Out there in the semi-dark are her twin sister, Tibbs; Tibbs's husband, Spoke, who's been skinny as a blade of grass since they were all nineteen; and Arley, the twins' younger brother. Arley is fifty-six years old. His wife died last year of sugar diabetes, and Roseanne and Tibbs try to include him in their family gatherings so he won't be lonesome.

Marian is there, too, Roseanne and Jack's daughter. Marian is thirty-three, has not yet married, and lives in her own apartment on the other side of the river. She is editor of a woman's magazine called *Women Anew*, and says she's always on the lookout for family stories. Roseanne still hasn't read a word of Marian's that has been recognizable or that has meant a thing to her own life. She and Tibbs think Marian is too serious; they'd like her to write something funny, something that shows the family sense of humour. Privately, to Roseanne, Tibbs says that the readers of *Women Anew* must think Marian comes from a family that's dead-from-the-ass-up. Roseanne can't say much because Marian is her daughter and she doesn't interfere. But Tibbs, the aunt, can get away with interference both moderate and outrageous. She sat Marian down two weeks ago and said, "Now I want you to promise that you'll write one thing that's funny. Just one. A story or an article for that magazine of yours. Something that will make me laugh, hear?"

Marian's feelings weren't hurt at all.

As for *Women Anew*, reading it doesn't make Roseanne feel

one bit new; she and Tibbs are the kind of women they are, not really old, certainly not new, just sort of stuck between what Marian's magazine says is happening and what their own lives really are.

When no one else is around, Roseanne and Tibbs have taken to amusing themselves by thinking up catchy titles for stories and articles. So far, anticipating rejection, they haven't shared these with Marian. Some of the titles they contrive are from items they read in supermarket tabloids: "Shrunken Human Head Found in Peanut Shell," or "Newborn Memorizes *War and Peace.*" Others, they just dream up, like "The Case of the Rolling Peas." One of their long-standing inventions is "Earthman Pointing," a title that makes them hoot with laughter because, in a harmless way, it both mocks and describes Roseanne's husband, Jack. No matter where they are—on holiday, in the backyard for a Bar-B-Q, at a wedding or a funeral, standing in the street—anywhere there's a group of people, Jack is always pointing. This is something to do with *Life*, Roseanne thinks, or maybe *Destiny*, she isn't sure. For years, this ritual of his has irritated her, even though she tells herself that at least he points in an upward, skyward direction; it's not as if he were pointing to a hole in the ground.

As for catchy titles, Roseanne favours "The Sardine Coffin," having read about designer coffins in Ghana. An old fisherman had told his daughter that, when he died, he wanted to be buried in a sardine. His older brother, a farmer, had been laid out in a carved shallot. Roseanne, if she had the choice, would choose a crane for herself. A whooping crane, elegant and nearly extinct. It would have to be carved thick across the middle, so she could fit inside. The fisherman's daughter in Ghana had told reporters that the sardine coffin was to let people know that her father was a proud and successful fisherman. Roseanne wonders what Marian might write in *Women Anew* about *her* mother, laid out in a whooping crane. Something humourless, no doubt. And what about Jack? What sort of coffin would he choose? Probably a long thick arm with a pointing finger.

* *

Right now, on the patio, they're talking about how a giraffe's blood gets pumped up into its head. "Their necks are over eight feet long," Arley says. "Must be a hell of a heart to get the blood all the way up there, to its brain." Then they switch to Tibbs's husband, Spoke, who, back in high school, had been nicknamed Giraffe. It's the Thanksgiving story; they're into memory lane now. Roseanne doesn't know how they move from one story to another so quickly. One thing she does realize, is that all of them—herself included—talk about their past as if it were cut from fresh crisp paper only yesterday. And they seem locked into a period that stretches from childhood to early marriage, and includes only events that can be made to seem hilarious. Nothing recent, nothing grim allowed. This includes the past twenty-five years.

In the Thanksgiving story, Spoke is standing on a dining-room chair screwing in a new lightbulb, or maybe unscrewing an old, moments before fourteen people sit down to dinner. Spoke loses his grip and the bulb explodes on top of the turkey, just taken out of the oven and set at the end of the table for carving.

Every time the story gets told, the number of people around the table changes and the person screwing the lightbulb changes. Sometimes it's Roseanne's husband, Jack, sometimes it's Arley, sometimes it's even the twins' Daddy, before they all left home and got married. Now, they're saying it's Spoke, and maybe they're right, for all that. Spoke, as long and lean at fifty-nine as he was in those early years when he and Tibbs started going out together. (When Tibbs first brought Spoke home, their Daddy took one look at him standing at the back door and said, "Who let the air out of you?")

What Roseanne remembers is that Thanksgiving dinner was at her house that year; that the turnips, mashed potatoes and gravy had not yet been put out, or she'd have had to dump them in the garbage. Cranberries and pickled beets did get dumped, millions of glass fragments glittering across Roseanne's sparkling white table. She and Tibbs ran every dish back to the kitchen sink for a rinse, wiped the cutlery, stood on the front step with their backs to the storm door and shook out the table-cloth. Inside, the men peeled the skin right off the turkey, gave it a few swipes with a dish towel, and served it up anyway. Under-neath the skin was another of Roseanne's perfect turkeys. Jack, in a red apron, posed at the end of the table for a photo, pointing to the ceiling with fork and carving knife.

* *

Roseanne is still listening at the window, all the while keeping an eye on Jack. So far—and for this Roseanne is grateful—Tibbs has held her tongue about Jack's drinking. It's part of being a twin, knowing when to speak your piece. Privately, Tibbs will no doubt invent some theory that will have to do with Jack's sixtieth birth-day coming up. She'll say that Jack missed his change of life earlier, and then she'll tell about Spoke who went through his, right on the stroke of fifty. She and Spoke went through their change together, according to Tibbs, and it wasn't all buttercups and roses, but they came out the other side. She told Marian she'd be happy to write a family story about *that*.

Jack wants another whisky; Roseanne can tell by the way he's pacing around the picnic table. He glances towards the window every few minutes, knowing Roseanne is at the sink, but he's unwilling to come in again after walking through the screen. Roseanne pours herself a glass of wine, curses the Big-Little book, wonders if Tibbs needs a refill, and hears Marian's voice. "Come on out, Ma, we're telling stories. Leave the dishes. We'll do them later."

"I'll go in and drag her away from the sink," Tibbs says. "She's up to her elbows in you-know-who."

Roseanne hears laughter and, by the splurt of it, knows right away who they're talking about now. That sort of outburst is always about Harold Beavis, who followed the twins around when they were in senior high. Harold was a dumpling of a man and, when he walked, what you saw from behind were the cheeks of his bum sliding, one up, one down, as if the two weren't connected. Roseanne and Tibbs never liked him, because crude words came out of his puffy mouth—smutty queries as he followed them through the halls.

Ten years after they all finished school, Harold Beavis drowned in the river that ran through town, just a block from where he'd always lived. His drowning is the reason Tibbs never drinks from the town water supply, even though the drowning was more than twenty-five years ago. The person Roseanne feels sorry for is Spoke. Ever since Harold drowned, Spoke and Tibbs have been hauling water from a natural spring, thirty-three miles out of town. Once a week they load up the car with plastic jugs and bottles, even in winter when there are treacherous ice slides around the spring. This has become a family joke ("Have you noticed Harold's been a little sweet since spring runoff?" "Is that Harold, dripping out of the tap?") Tibbs has been teased for years, but she's made up her mind; not one drop of fat Harold will get inside her, even on her teeth.

* *

Roseanne, believing this to be irrational, understands. Who could know Tibbs better than her own twin? And has Tibbs ever said a word to Roseanne about pork?

On her fortieth birthday, Roseanne started work as a part-time cashier at the Auction Barns. More money changed hands on paper at the Barns than she would have thought existed in the whole world. She got used to this, and the men liked her because she was quick and could keep up with rapid-fire transactions. At the Barns, which were on the edge of town near First Bridge, she was known to the men as Rosie. It was Rosie this and Rosie that. She stayed in that job for six years and quit on a Friday morning—the day the late Shank Brady's pigs were auctioned off. One of the men who worked the ring sidled over and said, "You see that big sow over there, Rosie? Who-ever eats a piece of bacon out of that hide will be eatin' a piece of Shank Brady." Sure enough, though only a few people knew, the pig had killed Brady, eating the guts right out of him when Brady had fallen into the pen.

Since that very Friday, Roseanne hasn't eaten so much as a slice of ham or bacon, or cooked a roast of pork. She eats beef and a little chicken, but every time she passes the meat counter in the A & P she thinks of Shank Brady head first in the pigpen, the old sow chomping on his insides.

Tap water and pork. These are the twins' deprivations.

* *

Roseanne slides back the glass door and lets herself out onto the patio where the others are sitting in a circle, slapping at mosquitoes. Jack sees his chance and shoots past her into the kitchen. Across the darkness, Tibbs raises her eyebrows, and she and Roseanne exchange meaningful looks.

Spoke is saying, "Purple martins aren't that easy to attract; I've been trying for years."

"The Darth Vaders of the swallow world," says Marian, blackly. "That's what they look like to me."

"Jack knows all about birdhouses," Tibbs says. "He built two last year. Put them too close together; Roseanne and I kept telling him. One of them blew down in a windstorm. The other is still attached to the tree."

Roseanne's version of this story begins earlier, though it's true that one house did blow down.

Jack built the birdhouses with holes so small, no bird could get in. He set the ladder against the tree, and climbed. He checked the measurements and said the holes were exactly right; if he were to make them larger, sparrows would take over. Swallows did try, but could get only head and breast in before they struggled and heaved and flapped back out.

After two days of watching unsuccessful entries, Roseanne convinced Jack to make one hole larger. Back up the tree he climbed, pointing his file skyward. He rubbed at the wood and came back to the kitchen to stand at the window with Roseanne. Just then, a sparrow flew straight into the hole, plugged it and stuck there. Feet and tail thrashed and flailed as the bird tried to dislodge itself.

Thinking of the bird's head in the dark, thinking of the descending lid of her crane, Roseanne said, "It's terrified, Jack. It's going to have a heart attack."

Out came the ladder again. Jack climbed, cursing all feathered vertebrates, and enclosed the bird in one of his large hands. He tugged it backwards out of the hole. The bird stilled; only its head emerged from Jack's curled fingers. Jack stretched his arm and opened his hand, pointing towards the sky. At first, the bird didn't move; then, it seemed to become an extension of Jack's fingers, and flew off. Roseanne felt the stirring of an old surge of affection for Jack that day, watching the sparrow in his hand, watching him set it free. A few hours later, the swallows returned and built their nest. But before the eggs had a chance to hatch, the house blew down.

* *

Jack must have slipped out the front door and sneaked around the side of house; Roseanne sees his silhouette near the tree. He's down at the end of the yard, acting like an alien who's lurking at the outer edges of a family gathering.

In the shadows, he raises his glass; for a moment, Roseanne expects him to point it skyward as he did the bird. He does not; he downs the contents, probably whisky again, in one gulp. And stays there, by the tree.

She sees now that making fun was the worst offence. She and Tibbs could have made the book and never shown it, and Jack would be none the wiser. It's all so much silliness, she thinks, all his damned waving and pointing and gesticulating. If he's that thin-skinned all of a sudden, maybe he *is* going through the change.

She wishes she could remember how she and Tibbs got started in the first place. Maybe they were thinking up titles for Marian's sour-grapes magazine. She remembers trying to match catchy titles to photos, but she can't remember whose idea the Big-Little was. All she knows is that in the afternoon she and Tibbs were sprawled out on the living-room rug, cutting and pasting, laughing until their cheeks hurt. It had not been difficult to find photos of Jack among the albums and cigar boxes. Jack, with a point for every occasion: an arm, an index finger outstretched, a stick, a hoe, a carving knife, a shovel, a baseball bat, a piece of driftwood, a fishing rod—pointing at, but at what? At the end of the driveway? At the hedge, the turkey, the flying saucer, the dunes, the migrating geese—the beyond?

What she and Tibbs had done in their great flush of laughter and craziness was to cull the photos and paste them onto construction paper, each photo having its own page. Jack's point was manoeuvred so that it was always aimed towards the upper right corner. They cut and shaped and produced their own Big-Little book, twenty-two pages long. They stapled the cover and printed the title, *Earthman Pointing*, with felt pens. And then, shrieking and holding their sides, took it to Jack to show him. The book had enough thickness so that when they thumbed the upper right corner, riffling the pages, the effect was that of Jack in rapid motion, Jack with finger in the air, swinging his implements of destiny.

But Jack had not laughed. Had not thought this funny at all. Something in his face tightened and, while Roseanne did not miss this entirely, she and Tibbs had gone too far to turn back. They flipped the Big-Little under his nose. Their laughter flattened—and died.

Yes, making fun had been the worst offence, and she and Tibbs had committed it. No wonder Jack is standing down there in the dark, drinking whisky beneath the tree.

* *

Roseanne looks at Tibbs across the picnic table. The storytelling has petered out; moments of silence are gathering before everyone starts picking up to go home. Tibbs looks back at Roseanne and raises her eyebrows and, with this exchange, Roseanne is caught off guard. Sometimes, looking at her twin is not unlike searching a mirror for her own likeness. Tibbs wriggles her eyebrow again, unnoticed by Spoke, by Marian, by Arley. She has a smirk on her face as she motions towards Jack, who has set down his glass and is pointing up to the black black sky.

Roseanne is angry: at Tibbs for making fun; at the Big-Little; at herself for taking part; at Jack, who sees something Roseanne does not.

Roseanne finds herself wanting, wanting to see, too. She peers down along the grass. She can't see the remaining birdhouse, just barely sees the outline of the tree. Darkness has settled. Roseanne no longer knows if Jack is even there.

The Eyes Have It

As he cuts into Ceese's left eye, the surgeon begins to sing. A low hum, rather than lyrics. There is a drape over her right eye, over her entire face, and she can't see him or the nurse, above her. Ten minutes earlier, she had been sitting on a chair in an outer room while the anaesthetist inserted a needle between her cheekbone and lower lid and injected the contents of the syringe into her. When he wheeled her, on the stretcher, into the operating room, he asked how she felt.

"Sacrificial," she said.

His upside-down face had seemed puzzled. He was the kind of anaesthetist who tried to hide the needle and syringe from his patient—trying to spare her—but her glance had been quick.

"You might be treated to a colour and light show," he said, as if he thought this would be encouraging. "Some people are. During the operation."

"What if I move my head?" She was keeping her cataract eye open until the last possible moment. That's how she thought of it, her cataract eye. Not that she could see out of it, at this point. The drops that preceded whatever he'd shoved into the space above her cheekbone had made the wall appear foggy, moveable. It was shifting, behind him.

"Move your head?" Again, he had seemed puzzled. "You're the one in control of that," he'd said. "Don't."

"Spanish Eyes," she thinks. That's what the surgeon is humming. Doesn't he realize?

But Ceese does not bring it to his attention. She wants him to focus, no interruptions. She doesn't want to jar him with a thought that will cause his hands or his miniature eye instruments to shift. She suppresses the impulse to shout, "This man engages in painless torture!"

Instead, she tries to figure a way that will help her to bear this. *He's scraping out the old lens (already it's the old lens).* How did she *think* she was going to bear it? When she walked into the hospital at seven in the morning, she had no plan. How can you plan for something as outrageous as another human being picking up a blade and slicing into your eye?

Tai chi, she decides. I'll do the set in my head. Meditation gets me through anything. She does the bow, turns her inner self to the right, turns back again for *single whip.* She tries to close the inner eye. Not easy when the covering of the outer eye has been peeled back. It is open, helpless. Flayed. *Flayed?* The word pops into her head. She'll look it up when she gets home. If she is ever able to see again. Not out of the eyeball that's flayed, or displayed, or whatever it is that's happening up there on the other side of the sterile drape. Exposed. That's how she feels. A truly terrible violation is going on and she is here beneath it. She has even agreed to it. A form of madness, like eye-rabies, must have bitten her, and there is nothing she can do. If she moves, all is lost.

Somebody stop this man.

She goes back to the beginning of the set. Recites to herself, deliberately, controlled, the way she instructs her tai chi students on Wednesday nights. She gets as far as *single whip* again and tries to push through to the next move. The digging inside her eye is robbing her concentration. The humming of "Spanish Eyes" has stopped.

Ward off, slanting upward.

She's forgotten the move between. Never mind, keep going. *Step up and raise hands.* And then, she glides into a perfect *stork cools wings,* her favourite. She thinks of waterfalls, a single and elegant raised wing. Once, she read an entire book about dancing cranes. The writer believed, after years of photographing cranes, that they danced only for the sake of dancing. The act was unrelated to mating or acquiring food. Related to nothing, he believed, except play. Ceese believes this, too.

"Ceese," a man's voice says, and she remembers the stranger, above her. "What kind of name is that?"

"As in . . . and desist," she says, and regrets this immediately. *Don't irritate the surgeon.* "It's short for Cecilia," she adds, trying to placate.

He hums a few notes and says, "Almost through—four or five minutes more."

She still has her other eye. Which he will never get near, she has already decided. Even if the artificial lens he's now implanting gives her 20/20 vision in the left, he'll never get his teeny eye spades into the right.

She wonders if her legs will buckle when she tries to stand after surgery. She realizes that her tai chi has stalled again, that her legs might already have buckled. *Inner legs buckle.* She could invent a new move and call it out on Wednesday nights, and the insides of all the people in her class would cave in.

She gives up on tai chi—requires too much concentration— and switches instead to the sword set, one she learned from a Chinese master but knows only imperfectly. Nonetheless, if the surgeon misses, or offends, or even hurts—God forbid that the local anaesthetic wears off—she'll tap her inner sword to her forehead and thrust. *Three rings encircle moon.* But more footwork is required, more than in tai chi. She reaches *swallow skims water* and has to give up the sword set, too.

She now decides—how else will she get through these last minutes—that she will look out of the eye he's working in. It's open, isn't it? *Small supreme star*. The moves in the sword set have wonderful names. Her favourite is *Immortal directs the way*. She wills herself to stare upward but there is only brightness. She sees no image, no shadow, no face peering into her head, no colour and light show, no fingers, no Lilliputian probe. This causes a profound and generalized panic.

Cataract: A descent of water over a steep surface; a waterfall; a furious rush or downpour; a deluge.

Not.

(Except, perhaps, a deluge of tears.)

Cataract: Abnormality of the eye, characterized by opacity of the lens, usually associated with aging.

She is fifty-four.

"No matter," the surgeon told her, before booking the operation. "Some people have the misfortune to develop cataracts prematurely."

Fortune and misfortune. Her son, when he was four, held out his empty dinner plate and said, "I'd like a medium fortune, please." Which made Ceese think that perhaps portion and fortune were one and the same.

The body fails us in miserable ways. Every friend she has is trying to ward off something. Ingesting Vitamin E. Drinking cranberry juice and decaf green tea. Worrying about roving free radicals. Ceese knows nothing of radicals except what she remembers from the sixties—some of her friends still haven't moved on. People she knows are obsessed with stroke prevention, diabetes, too much salt. Her closest friend, Lucy, weighs every item before she eats, including crackers. It is Lucy who is coming to the hospital to escort her home—an hour from now, O blessed hour! She allows herself a wedge of hope. She'll hug Lucy and thank her, lock the door, draw the shades, bar the light, collapse.

"Not your husband?" the admitting clerk had asked, before surgery.

Was this reproach, censure? The clerk looked fourteen; surely, she was older. Her brown eyes reflected boredom.

"He's out of town," said Ceese. "A friend will come to drive me home." These husbands who run off on extended jobs—no, she will recover alone. When the hospital had called with the scheduled date, she'd told Evan not to cancel his trip.

The clerk had ground her teeth, audibly. "Then you'll have to give me your friend's number. She'll have to bring you back tomorrow for your bandage removal and post-op check."

Did she think Ceese had not made the arrangements? But Ceese did not retort. Save your energy, she told herself. You're going to need it. She thought of her late Granny MacCallum quoting Ezekiel: "The fathers have eaten sour grapes, and the children's teeth are set on edge." This child-clerk must have a sour-grapes father, or maybe she is an unhappy child-bride— Ceese thinks she remembers the flash of a ring. But no flash of sparkling eyes. Only dull brown, belying boredom.

"Perfect." The nurse's voice speaks, above her. The surgeon hums assent. Ceese hears a crackling noise and smells burning flesh. Her own. Cautery. She wants to wince but can't. She tries to scrunch her thoughts, render them minute. She tries to stay in the shrunken space where she has removed herself.

When she was a child, every night at the dinner table during summer, the sun shone through the window in exactly the same spot, directly into her face, blinding her. Every night, her mother stood on a chair and pinned up a corner of the curtain to block out the sun.

* *

"Finished," says the surgeon, a flourish in his voice, and lifts the drape. *The curtain rises.* Ceese's last image while on the table is the one that stays in her mind's eye: limitless white, milkiness, unseeing, blind.

* *

Why is it that everything she reads, hears, sees with her right eye—now alarmingly bloodshot like the left—why is it that everything has to do with *the eye*? Or was it all there before and she hasn't been looking? "There are none so blind as those who *won't* see," Granny MacCallum used to say, usually to close an argument.

A postcard invitation arrives in the mail—sent by the Postal Museum—and bears two eyes captured by a shaded oval, the eyes trapped in a frameless rear-view mirror. Two larger eyes stare at Ceese from the cover of a glossy magazine. She turns on the radio, only to hear an item about Peeping Toms, eyes staring in from the dark. She remembers living in a ground floor apartment, a young couple banging at the door to tell her they'd been out for a walk and had seen a man standing at her kitchen window. The man had run off when they shouted. She thinks of Cheever, and Uncle Peepee Marshmallow in *The Wapshot Chronicle*. She thinks of a man with a white dog who once left footprints outside her bedroom window, in the snow.

Ceese's older brother phones from Vancouver. He asks about the surgery but before she can reply he says, "I don't want to hear." She doesn't blame him. Doesn't he have his own future to consider? Don't cataracts run in families?

Evan calls, from the opposite edge of the country. She is determined not to feel sorry for herself. She tells him she was at the library the day before surgery—Main Branch, the selection is better—and borrowed fourteen books-on-tape to get her through the healing period. She tells him she's been lying on the living-room floor, listening to professional voices. She doesn't tell him that the first book she listened to was Toni Morrison's *The Bluest Eye*. She doesn't shout at him to come home.

She doesn't tell him, either, that now that the bandage is off and she is applying compresses, she can't bear to look in the mirror at her bruised eye. Battered, she's been battered. She doesn't tell him that she feels small.

Their son calls, from Toronto.

"I'm supposed to put drops in my eye," she tells him. "Every six hours. But I'm having trouble finding my eye."

"Is this some philosophical problem?" he says. "Where is the I?"

She laughs, first time since surgery.

She stumbles from one room to another and goes down to the basement where she bumps into the ironing board. The iron falls, tinny pieces of its dial clinking on cement. She leaves the pieces where they scatter.

* *

At night she wears a hard silvery patch surrounded by fluorescent pink foam, to keep her fingers from tentacling upward in her sleep and rubbing the eye. Every morning she takes the patch off and peers into the mirror. The woman who peers back looks as if she hasn't slept for weeks. It is impossible to wear glasses; the old prescription doesn't fit the new eye and she can't get a new prescription until the eye has healed for four weeks. Although she had no fear before surgery, now she is petrified that her vision won't be restored, that even her good eye will somehow be robbed of sight. *Good guy, bad guy; good eye, bad eye.*

Terror follows, she writes in her journal, keeping one eye closed. These are the only words she can muster. She has trained her eyes to work independently. She alternates: one eye open, one eye closed. Her eyes work in opposite directions under opposing orders. At the bottom of the page she draws a human eye with wide-apart lashes and a morose brow. Beneath the picture she prints: *The victim's version.*

One afternoon, strain in one eye, seeing double in the other, she lies on the rug, puts a compress over both eyes, and listens to a tape of the stories of Oscar Wilde. In the first story, the statue of the Happy Prince commands a little swallow to swoop in and pluck out one of his sapphire eyes. The next night, the little swallow is told to pluck out the other. Ceese removes the compress, takes out the tape, and understands that there is no escape.

She decides to check e-mail, turns on the computer, squints at the screen. A message from Lucy pops up, with the heading: *I spy with my glitter eye.*

I know you want to be left alone, she writes, *and I don't want to be annoying. I'm just checking, to make sure you are all right. Call if you need me. Or send a message. Guide me through this. You can be the seeing-eye . . . well, never mind. Don't be an EYE-dealist.*

Ceese sits back and laughs, second time since surgery. She remembers the evening she and Lucy attended a foreign language film—Danish, with English subtitles—and just as the lights went down two women took their places directly in front of them. The elder of the two was blind and accompanied by her seeing-eye dog, which settled obediently at her feet.

But the blind woman did not understand Danish, as Ceese and Lucy had naturally assumed. Which meant that the companion had to read out the subtitles, and this she did in a loud voice. Even more perplexing, every time an actor laughed, the companion interpreted by saying "laughed"—or "coughed" or "snorted," although bodily functions could easily be heard from the screen, comprehensible in any language. Patrons around were shifting uncomfortably but no one worked up the courage to comment. The seats were full, and there was no place to retreat.

* *

By the end of two weeks, Ceese has seen the surgeon twice. She no longer wears the patch at night. Every morning when she wakes, one eye opens and then the other, as if they're no longer friends. She picks up the morning paper and reads the caption, *Heights of danger*. She's still seeing multiples; there are one and a half captions now. She has a sudden insight, pops the left lens out of her old glasses and reads with the right. This works, as long as she keeps her left eye closed.

She reads that a passenger liner at sea has encountered a giant rogue wave. It was, the captain reported, eye level, the bridge being ninety-five feet. Other height danger is reported in the same article. Volcanoes can blast clouds of rock so high, the rock drifts around in the sky. You can be buckled into your seat in an airplane, flying high, and look out the window, and there will be ash and rock, spewed up from below. Fifteen hundred passenger lives have been at risk in recent years, the report asserts, with authority.

Are we safe anywhere? Ceese recalls reading two large-print headlines from a prominent poster on the wall of the Breast Clinic, the last time she had a mammogram. The first was: WATCH FOR ASYMMETRY AND SKIN CHANGES. The second was not addressed to her at all, although it was part of the same poster. It read: MEN, KNOW YOUR TESTICLES. Ceese has never seen a man at the Breast Clinic.

Evan phones, in the evening. She looks at the receiver as if it holds the voice of a stranger who knows things about her family. "I'm about to start driving again," she tells him, and realizes that after she hangs up she will weep. *I want my husband, my companion. I want my old life.*

She has nothing, really, to cry about. She doesn't even know if the new plastic eye is capable of allowing tears. She sends a message to Lucy, who replies: *Your NOT-crying is like the movie stars who keep smiling through the picture. They put Vaseline on their teeth. And then there's you: 'I vow not to cry. I vill not cry. I vant to be alone!'*

* *

Ceese's vision is less blurred; her four-week follow-up appointment is looming. Evan will be home the same day as the appointment, as it turns out. By the time he arrives, she'll have a new prescription; she'll have ordered new glasses; her eyes will welcome symbiosis and binocular vision.

She thinks of how, in dim light, a tiny crescent moon appears at the edge of her peripheral vision; how she changes position quickly to make the moon go away—just in case it means that something's wrong. She has read that her implanted lens is made of the same material airplane windshields are made of; that it will last fifty to sixty years. This is comforting. When she sees the surgeon for her final appointment, he tells her that the eye is healing. It's just fine.

"Any questions?" he asks.

"Where do you store the replacement lenses?"

Surprised, he tells her that they are in cabinet drawers in another room.

"How big are they?"

"Small, very small. They come in different sizes."

But she doesn't want to see. In any case, he doesn't offer.

She clutches her prescription in her hand and puts on her dark glasses. (*You must wear dark glasses, even to hang out the clothes,* she has read, but who has a clothesline in the city?) She heads out into the sun.

As she walks towards the Eyewear shop, she is arrested by a

blaze of greenery in a small park. Her feet won't move forward. She raises her sunglasses the tiniest bit. The verdant colour rushes into her eye, her plastic eye. She has forgotten that this is July, that the visual world is rich, so rich. That flowers can slip their images through your tiny pupil and make their assault in scarlet and vermilion, in ruby and crimson.

O, the wonderful sights to see. She walks along, more slowly now, and tries to think of the most beautiful sight she has ever seen. But all she can think of, all she can remember, is a Saturday morning in May when she and Evan were having breakfast at a café in the market, sitting on an outdoor balcony above street level. She looked down at the crowd below and watched the lights change at the crosswalk, half a block away. And then, a giant box of French fries on legs—perhaps seven feet tall—crossed the street and began to walk towards the café.

She'd laughed and laughed as the fries approached, individual fingerlings flopping side to side as they jutted out of the box. There was no sign of a head above or a body below—only legs and the box of fries jaunting along through the market crowd. The sight was so absurd she couldn't stop laughing, waves of hysteria rolling through her.

Evan, bemused, said, "Get a grip, Ceese," and sipped his coffee. But she was choking on hers.

Maybe it was the funniest, maybe the most bizarre sight she has ever seen. She didn't know then and she doesn't know now. For now, it's the only scene she can call up. She'll remind Evan when she picks him up at the airport. See if he remembers.

And then she'll say, "The ayes have it." And the best thing about this—she won't have to look him in the eye—is that Evan (she hopes, she prays) will completely understand.

Man Without Face

There is a man in one of my old childhood comics and, in the story, the man has stopped overnight at a hotel in an English town. One of those towns with narrow red brick houses and unfriendly, ruddy-cheeked citizens; a town where men wear tweeds and black scapulars as they stride over cobbled streets.

In the morning, when the man goes to the sink to wash and shave, he looks in the mirror but *he has no face*. Where eyes eyebrows nose and mouth had been, there is only an oval of smooth blank skin. Did his face rub off on the towel? Did I then ask myself: how can he see his no-face if he has no eyes? How can he breathe with no nose, no mouth? By some leap of faith into true horror, the man at the sink and I knew and believed that all of this was possible.

Why do I think of this, why, when I think of my own father tripping off my front step and falling flat on *his* face on the newly cut grass? Always one to cover his tracks, he picked himself up and stepped, even nimbly, into the waiting taxi. Nothing was said. Perhaps, at the hotel the next morning, he didn't remember. That's the part I never knew and never asked. How much did he remember?

Just before Father fell on his face, he'd been sitting on my living-room rug trying to organize a singsong. He was wearing a summer shirt and khaki shorts. His cheeks were flushed, and he was slapping his bare legs against the rug as he roared through the lyrics of "In the Summertime," a song he knew well but that none of us did. Not that we could have sung with him anyway. Not I, nor my husband, nor our children, nor my twin sister, Beryl, who lived in the same city. Not one of us sang with my father.

* *

Burr and I lived with our parents, a mile and a half from Greenly. We had no family car, so to do our shopping we had to take the bus that rattled past our house on the dirt road. There was little traffic, but occasionally some old car bumped by and raised a cloud of dust. Father would say, "There goes Percy to take salt to his cows," or "Mrs. Leary must have run off on Telly again. Serves him right, the damned fool."

Behind our house and beyond a fold of hills, there was a rocky place thick with trees. A ten-minute walk past that took us to a waterfall that cut its way down a narrow gorge and opened to slow rolling farmland. The place we lived in was not like that. Thorn and crabapple and chokecherry grew close together and dust blew in off the road. That's how I remember it.

Burr and I made our way as often as we could to the waterfall. The climb was steep, but midway to the top and, behind the water, there was a kind of half cave, a niche where we could hide away without getting wet, where we could bring our comics to read, where we could watch the water tumble down—and discuss our father. His drinking was the first topic before we got to the second. Why did Mother marry him?

"Why does he drink?"

"How should I know?"

"Do you think he's always been like this?"

"If he has, why would she have married him?"

"Why did they have *us*?"

We broke off pieces of limestone from the sides of the cave and tossed them through the waterfall. If Father had known where we were, we'd have been in trouble.

"The old fart," Burr said, daring, watching to see if I'd react.

"Old fart," I said back, and threw a chunk of stone.

"Old fart, old fart." We chanted into the back of the waterfall, louder and louder, until we were shouting above its roar, holding our sides, amazed at the release of our own laughter.

We became serious again.

"What about Mother? Why does she put up with him?"

"She's trying to keep the peace."

This was an expression our mother herself used. In tight-lipped grimace, she said, "Try to keep the peace," as she fed us early on a Friday night before he came home from the tavern where he'd already begun his weekend binge after leaving the cheese factory. Dressed in his old suit, shirt and tie, he'd just performed his week's work, keeping the books in a tiny office that reeked of curds.

Mother invented errands, sent us outside. Never, as far as we could see, tried to alter his behaviour. No, that's not true. There were a few rare times when Burr and I were witness to whole bottles of whisky being poured down the sink, a prelude to Mother fighting him for all she was worth.

Behind the waterfall, we tried to understand what we had done that had landed the two of us into a family as godforsaken as ours. We thought we were born realists, something we'd heard Mother call herself. If we had to take after someone, we said, it wasn't going to be him. It never occurred to us in any realistic way that there might be any other sort of father. He was the one we had.

"Why do they fight?"

"Maybe they hate each other."

"They got married, didn't they?"

"Maybe he didn't drink then."

"Maybe he started drinking after they had *us*."

One time, we went home and sneaked into a silent house and opened the glass door of the china cabinet. We lifted out the charcoal-covered prayer book and searched for the passage we wanted and laid the book on the dining-room table. A frayed silken cord kept the pages open at the marriage vows. But the book silently found its way back to the shelf behind glass before we were up the next morning, and we did not know who had replaced it. This disappointed us because we wanted the two of them to know that we were part of this, too. That we had to shift and bend with every ripple the two of them made.

The summer we were nine, the daily paper ran an article called: *Take this test to see if you're an alcoholic.* Burr and I cut out the article and administered the test—not to Father, but to each other. Behind the waterfall, we learned the questions by heart. *Have you begun to invent excuses for having a drink? Do you try to push drinks onto others?* No, no, we answered. *Do you drink to forget your troubles?* And the most ominous of all: *Do you drink alone?*

After we'd given the test to each other, we answered for Father. Three truthful yes answers meant a drinking problem. But unlike the marriage vows in the prayer book, we did not leave the newspaper test lying around on the dining-room table. We couldn't go that far. Because Father's drinking, except between Burr and me, was never discussed.

* *

There was always the next day. The real morning after. When living people rose from their beds and had breakfast and stayed in or went out—to school, to work, to play—and carried on with their lives. Even born realists who lived together and looked one another in the eye and spoke the way they believed other people spoke. But did not mention, no, never mentioned the night before, the day before, the weekend of stumbling, of spilling, of drunken singing, of maudlin tears. Never mentioned Father falling into the empty tub and, arm outstretched, halfway through the bathroom wall; never mentioned the broken glass, the stains on the rug, the holes in the plaster, the lawnchair collapses, the slips on the ice, the broken ribs, ankles, bones. The weeping red-rimmed eyes.

How could we get up in the morning and never mention any of this?

Because these were our real lives.

Because Father got out of bed Monday morning, put on his old suit, stood on the dirt road to be picked up by the factory truck—and went back to work. In some wild and implausible way, he convinced us that he could function. And Burr and I returned to school, pushing down the fear that had knotted in our stomachs like a lurking tiger, since Friday afternoon.

* *

Christmas: Burr and I are ten years old. Father lifts the tree with one hand. He storms through the living room, out the front door—bulbs attached, cords frayed and flying—and plants the tree in the snowbank.

Who brought it back inside? Rescued the surviving bulbs, the frosty angels? Who went down on hand and knee to shake the snow from bruised needles and limbs?

Christmas Eve: Burr and I are eleven. Father sits in his green chair in the living room and begins a slow and steady binge that will last until New Year's Day. He holds his glass in a salute to anyone who walks through the room, and sings:

Hither, page, and stand by me,
If thou knows't it telling,

Yonder peasant, who is he?
Where and what his dwelling?

He tries to whip up speed in the lyrics, but his tongue thickens and he's lodged in his chair and only one arm is able to beat itself against the upholstery.

The last three days, he carries his whisky to his room and stays there. Mother comes downstairs to sleep on the couch. On New Year's Day, he emerges. Showers, shaves, and comes into the living room, whistling. It's as if he's been away on a slightly wearing trip. He reaches under the tree and pulls out our gift, the one he's refused at Christmas. It's a photograph of Burr and me, taken at Woolworth's in Greenly and framed by ourselves. He rolls his eyes towards the ceiling as if to a distant agreeing oracle and says, in a way that only he seems to understand, "By their fruits ye shall know them," which drives Burr and me back to the cave, despite the icicles and the slippery climb.

"Do you think we're like him? That we'll turn out like him?"

"We'll leave before that can happen," says Burr.

Where was Mother during this time?

She was keeping the peace.

* *

There were acts of Mother's that we admired. Her capacity to avoid argument. Her ability to feign sleep; so practised was she at this, she was able to fool Burr and me some of the time. We admired her resolution. Four days a week, she took the bus to Sadie's Dress Shop on Greenly's Main Street where, from the day Burr and I began school, she was head seamstress. Mother, in fact, had a narrowly circumscribed life of her own. She had a small income; she had a few friends who, like herself, worked at the shop and with whom she went out occasionally, but whom she never invited home. This, Burr and I understood; our own best friends were more or less kept in hiding over a period of fifteen years.

Long after Burr and I left home, we phoned each other, going over and over the same ground. By then, we were married and had children of our own. But we talked as if there was still something we could do about Father's drinking: acknowledge it, make it public, somehow. To free Mother, we said. To free ourselves. "The patterns are entrenched," we said, into the phone. "Thank God we got out. But how can she put up with him? How can she have stayed with him all these years?"

"Too late to leave," said Burr. "Neither of them can make a move now."

We sent each other identical newspaper clippings: *Nine out of ten wives stay with alcoholic husbands. One husband in ten will stay with an alcoholic wife.*

Once, we went into hysterics when Burr, having put her children to bed a few minutes earlier, told me she'd just poured herself a sherry.

"Do you drink alone?" I said, in my behind-the-waterfall voice.

* *

We continued to make the climb in good weather, even after our bodies had grown too large to fit the cave. During our early teens, we sat on the ground at the bottom of the falls and scratched boys' initials onto flat layers of rock. We knew we were too far from home to be found; in any case, there was no one to come looking. Mother was at the shop until five; Father at the cheese factory until six when the truck dropped him off.

Some days, he brought home a block of cheese, which he stored in the root cellar, the entrance of which was a double trapdoor around one side of the house. Burr and I seldom lifted those wooden slats; a few times, while Father was at work, we did so on a dare, and descended the wooden ladder. Once down in that stifling space, we had to hunch shoulders and bow our heads. Father had run a wire through the floor of the house and hooked up a swinging socket, but this rarely contained a bulb. Burr and I encouraged each other to hold our breath so we wouldn't have to inhale the underground. I believed the place was alive. Burr called it the rat cellar instead of the root cellar.

While we were there, we inspected Father's whisky, for this is where he kept his stash. He'd banged shelves into an earth wall. One shelf held aging blocks of cheese. Surprisingly, there was little dampness in that room underground. Another shelf held his whisky—five or six bottles at a time. Never fewer than three. The store, he called it. Go down and see what I've got in the store. And Burr and I, even though we might know the answer, would hold our breath and go down.

* *

Father walks through the back door each evening and reaches for the bottle he's brought up the night before. He's taken to announcing in a loud voice, "The bar is officially open," as if granting himself licence. As if this is a safe joke, an opening line to which there is no reply.

How does he know we won't speak? That we won't scream, throw plates, dump whisky down the drain. That we won't cry or despair or quietly plead, "Please go somewhere and get help. You have a drinking problem."

How can he count on our silence?

This is the part that is most difficult to understand.

Father has to take only two drinks now, before he starts to weave his way across the room. "I can hold my liquor," he says, but doesn't look us in the eye. "Don't ever think I can't hold my liquor."

We hear him from the green chair:

O Mother, O Mother, make my bed
Make it both long and narrow.

Then, silence. We don't need to see his face to know that he's
begun to weep, as he often does, now.

* *

"Think of his face," I said to Burr one day when I was sitting in
the kitchen of her apartment.

Burr looked over, saw me as I saw her, saw the cold stone that
lay at the bottom of our lives.

"Flushed," she said. "Moist eyes." She sat down.

"Moist around the lips," I said. "Soft chin. Wrinkles from the
corners of his mouth up across the cheeks."

"Extra folds of cheek."

"A wonder, really." We knew plenty of statistics. "He should
be emaciated, malnourished."

"Mother keeps feeding him, meat and potatoes."

"What's she supposed to do? Let him starve?"

"Maybe," said Burr. "I mean, think of his liver."

We giggled dangerously, as if Father were in the next room.
And then found ourselves doubled over.

Burr stood up, held onto her chair, addressed an unknown
audience. "If you wonder why we laugh," she said, "if *you'd*
spent the first fifteen years of your life edging away from tears,
you'd laugh, too."

She sat down. We stopped laughing, but continued to wipe
our eyes. We were in a place we hadn't allowed ourselves for
years. But the place still had no outlet, no escape.

"Enablers," I said. "That's what we're called now."

"The people who made up the word never had to look Father
in the eye."

"Did *we*?"

* *

Father has become tricky. We know this, but we never say it. It's something about his eyes, the red horizontal streaks through the whites, the narrowing of focus, the pulling of the look into himself, fast, so we get just a flash, a quick hint of what he might do next. This is our cue to move sideways, exit, make a swift get-away. Sometimes I wonder if, from above, we look like a family of crabs, picking our way sideways to get around one another.

By now, he has bought a car, a second-hand Pontiac with a stick shift behind the wheel. The car is two shades of green and breaks down a lot, but Father manages to keep it going and no longer relies on the factory truck to travel back and forth to work.

During summer evenings and weekends, before *the bar is officially open,* he teaches me to drive on the dirt road. Burr and I are fifteen. Burr refuses to learn. I see it as a means of escape. She sees what's coming next.

And what's coming next is this: Father, on Friday nights after work, drives home and drops off the Pontiac before he heads now farther afield to do his drinking. He's picked up by the men he calls his drinking partners, but tells us he's too smart to drive home with them. "They're all pie-eyed by nine o'clock," he says. "They can't hold their liquor worth a damn." But he, he wouldn't get behind the wheel after three drinks. To ensure that he gets home safely, he's decided that I will pick him up when he's ready to come home.

"Don't do it," says Burr, upstairs in our room. "I wouldn't. You'll only be helping him drink as much as he wants."

This is decades before the words *emotional blackmail* begin to appear in the articles we seek out and read.

Friday nights, Saturday nights, I don't know how long it goes on, Father phones when he is drunk and ready to come home, and I climb into the Pontiac and edge my way close to the shoulder of dirt roads and back highways, and collect him. I am always to wait in the car and this I do, watching for his swaying figure in doorways of hotels, houses, bars. A greenish sort of light shines across these openings; music blurts into the air with a suddenness that surprises; voices erupt and subside as if severed by the closing doors.

My father reaches out to steady himself against the passenger side. He slumps rather than slides in, and as soon as the door is shut he raises his head and begins a conversation as if it's normal for us to converse. Truth is, at home we hardly ever speak. The two of us face forward in the close, whisky-breath space of the front seat. I can escape him no more than he can escape me. His slurred questions are barely understandable; they don't seem connected to my life or his. One night, he reaches into his pocket and pulls out a handful of coins, which he says are for me. When we get home, he scatters them over the front seat. I wait until he goes to bed, and then I go out and scoop up the coins, wondering if he'll remember and take them back the next day.

Each time I get him home, I believe I have saved his life. It never occurs to me that if he is at the wheel, he might kill someone else. I concentrate only on him and me: if he drives, he might die; if I drive, I keep him alive.

He is my father.

* *

The summer we finish high school, a Saturday, Burr runs away. Father, who descends to the rat cellar and comes up bearing a bottle, opens the bar early because it's the weekend. After two drinks and some prowling around, he comes upon Burr's diary and reads portions of it aloud, making fun. Burr is furious. She will never forgive him, she says, never.

I know where she's gone, of course. Not far. There's only one place to go.

Father walks out to the road a couple of times, glass in hand, looks both ways, comes back to the yard and leans into the Pontiac.

"Where's your sister?" he says.

"I don't know."

"Where is she?"

"How should I know?"

He rolls his eyes, and when he does this I'm reminded of the New Year's Day he surfaced to open the framed photograph of us, his children, his twins. *By their fruits ye shall know them.* I'm possessed of a rage I didn't know I contained, a rage I could not have let fly even moments before.

"It's your fault she ran away! It's your bloody fault!"

Me. Shouting at Father.

"What the hell are you talking about?"

His rage is greater than mine. His stance threatening. It stops me. Right there. The closest I've ever come to naming it, naming him. I have a momentary insight into how Mother must feel. The reasons she leaves him alone. The incident closes over the way water closes over a mudhole.

I sneak a chunk of ham and two apples out of the fridge and take them to the base of the waterfall. Burr comes out of hiding and I tell her that I've shouted at Father. I've come close to calling him—a drunk.

"But you didn't," she says, and her voice is flat. "Did you."

At the first sign of shadows in the fields, we walk home and go up to our room, unchallenged. Leggings over psoriasis: like every other encounter with Father, this one is never mentioned. After we leave home, we say to each other. After we leave home if he so much as touches a drink in our presence, *we'll tell him.*

But after we leave home, nothing changes. Except that Burr and I move away. Mother stays; they go on living together as if there's no escape.

"He's coming here," I tell Burr. "They're both coming for a visit. Only one night, and they'll be staying at a hotel."

"So he can drink without censorship," she says, on the phone.

"Do you realize that this is the first trip they've taken away from home?"

Burr and I have distanced ourselves, put a hundred and thirty miles between us and our childhood home. We can visit, but we can also get back to the city quickly. I think of the old dirt road, dust rolling in over the fields and settling on the long grass. Greenly has stretched out to the country now. It has surrounded and encompassed the waterfall—now a picnic site—and our parents' home, which is part of the town. I think of the cheese factory, shut down years ago. I think of Father's stash under ground. Is it still there? Who buys the whisky? We know, of course, that Father doesn't drink the way he used to. Can't. Indirectly, Mother has let us know this as his health has become worse and worse. She does all the driving now. The bus service has stopped; the roads are paved. And she, too, has retired.

Because Burr's apartment is small and located on the outskirts of the city, we decide that it will be easier to have the family meal at my home. Burr's family will stay overnight. "I'm not serving liquor," I say. "One bottle of wine for the adults, and that will have to be shared. He can't get drunk on that."

Father brings his own. A large bottle of cheap red wine, which he sets at his feet under the table. Before dinner, he pulls two miniature whisky bottles from his shirt pocket, and drinks the contents of those.

Burr and I are mute. The children chat with their grandmother and, after dinner, go out to play. Our husbands have heard our stories over and over again, but they're not entangled the way we are, in our past. No one interferes with Father, who stays aloof and sinks into silence at his end of the table.

Until the momentary flush of rowdiness when he tries to raise a singsong after dinner, slapping his legs against the rug. Mother has already slipped quietly away, and has driven herself back to the hotel. She kisses Burr and me at the door. "He'll come by taxi, later," she says. "We'll stop by for a few minutes on our way home in the morning. We can say goodbye then." And when Father leaves, not more than a half hour later, he falls flat on his face on my front lawn.

Burr and I lean against the door and curse and laugh in outrage and relief after the taxi pulls away. I swear to her that I'll say something the next day. Not when he's drunk, when he's sober. I'll let him know—no shouting or screaming—that it matters to us, that we're all in this together, that we, they—I don't know what I'm going to say.

In the morning, Burr and I stand on the step to greet our parents. Strength in numbers, we say. My heart is fluttering wildly. "Steady," says Burr, "steady." If I don't speak, will she?

Father slides out of the passenger seat and shuts the car door, but just as he begins to walk towards us, the children swoop around from the backyard, having heard the car. He looks down at his grandchildren, scoops up the youngest and swings him to his shoulders. There's an outcry from the others; they all want a ride. Father will not be looked at, face to face. He could be anyone's grandfather, some pleasant old gentleman romping with his grandchildren before he sets off on his journey home. Has he erased himself so thoroughly? Or have we done it for him?

Maybe he really doesn't remember.

* *

One last scene. After Father's death, I have a dream, and I phone Burr to tell her.

A group of people has gathered at our childhood home. Family, friends, workmates of Mother, even drinking partners of our father. We are there to celebrate, though what we're celebrating, I don't know.

When Burr and I walk through the door, we don't see Father. We begin to look for him, upstairs and down. "I'll bet he's in the rat cellar," says Burr, and we go out and walk around to the side of the house. We have to push back the bushes because spiraea has grown over the double trapdoors. We raise the slats and descend the ladder; look at each other and prepare to hold our breath. But here, something happens. The earth cellar opens into an amazing network of underground rooms. We understand now that this is where Father lives. He's been bringing down odds and ends, bits and pieces, for years. He's constructed extra rooms, three of them, and these have ceiling tiles and are lined with wood. Old linoleum has been spread across the floor. There is a chair in one corner, even a second-hand fridge. I think of the hanging socket and wonder if the fridge has been plugged in.

And now, we see Father. He is standing in the middle of the first room, an overflowing bottle in one hand. Champagne, something we've never seen him buy or drink. From above, there are noises of celebration—people shouting, congratulating, many voices. Shall we stay down here to celebrate? There is a moment when we must decide.

I marvel at how much work Father has done to the place. The shelves are neat; the ceilings tight. I move into one of the bedrooms and reach out a hand to smooth the spread, an old one, made of ribbed chenille. I give it a shake to show Burr that, look, Father has even carried a mattress down here. But there is no mattress. As I lift the spread, I see the decay, the disintegration of all that lies beneath. In that single moment when I lift the spread to give it a shake, it becomes clear that everything has been eaten by insects, is in shreds, or has rotted away.

But his face. I see Father's face. He has turned towards us while champagne flows over his hand and runs down his arm. He's looking at Burr and me, and he's about to celebrate, and we clearly see the expression in his streaked and watery eyes.

Sarajevo

∞

During takeoff, Marta called up her angels. Morav, she said to herself. She closed her eyes. Daddy. Aunt Elspeth. Uncle Harry. Jill, who died before me and was too young. She forgot Grandmother O'Hare, and was reminded later the same night. Grandmother O'Hare walked into her dream and stood with a pinched face, severe, silent because she'd been left off the list.

There was a windstorm in Frankfurt, but flights had not been cancelled. Marta felt the wing outside her window tip to the left, as if she'd caught the plane in the act of tumbling over. Tumble. Drop. She'd gone through this so many times in her mind, for so many years, she knew the sequence.

It had been bad enough getting herself across the Atlantic. An act of faith she did not believe she could raise each time she flew across an ocean. Acts of innocence and faith to believe, as the plane drifted away from one continent and entered the abyss over cold bottomless Atlantic, that it could and would reach the opposite shore. Always night flights. Flying out over darkness. Hard cold ocean with creatures great and small, lurking below. Never, when she set foot on a plane, did she have a single expectation of arriving at destination. If it happened, it was a gift, a blessing, a miracle.

Between Frankfurt and Zagreb, the Croatian attendant presented a meal heavy with meat, a layer of cold grease visible.

Marta rejected the food, turned away, wondering how, why, she had entered this new set of risks and possibilities. War. Warriors. She was married to a man who'd been away from home for almost a year. That was why she had left Frankfurt in a windstorm, and was headed for Zagreb.

* *

She phoned her friend Marion before leaving.

"Marion? I've got my ticket."

"You're sure you want to do this?"

"Want has nothing to do with it. I have to do this. He's out of Bosnia now. He's living in Croatia. But he goes back just about every week. The last time I talked to him, a Serb had held a gun to his head."

"What did he do?"

"He said to the Serb's companion—another Serb—'Ask him if it's because he has such poor aim that he has to stand this close to shoot me.'"

"Was Geoff armed?"

"No. He hates wearing a gun. I don't know what he's thinking, but he's not afraid. He believes that *right* not *might* will have its way. He truly believes that. Despite what his eyes are seeing."

"He doesn't think about death the way we do," said Marion.

"How is that?"

"I don't know. Fear, I guess."

"He doesn't think about it at all. He says if he were to think about death in the middle of a war, he'd already be dead."

"He's probably right," said Marion.

* *

A week earlier, a UN soldier's face had been carved with a knife, at gunpoint. And snipers, there were always snipers. They picked off whomever they could—their own civilian population, UN peacekeepers, aid workers. In downtown Sarajevo, old women out for firewood or water were shot at for target practice. Cowards. Cowardly men hiding behind guns, shooting at their own elderly, their own children. She hated, detested Geoff being there. Last year, his arm had been broken when a Croat had tried to kidnap him. Geoff had not been shot, nor had he been kidnapped. But he'd walked away from a cocked machine gun. He believed in his work. He didn't see Muslims, Croats, Serbs. He saw humans needing help. Children—many children. Orphans. Women. Some men. The old. He knew individuals. Friends. Teenagers. Victims. All of them victims of their own war. There were days, nights, when she regretted loving him.

* *

Days and nights were all alike in the hotel. They lived in the countryside, outside Zagreb, a rural stretch of four-lane dusty highway. The hotel had been taken over by the United Nations; from the outside, it was baby blue, a long flat building, concrete and glass. She felt like Rapunzel, alone all day on the second floor. Croatian police guarded her from outside. They swaggered into the bar in the morning where she, the only customer, sipped bitter coffee and kept watch over knives and guns strapped to their waists. The waiters wore blousy shirts and in halting English spoke with her about *gut Geld* in Toronto and Frankfurt. Every one of them had a brother, an uncle or a daughter in Canada or Germany. No one, it seemed, wanted to stay in Croatia.

In the evening, the warriors came back from headquarters, lining up their white vehicles like cardboard jeeps in the parking lot below. They were from many nations, European and African. Geoff was the first to leave in the morning and last to return at night. He flew in and out of Bosnia by helicopter, by small jet, continuing his journeys in open jeeps or armoured personnel carriers for the final leg. One morning, a bullet ripped through the cockpit of the plane as the pilot landed. Geoff was sitting behind the navigator. The bullet exited inches from his ear. In their hotel room, he painted his blood group on the back of his blue helmet—large permanent felt tip letters, so there'd be no mistake.

Some part of him, she knew, had been drawn to the danger. He talked with resignation and inevitability about the violence. He told her of thugs who'd emerged from the deepest crevices of the earth when war began. Territories had been drawn; the slime-balls, as he called them, would stop at nothing to keep their guns, their endless supply of liquor, women, money, drugs. Their power. War would not end, not with signed agreements in Geneva, London, Sarajevo. No, it was already far beyond three political parties lining up continual complaints to make one another look bad.

She could not speak to him of home, of their children. She watched, waited, trying to learn what he was dealing with. Sometimes he stayed in Bosnia several days at a time. He left his gun locked in a trunk in their room. His friends were in Sarajevo. He'd left them behind. He could get out. He was alive. Word of the killings always reached him. Another soldier, another interpreter, horrible, intentional murders. He shook his head, talked to her as if the dead were still alive. Some, a few, had got out. He'd helped. He received letters at the hotel, passed through many hands, filled with tears, with kisses, with love. When he returned each time from Bosnia, his back was soaked through under the armour he wore. The equipment too heavy to carry. He removed it piece by piece in their room, stacked it in a corner, the blue helmet placed on top with his blood group showing, reminding them of what was necessary, of what might be.

* *

During daylight, she walked for hours along an open four-lane highway where she would be safe. Past dusty cornfields, flat and plain. Men looked at her with anger, knowing she was a foreigner. She wore old clothes for walking. Found paths through the field gardens, greeted women bent double over small patches of earth. No one ever returned her greeting. The women were hostile, suspicious. She returned to the highway, ignored the horns of trucks. She sat at the window and watched the Croatian police below. Wrote long letters to Marion, who wrote back to what she called the land of Godforsake. Marion was her thread, joining her to Canada, to home.

Geoff brought food to the room. Bottled water. She went into the city and sat in cafés. She walked everywhere. The faces in the city were the same: sullen, silent, grim. Grim described everything, everyone.

She had spoken to Geoff by telephone the night he'd moved from Sarajevo to Zagreb. He'd been sitting on the steps of *the Residency*, he said, waiting for his driver to take him to the airport. Branches were snapping off trees above him in the garden. Bullets.

"Didn't you think to go inside to wait for the driver?" she said. She'd held her breath in their kitchen, in Canada.

"No." His voice was thin. "The bullets were higher; they were over my head."

* *

The two of them were invited to dinner in the old city, on one of the wooded hills of Zagreb. The general and his entire staff. The French were polite, tugging sideways at their blue berets when they saw her, shaking hands each time they met in the lobby or the bar. The general jogged each morning, accompanied by his four bodyguards, guns strapped to pouches on their backs. The dinner party was pre-arranged; several days earlier, the bodyguards had driven to the ancient hill to inspect the premises. She said to Geoff, "Isn't it rather a giveaway, to let people know we're coming?" But he shook his head, no. This was Zagreb, not Sarajevo, after all. Still, precautions had to be taken.

They drove into the wooded area on a Saturday night. When they stepped from the Land Rover, she heard Greek music, Theodorakis, from the front of the restaurant, the public part. Their dining room was behind: a private closed veranda, partially screened, up three wooden steps. Separate entrance. She and Geoff were last to arrive. The party, seated around a long narrow table, rose to its feet. Only a few had known she was there, living among them at the hotel. The interpreters were there, too, and office clerks, French and Belgian and Canadian officers, body-guards and drivers. Eighteen at the table. Several languages spoken. Croatian waiters carried in tray after tray of brandy, slivovitz, red wine. Creamy cottage cheese and plates of ham and dry bread. Before the main course.

The general laughed and parried. His eyes dark. All conversa-tion centred around him. He was used to command and control. Expected nothing else, nor did anyone, at the table. She spoke to the UN interpreters, learned their backgrounds, asked ques-tions. Several hours had gone by when she noticed two empty chairs at the far end of the table, to her right. Moments later, the general stood, a small man. The table rose to its feet. Armed bodyguards surrounded him; two white cars with black letter-ing waited at the screen door. The general slipped into his vehi-cle; the car roared off into the night. The Land Rover followed; more bodyguards. The party was over, instantly.

"What," she said to Geoff, "what have we just been a part of?"

The remaining few drifted towards their own white vehicles, parked along the shoulder. A soft fall night. The air was good here, in the woods. "Why were the chairs empty, at the end of the table?" she asked Geoff. "Two of the bodyguards slipped out," he said. "Half hour earlier than everyone else. They had to check the general's car, every inch, above and below, with mirrors, for bombs."

She tried to think of home, of her giant shadow legs striding in the sea at sunset, of the undulating lines of migrating cormorants and geese along the shore of Prince Edward Island. If she ever got home, she would give thanks for being, for belonging in that wondrous place.

* *

After Samobor, she began to talk to Geoff about home, about their children, their family. They drove to Samobor during his first break in more than three months. It was a Sunday in September; he hadn't had two hours off since June. Because he would have to return to work in the afternoon, he remained in uniform. Samobor was a fifteen-minute drive from the hotel. The front lines had changed since she'd arrived; they were always changing. The southern outskirts of Zagreb had been hit by rockets the week before. She'd been writing to Marion, when the windows in her room began to rattle. Shelling went on most of the afternoon and all night. She and Geoff slept to the sound of guns, not so distant, nine kilometres away. Samobor had been hit. They'd been told it was the most pleasing village in the area: beautiful, ancient, quiet. Narrow streets, woods, castle ruins above the town.

A mistake. There were no signs of shelling, but the people were angry. Youths began to circle. An old man turned and shouted at Geoff. They had left their vehicle on the main road, in the centre of town, along a meandering canal.

The people hated the UN. They knew nothing of those who'd been helped, those who'd been saved. Each party angry because the UN would not take its side. So far, Zagreb had stayed out of the physical war. Samobor had never been touched. Until the rockets. She felt something rising inside her, a state of readiness, she was not certain what. She asked Geoff; he felt it too. Hate all around them. Hate and anger that could turn at any moment.

Flick, she thought. Flick, and we are into chaos. They returned to their vehicle, aware of each careful step. They left the village and went back to the dreary hotel. She knew then, that she was going to leave. She'd been in Croatia for months, and now she wanted to go home.

* *

A small jet was returning to Canada, a visiting commander. They were offered seats, and they accepted. Geoff would take his leave. He would never be able to use up all that was owed him, but he would, at least, take leave. He now had a broken rib. MASH had x-rayed him after a jeep accident during his last trip to the front lines. The rib had snapped in two, would hopefully mend on its own. I will, she wrote to their children, get him out of here, but it might not be in one piece.

The dreams of flying began again. Nightmares lined up, ready to assume their place. Geoff told her that she had too much imagination, as if this were some extra affliction she carried. It was true that she could imagine anything. At the hotel, the navigator told them they'd fly first to Italy, staying overnight; then, to Iceland, then Halifax. The more luggage they carried, the more often they'd have to stop to refuel. She began to dream about Iceland, about drifting over open water, the engine chugging its last before the plane could reach Newfoundland. They were to depart in two days. She had never crossed the Atlantic in an eight-seater plane.

They flew to Ancona first, on the coast of Italy, and spent the night. She saw Geoff smile, heard him laugh for the first time in months. Flowers bloomed in Ancona. Voices lifted in ordinary tones, which she thought of as celebratory. She realized she'd lost the sound of normal conversation. She felt as if she were rejoining life after a long time in a darkened tunnel.

When they left Iceland, last chance to refuel before Canada, her thoughts, chasing one another, broke to pieces. She did not want to have to call up her angels. The night before, in Ancona, after a long walk on the beach, a long wonderful meal, she'd dreamed this tiny plane. Inter-city trains had roared below their hotel, between gardens and beach, close enough to keep her awake most of the night. She had heard the co-pilot say, before she'd boarded in Italy, "Oh, haven't the brakes been fixed?" and knew this had been intended as a joke. She was not able to laugh. They were on the military side of the airport and, while waiting to board, she had been free to wander through the cluster of canvas tents set up like a small village, boardwalks linking one to another.

Burned and blistered children had been arriving on stretchers, IVs dangling above them. Sarajevo to Ancona. A few were getting out. A country here, a country there, accepting them. She'd talked to some of the Canadian soldiers working there. To them, Bosnia was a place of bloody war, unseen, which sent out its children on stretchers, innocent and wounded. That was their portion, their reality. At the end of the working day, these Canadian men and women slept in clean hotel beds and drank cappuccino and ate good meals. They loaded tons of flour, stacked like sandbags, and worked in tents lined with maps and makeshift comforts.

Everyone's reality differed. There was no use breaking anything down to its simplest parts. She'd heard Geoff laugh, the old remembered, unrestrained laugh that released the tightened lines of his face. He'd laughed only once, but it was a beginning, after Sarajevo. If death came at you unexpectedly, she thought, okay. But not from guns behind buildings, from snipers high on dope or slivovitz. Murderers who were not even your enemies. Who did not know the expressions your face was capable of, or the shape of your fingers, or the colour of your eyes.

* *

She stepped inside her house. *Her* house during the past year, *their* house now. Left the luggage in the living room, was not interested in opening suitcases or hanging clothes. She knew there was a bottle of champagne in the refrigerator. Good champagne. Dry, the way she liked it. Geoff walked from room to room, every room, upstairs and down, examining as if he had not believed anything would be here when he returned. He lifted a dish, opened a cupboard door, peered into framed photographs of the children. It was late, they'd been travelling fifteen hours. They drank champagne and hauled out the sheets and made the bed.

It was then that she began to tell him all that she had imagined before they left and all that she had imagined during flight. The sounds she'd heard, the expressions she'd watched, her head filled with details she'd been afraid, until now, to release. He began to laugh, great shaking laughter. She began to cry. Her sobs defeated him. Then, they both laughed and cried together.

"Why," he said, "why are you crying like this?"

"Because I've earned the right," she said. "Because I've earned the right to cry this hard."

In the Name of Love

❦

1993: It was her birthday, and Jule was sitting on a hard-backed chair in a hotel room in Croatia, eating a fried-fish sandwich. The fish was cold but it was the best she could do. She propped her feet on the desk and leaned back, trying for comfort. As she bit into the sandwich, she wondered what Carl was eating in Bosnia. *Not* the sardines. Ten months ago, when she was at home in Canada, she had included a tin of sardines in a care package—knowing that Carl was stopped at checkpoints on Bosnian roads, or stuck inside an armoured personnel carrier, or in a bunker while shelling went on for days. He had not eaten the sardines, but had tucked them into his shoulder bag, just in case. "I'm saving them for an emergency," he told her. But emergencies had come and gone. The reason he hadn't eaten them—she was sure of this—was because they'd been a gift from her. This was what war broke down to: an endearment between two people became symbolized by a tin of mustard-flavoured sardines.

Jule switched on the TV. If she wanted to know Carl's where-abouts, she watched CNN. Sometimes she caught a glimpse of him in Sarajevo behind the warring leaders who, surrounded by bodyguards, strutted in and out of the peace talks. Or she saw him in the same frame as a visiting Cabinet minister from

217

Canada who sat before a microphone, being prompted from behind.

Carl entered the room at that moment, double-locked the door and slipped the chain. He removed his jacket and bullet-proof vest and set them in the corner.

"I've been keeping track," she said, by way of greeting. "Six hundred and four years ago, the Battle of Kosovo. And seventy-five days. Do you think we'll ever get out?"

The windowpanes rattled in answer. Karlovac had been shelled by the Serbs the night before, and the night before that. Alone at the window on the third floor, she'd watched flashes light up the southern sky. When she'd first arrived from Canada, the front line had been fifteen miles away. Now rocket attacks were occurring five miles from the hotel.

Carl stood behind her chair and leaned forward to rest his chin against her hair. She could tell by the gesture the extent of his fatigue. But he pushed away the fatigue and lifted a bottle of champagne from his duffel bag. He grinned, and set two plastic cups on the dresser. "My French colleagues came through," he said. "Happy Birthday, dear wife."

They clicked plastic and drank.

"How did you manage? I wasn't expecting you so soon," she said. She drained the plastic cup.

"I told the warring parties it was your birthday."

"Seriously."

"It was deemed safe to fly out before dark so I grabbed the one available seat." He pulled a chair nearer the dresser, and sat down.

She shifted her own chair close, seeing the lines of weariness on his face. "Did you come in from the coast?"

"I did," he said. "We were in a Russian jet, a 24-seater. It was *not* a luxury plane."

"Was there any peace today?" She was sorry as soon as she'd asked. The question was a bitter joke.

"It was gruelling," he said. "An all-day session—with aides and bodyguards and interpreters and UN people. At the end of the day, the leaders and their entourages poured out of the sandbagged building to greet the media, and a shell lobbed in. If it hadn't been so horrible, it might have been funny. The timing was astonishing. What was more astonishing was that no one was hurt. There were a few black remarks over that."

Jule knew all about macabre humour that surfaced during war. She was surrounded by it. The fact of her being in Croatia at all was perhaps the blackest humour of all. *Extricate Carl,* she'd printed on a notepad the day she'd arrived. She'd placed the note on the bedside table so that there would be no misunderstanding about the reason for her presence. That evening, the note was buried under Carl's papers. The next morning, she placed it on top again. By nightfall it was buried. No mention of it was ever made, but neither did the note entirely disappear. A hint of the lunacy we are a part of, she thought. And that includes the lunacy between us. I am as much into it now as he.

"You're pretty serious on your birthday," said Carl. "Where's all that humour you've always had?"

Where, indeed? Most of the time, she felt like throwing her hands in the air and wailing. But she held back, reminding herself, *Cry on your birthday, cry all year.*

* *

After Carl left in the morning, Jule went out walking. She'd found a way to stay near the fields and gardens where she could smell fall, smell earth, yet still be in the open. Sometimes she hiked along the side of the road, circling in a wide arc around the nearby customs building, which was built of pink concrete and could be seen for a mile across the plain. There were hills in the distance but Carl had warned her to stay away. What I need, she thought, is a *Schutzengel*, a guardian angel. But Carl's need was greater. He'd been transferred to Croatia, yes, but he still travelled in and out of Bosnia, sometimes daily. She tried to invent, to call up a *Schutzengel*, for Carl.

She turned away from the highway and crossed the ditch on a plank that led to a path. Two men were working at the edge of the field. When she was within a few feet, they unzipped their trousers and urinated beside the path. She kept on without changing her pace, not wanting to show fear. They were letting her know that they were in charge.

She thought about an evening the week before when she and Carl had walked together after dinner. A rare evening, because he'd managed to get back to the hotel before dark. They'd taken a service road, and had strayed in a direction she'd never taken alone. It was almost dark when a long sleek car approached and stopped near an abandoned farmhouse, ahead. The headlights went out. A man appeared as if he'd sprung from the ditch, and began to load crates from a wooden cart into the trunk of the car. It was not difficult to see that this was an arms transfer. Carl took her hand and said, "Turn slowly and don't pause. Keep walking at the same pace until we're back."

All that night she dreamed, but her dreams were of visions she herself had never seen: the big guns, bodies in the streets, buildings crumbling. It was as if Carl's head had transferred images to hers. She tossed for hours while, beside her, Carl slept a deep and peaceful sleep.

She continued her walk through paths of dirt and dust. She would be glad when the weather cooled—any day now, a hotel clerk had promised. She reached the blocks of flats, miles of them, which stretched, after another hour's walk, into the centre of Zagreb. She looked up to the windows as she passed, rarely seeing another person.

She veered towards open fields again and walked another mile, arriving at a cluster of houses joined by grape arbours and surrounded by pens holding hens and geese. She nodded and spoke to several women and children, but no one returned her greeting. Two uniformed soldiers were working on a military jeep in the hot sun. There was no mistaking the red and white chequered shield, the *Sahovnica*.

Jule wondered if she should turn back, but by this time more people, men *and* women, had come out of their houses and now stood at the fences. The road dwindled to a path, and her heart sank as she saw that she was approaching a dead end. She circled a small grotto and, striding purposefully, returned the way she'd come. There was no other way back. When she passed the gauntlet of hostility a second time, she felt as if she'd been spat upon.

* *

During her trips into the city, whenever she was alone, Croatian men walked up to her as close as they dared, always approaching from behind. They murmured angry words, unmistakably sexual words. She was forced to keep separate, to watch and listen at her back. Whom did they believe she was? Or was it just an insult to the foreigner?

One day, she descended from Strossmayer Satellicta above the old town, taking the cobbled street that wound through a shrine built beneath an open tower. Women were praying in the outdoor pews. Smoke had blackened the inside arches of the tower, and rivers of melted wax meandered like lava through a sea of candles. When she reached lower town, she crossed two sets of tram tracks and sat in the sun at the foot of Ban Jelacic statue in the main square. Everywhere, she saw Croats in combat uniform. To her they looked like bewildered young men,

not the men she read about who committed atrocious acts—
acts that were not limited to any one side. She felt a hand touch
her neck, and turned, startled. An older woman sat close beside
her on the cement wall. Jule shifted over. The woman spoke
German in low hurried tones.

"My husband is twelve years dead," she said. "I live on small
pension." She hauled up her wool skirt to show wide runs at the
top of her stockings. She reached for Jule's neck again and fin-
gered a Celtic cross Jule was wearing on a chain.

"You are good Catholic," she said. "Give me dinars. I need
dinars."

But Jule did not give her money. She stood, and began the
long walk back to the hotel. On the way, she was stopped by two
boys who rushed at her from behind shrubbery. "*Geld*," they
shouted. "Five *Mark*. One dollar. Give sandwich." They roared
off, laughing.

Jule thought of the faces of the women at the shrine. Every
evening on TV, she watched the stooped controlling presence of
President Tudjman in front of the cameras. The clips were
repeated until she knew them by heart: burned bodies, bluffing
soldiers, women clutching children and shouting into the lens.
She thought of the police barriers surrounding the *Sabor*, the
parliament, and the silent square above the old city. She felt like
shouting, *Abandon all hope!* and cursed herself for considering
such a thought. Later, when Carl was sleeping a deep sleep beside
her, she rolled on her side, propped an elbow and said to his sleeping face, "If you don't open one eye, I'm going to leave you."

* *

At the hotel, she ate a makeshift lunch from the tiny bar fridge,
which she and Carl tried to keep stocked with supplies. The closet
shelf contained English cereal Carl had bought from the British
NAAFI; cartons of H-milk from the Americans at Pleso Airport;

bottled water; a few cans of Tuborg from the Danes. When Carl's French friends learned that she was at the hotel, they sent grapefruit juice and, one day, even a fresh chocolate éclair.

On the occasions when Jule was able to get to the centre of town, she purchased brown bread and cheese. Once, she found a can of tuna. She bought an American kettle, which Carl's electrician friends rewired to fit the outlets. All in all, she and Carl managed, in a ten-by-ten-foot room, to live, to love, to work—for she had brought her work with her and was sending articles home.

With the TV on in the background, she began to practise German. She was willing to watch or listen to any program except *Der Preis Ist Heiss*. As she did not speak the Serbo-Croat language—now called Croatian here—German was the language that moved her about the city. If the shelling got worse, she would head for the Austrian border. She was four hours from Graz, three hours from Klagenfurt.

When Carl came in, Jule decided to remind him again that there was a world outside these borders. But Carl had turned into the war. "There's work to be done," he said. He hadn't had a day off since last winter, but she could see that the stress of the year he had lived in Sarajevo—before she'd even arrived—had already done *its* work.

"You've lost perspective," she told him. "You're out of touch." But he stood blinking at her as if she were the one who was out of touch. *Extricate Carl,* she repeated silently. *Open one eye.* She would find the note again and return it to the top of the heap on the bedside table. Or maybe she would just go home by herself.

* *

Sunday, Jule managed to get a call out to their daughter, Alex. Usually the phone system was crippled by long waits and frequent disconnections. As she talked, she stared out the hotel window at grey smoke in the distance. Carl had been back in Bosnia for three days, and Jule did not know when he'd return.

"Work," said Jule. "Work keeps us sane. Thank heavens I've brought my own. I've sent two articles back so far, and put my name in with aid agencies. I've taken typhoid pills, had hepatitis shots, whatever I need."

Alex was working, saving money for graduate school. She passed on her own news. As they hung up, Jule felt a sudden sense of danger. She did not understand why, but the chill that coursed through her was real indeed. She was thankful that she loved life, loved Carl, loved Alex. But there were no rituals here, no daily events to help preserve the ordinary nature of things. Everything was drama and violence and force. Even within their hotel room, grimness had set in. It was becoming more and more difficult to laugh, even to smile. *Make no mistake*, she told herself—allowing a momentary glimpse of home—*what we do in the name of love is also done for the sake of ourselves.*

What will I do, she thought, if a rocket explodes while I'm in the city? She already knew the answer. Half-torn shelter signs were pasted to buildings everywhere—stick figures chasing after arrows. In a city of one million people she would throw in her lot. She would go to the nearest shelter and help those who needed help.

"Danger! Danger!" Alex used to chant as a toddler. These warnings had accompanied her own precarious climbs. Sometimes she would reach a top shelf and perch there while Jule, hearing her call out, would feel her heart stop and would run towards her. They'd lived within the walls of one house then, the three of them. It had been easier to believe that one of them could enact a rescue.

* *

Jule had still not heard from Carl and was becoming uneasy. She could find nothing on CNN about peace talks or convoys. Though the phone lines were usually down, he sometimes managed to get a message to her by begging time on a journalist's satellite hookup. She thought it prudent to go back into the city. To find the Canadian Embassy; to register there. Newly opened in the summer, the embassy rented rooms in an expensive downtown hotel. A Croatian clerk—the only person there—advised her about travel to Austria. She would need a multiple entry-exit visa if she left Croatia and wanted to return. The clerk wrote out a phone number and said, earnestly, "You must ask for the Department of Strangers." In any other circumstance, Jule would have had to fight a grin. She did not go to the Department of Strangers. Thoroughly depressed, she sat at an outdoor table in a side street and ordered pizza. Though she and the waiter had no common language, she asked for *champignons* and *fromage*, the only words she'd discovered so far that seemed to be universal, a kind of pizza Esperanto.

A young American woman made her way through a maze of tables and asked if she could sit with Jule. *Am I so obviously the foreigner?* thought Jule. But she was glad of the company. The young woman, Kristen, was from Boston and taught at the American School.

"How does the war affect the school?" Jule asked, hungry for news of other humans.

"I don't know," said Kristen. "I hate thinking about the war. It's too awful."

"But the front line is only twenty minutes away." Jule was startled by Kristen's indifference.

"Is it? Well I don't think about it at all."

* *

Jule decided to walk the long route back on the dusty highway and was passed by four screaming ambulances along the way. When she approached the pink customs building, she saw rows of European transports lined up, the drivers waiting to have their loads sealed so they could continue their journeys. HOLLAND was painted across the cab of one of the trucks. She wanted to shout at the driver, "Edam! Gouda! Take me with you!" Could the whole of Europe be three hours away? An entire population where people actually chose the places they wanted to go?

She entered the hotel and went directly to the café-bar on the main floor. As she sat down, the windows rattled furiously. The bar was empty—UN workers were always away during the day. But within minutes of the shelling, the room filled. Not with strangers, but with Croats—men and women in business clothes. *Where had they come from?* While everyone was ordering strong coffee, Jule sensed tension, a heightened alertness.

She drank her own thick cappuccino and went to her room, wishing that Carl would return. The windows shuddered so violently she willed herself to stop hearing. She lay on the bed and pulled up the covers, though she was fully dressed. She thought about the past winter, ten months ago, when Carl had come home to Canada—his only leave. They'd had six days together and had unplugged the phone and locked the doors. A storm had raged outside and, after two days, snow drifted past the windows. They called no friends, read no papers. Their lives had been suspended, temporary, as if the two of them were playing house and the props would disappear if they let down their guard. Carl never once relaxed; he would be heading back to the war, back to Sarajevo, in less than a week. It was his way of ensuring that he would stay alive.

On the seventh morning, Jule drove him to the airport. As

she watched him disappear into an oblivious holiday crowd, a woman she had not known was inside her raised her head and began to listen for bullets.

* *

Was Carl alive? Was he being shot at right now? She tried to watch CNN, but fell asleep in the middle of the news. She was turning off, like Kristen from Boston. She went out in the early morning and hiked around the old town. She entered the Ethnographic Museum, but two guards tried to separate her from her passport and she left without seeing the exhibits. "Sorry boys," she said, and ran down the stone steps. She resolved to start wearing her passport inside a travel belt on her body.

After ten days and without warning, Carl walked into the hotel room in the early morning. Jule saw the change even before he spoke. He sat on the edge of the bed and told her. A friend and colleague, Maria, the interpreter he'd worked with on and off during the war, had been killed by a sniper while in the cab of his truck. They had been leaving Sarajevo, part of a convoy carrying medicine and food, headed for two refugee camps. Maria had worked selflessly since the beginning of the war. She'd been the sole support of her own family, two young sons, and had lived with the boys and her mother in the basement ruins of a flattened apartment. The single bullet had been accurate, entering Maria's skull.

Carl was tired. He was angry. He was ready to take time off. No matter what anyone did, war went on with its violent desecrating acts. Maria had been pulled into the maw that had swallowed thousands of others.

Jule made arrangements for her and Carl to fly to Frankfurt and on to Canada. She located and tore up the *Extricate Carl* sign. Carl might return to Croatia and even Bosnia again, but she knew that she never would. For now, they would get through this the way they always managed to get through. One step followed another and another. She packed her clothes, and Carl packed his—along with the unopened tin of sardines.

* *

They had one day left in Zagreb—a Saturday—and in late afternoon they took a taxi to the old city, circling the cobbled road Jule had trekked many times on foot. As Carl had never had a chance to visit the Lotrscak Tower, they climbed the fire lookout and circled the platform, looking out over the range of hills, the river valley and flat plain, twin spires of the cathedral, onion bulbs, crosses and domes. They took a few steps back into the tower and a sudden hailstorm descended, so they sat inside on a stone bench, leaning against the wall, waiting out the rain. They did not speak while the storm crashed down around them.

By five o'clock the sun was beginning to shine. Far below, the cobblestones were wet and sleek. Just before leaving the tower, Jule stepped out onto the platform again and looked down. A sudden cacophony of unleashed sound confused her, and she quickly tried to locate its source. She moved from railing to railing, peering over, and saw wedding parties approaching the main square from three directions, as though along spokes to the hub of a wheel.

First came soldier-grooms and, with them, young men who waved oversized Croatian flags out the windows of small cars. There was considerable competition for parking space and much honking of horns. The bridal parties followed on foot. Brides were dressed in long white gowns, and their skirts were hoisted above their knees as they crossed the wet cobbles. Their attendants fussed and shouted as they tried to keep long trains of lace from dragging through puddles.

Catholic and Orthodox churches were holding simultaneous

ceremonies in buildings that faced each other across the square. Civil ceremonies were conducted in a government building nearby. As each party entered, more people arrived and waited in nervous semicircles at the entrances outside. One wedding replaced the next, as fast as the ceremonies could be performed. As Jule watched, she had a sudden flash of memory: Alex as a small child playing with her dolls, inventing a game she called *Bride and Gloom.* Jule could not have predicted the gloom she now felt, watching these celebrations.

She and Carl descended the tower steps and, gripping hands tightly, found themselves mingling with wedding guests in the narrow streets. Staying together and inching sideways, they manoeuvred their way to the edge of a cobbled path that would lead them down again, to the old town. Jule glanced over at Carl and saw that he might cry. *There are other places in the world,* she told herself. *We'll get out of this one together.*

Carl read her thoughts. "It's about what we can live with and what we cannot," he said. He did not try to explain. "It's about what we are left with, in the end."

Jule looked back at the wedding couples with their friends and families, as she and Carl pressed together and made their way. The chaos of the scene stayed in her head: uniforms and flags, cobbles and puddles, shouts and cries, suits and gowns. But it was individual faces she most clearly remembered. She'd been searching those faces for signs of hope. Laughter. Even prophecy. In the midst of war, she had been looking for signs of love.

The Thickness of One Sheet of Paper

Tosh had his hand on her belly. They were at the back of the motionless bus, and neither had noticed the man from Marseilles until he twisted into the seat beside them.

"*Pardon,*" the man said, his face flushed.

"*Oh, non,*" said Judith, and made a gesture away from and towards him at the same time. She wondered what he thought she and Tosh had been doing at the back of the bus while Teruko, their tour guide, was leading the others through the temple—their third that morning.

Tosh withdrew his hand, but his face was expressionless. The man from Marseilles stared out the window. Judith gave up the impulse to explain. She did not look pregnant, but was—five months—and she felt it in the September heat.

"My wilting gravid wife," Tosh had said, the night before.

"Don't talk to me about being gravid," Judith said. "I have to survive these temperatures. I'm not leaving this air-conditioned room, not if I'm dragged. Not even for dinner."

"You'll starve our child."

"Too bad."

But Tosh had phoned room service. And the unnameable efficiency they'd come to expect with both irritation and delight had produced a four-course meal, whisked into the room. The waiter tucked linen napkins into the necks of their *yukata,* dressing gowns supplied by the hotel. Judith removed her napkin as soon as he left, and placed it on her lap. She was trying her best to deal with the constant supervision, the scrutiny. *Gaijin*. She was the foreigner. *Hakujin*, white face. Nothing, nothing had prepared her for this. For being the only one.

* *

Their guide returned to the bus, leading thirty-one bedraggled men and women. Hours earlier, they'd been strangers to one another. Now, they were pitched together for a three-day tour by luxury coach. Citizens of nine countries—Judith and Tosh were the only Canadians—they were counted by Teruko each time they placed a foot on the steps of the bus. Teruko now fired a disapproving look towards the back. Judith, Tosh and the man from Marseilles had refused to visit a national treasure, *her* national treasure.

"I can't do this," Judith said, half-aloud, but only to Tosh. "I'm conserving my strength for Hiroshima this afternoon. I want to see the Peace Park, the museum. My clothes are sticking to my skin. I don't want my backache to get worse."

"Why are you feeling guilty?" said Tosh. "If you're falling down from heatstroke, what's the point?"

Judith settled into the corner of the bus. She closed her eyes and imagined their child. She did her best to pretend that this was not a land of extreme heat, not a land of ocean trenches, active volcanoes, ruthless, broiling sun. The man from Marseilles leaned sideways across Tosh, tapped her on the arm, produced a bottle of Vichy from his shoulder bag, and a paper cup. He patted his own tummy. Maybe he understood, after all.

* *

Judith had not considered this trip a pilgrimage until it had become one. A pilgrimage for Tosh, *Sansei*, third-generation

231

Canadian who had never been to Japan. For his mother, who died before her thirty-eighth birthday in a British Columbia internment camp. For his father, who, decades after the end of the war, had purchased a small orchard and owned, once again, a tiny piece of land. Especially for him, as he was the only real link Tosh had to his ancestral past.

His father. Who, during their summer visits to the Okanagan, knew no greater pleasure than to sit across from them at the kitchen table after a day's work, and instruct them in the history of his forebears. As he spoke, the muscles flexed and tightened in his arms and throat. Father, who'd been sent to Japan on a small boat with other *Nisei* male children of his generation for education in the pre-war years. Who, responding to some internal signal, rose abruptly from the table, clapped his hands to wake the gods, and offered a bowl heaped with cherries, or a fat, ripe peach from his youngest tree, and set it high on the altar shelf.

It was a pilgrimage, too, for *Nisei* and other *Sansei* whom Judith and Tosh were now meeting throughout Japan. They trickled into the mainflow from San Francisco, Honolulu, Kamloops, Saskatoon. Each had crossed the 180th meridian, losing a day in mid-air. In some unplanned way, for everyone, the trip had become a search, an attempt to make sense of an ancient culture, fragments and rites of which they half knew and which they were passing on to their children, or their children's children, with some loosely rooted feeling that they were right in doing so.

For Tosh, there might not have been a trip at all. Three weeks before departure, he'd received a letter from Ottawa telling him that he would have to change his name legally before a passport could be issued. The name on his birth certificate did not match the name on his application. Did the missionaries, said Judith, forget to tell the Prime Minister? That, in the internment camps

high above the Fraser, they'd renamed all the little Japanese children whom the Prime Minister had himself interned?

Decades later, the habit was hard to shake. Tosh dropped his English name, the one bestowed upon him in the camps. He printed
Toshio, the name which had been declared unpronounceable by
the missionaries, and returned the application. The passport
arrived two days before he and Judith flew to Japan.

And what of pilgrimage by association? Judith felt both
lightly connected and not connected at all. It was the way she
thought of the five islands, shakily attached to the Earth's core.
She was insider and outsider, mostly out. Away from Tokyo,
sometimes three or four days at a time, the only Caucasian face
she saw was her own, staring back from hotel mirrors. Tosh, on
the other hand, and for the first time in his life, was slipping
into physical harmony with his outer world. Some shadow of
himself left her side again and again, as he mingled with clerks,
travellers, pedestrians. Her husband, the stranger. Judith watched
the unmistakable human exchange, from which she was
excluded, take place in streets, in lineups and crowds, in subway
cars. Tosh was expanding, while she was shrinking—despite the
newly forming child inside her.

She was also aware of a hint of meaning, a cause. But what
cause? It was like being on the edge of a society that was
immersed in anonymity. Manners were held in place by invisible controls as fragile as the breadth of a hair. Controls that
could momentarily give rise to panic. The absence of chaos was
what made Judith aware of a subterranean rumbling, a deep
muttering beneath the surface.

* *

Before Honshu, before joining the tour that would this afternoon arrive in Hiroshima, Judith and Tosh had travelled on
their own up the Inland Sea, staying at various places on the

Island of Kyushu. They'd stopped over in a village of cultivated hills and raw coastline. Climbed to the top of a hill, where they'd been greeted by a Shinto priest on the open veranda of his outer shrine. A weathered *torii* gate, brilliant in lacquered vermilion, reared itself in brush strokes against the sky.

The smiling priest was directing visitors to put coins into a mechanical dispenser. He intercepted and distributed the folded papers as they fell out of the slot. Judith deposited a coin while Tosh went off to see the gardens. The priest assumed that she did not speak Japanese, and began to read aloud, translating into English.

The smile fell from his face as if he had slipped behind a mask. He stared at Judith and, once again, she became aware of a subterranean rumble of panic. The priest shrugged.

"I do not understand. This is unlucky fortune. There will be a difficult labour."

The priest could not be blamed, after all. How could he know about the floating cells curled inside the womb? Judith accepted the folded paper. The priest turned his attention to the young man who was next in line, awaiting translation.

She found Tosh beside a stream in a remote part of the garden. A cupped bamboo pipe clicked as it filled and tipped, filled and tipped. Did Tosh leave her side this often when they were at home, or was it only in Japan that she was noticing?

"That's only the first part of the ritual," Tosh said, when she blurted out the priest's translation.

"What do you mean?"

"You have to tie the paper to a branch. To close the circle, to complete the fortune. A branch of a *sakaki* tree." He was concerned and amused at the same time.

"So?"

"Interrupt the rite."

"Don't tie the fortune."

"Something like that."

"Cross-fertilization, confusion." Judith had a sudden image of purging herself of the unlucky Shinto paper at a Buddhist temple. She would tie it to a Buddhist tree.

On the way down the path she walked grimly past the *sakaki* tree, where paper hopes and knotted dreams fluttered in the hot breeze.

During the next few days, she had carried her own folded paper as if it were a living object at the bottom of her purse. A threat of gloom, a curse, a piece of paper two inches long weighing her down.

Tosh teased her at the hotel. "Don't be so serious. The person next in line might just as easily have been given it. It might have been a man. It probably means something like *labour diligently*, something as mundane as that."

"A man didn't get it. I did. I'm the one who's pregnant."

"Why don't you take it down to the desk and ask for a second translation? Maybe the priest used an indefinite article by mistake." Tosh spoke Japanese, but could not read the written language.

"No," Judith said. "No and no. I'm the one who looked into the priest's face. I'm the one who has to thwart fate."

* *

Now, they were part of a group. And, since six o'clock in the morning, they'd been led by a fraudulently cheery Teruko, to three of the four temples she wanted them to see before the bus continued on to Hiroshima. At the fourth, while the others milled about the low temple platform, removing shoes, sliding their feet into paper slippers, Judith left the bus and hurried around to the rear of the building. The path was lined with rugged stone lanterns, which hugged the ground as if they'd blundered up through the earth. Cicadas shrilled against the bark of trees, but could not be seen. She pulled the twisted paper from her bag and looked around to ensure that she was unobserved. She tied the fortune to the twig of a thorn bush, and fled. Her body was light. Free. Teruko's face closed when she saw Judith join the group, late. Judith smiled sweetly.

* *

Teruko was talking about masks. She had herded the group back onto the bus and now held a microphone in her hand. She was excessively thin, and wore a navy blue suit that seemed to be a company uniform. Her glistening black hair was pinned at the back of her head, but it wobbled as she gave what was a formal explanation. Perhaps she'd memorized the words, Judith thought.

"There are many kinds of masks. They have fixed faces; these are guardians of the temple. Dogs, devils, animals, even a man-beast. Evil in concrete form is able to repel evil itself. But masks," she added, "are also used for gentler purpose. A mask can still the spirit inside. The blank face reveals only what it chooses to reveal." She was not looking at Judith. Deliberately, Judith thought. "When the mask is used in art," she went on, "it is placed between the eye of the beholder and the spirit of the object."

The mask might represent multiple faces, Judith thought, but if it's left to the beholder to supply meaning, then meaning will never stop shifting. Why were the Japanese so preoccupied with masks in the first place? Why the preoccupation, through centuries of art, when the living face was so accomplished at drawing every expression into one? Had she not lived with Tosh for many years? For one disconcerting moment, she believed that her own face revealed everything.

Teruko's expression shifted to a place between forced politeness and disdain. Teruko had two and a half days left to lead her tourists from one landmark to another—*gaijin*, foreigners, every one.

* *

When she stepped off the air-conditioned bus into Hiroshima heat, Judith recoiled as if flames had waved her back. The driver had parked at the edge of the Peace Park, beside three other motorcoaches. The group formed a huddle on the cement, trying to stay in the shade beside the bus. Teruko raised her hand and commanded silence. She announced that tourists from all over the world visited the site every year, that the stone chest beneath the sheltering curve of the cenotaph held the names of the victims, now close to two hundred thousand. She told them abruptly that they should be back at this spot by five o'clock. Departure would not be delayed for latecomers. Pamphlets in many languages were available. The bus driver handed Teruko a Coke, and the two, without a backward glance, walked off towards a staff building outside the entrance to the park.

At first, no one in the group made a move. There seemed to be a collective reluctance to go forward, to see what had to be seen. The foreigners were on their own. Judith opened a bright red umbrella she had borrowed from a cache at the front of the bus. Earlier in the day, Teruko laughed outright when Judith used one of these in the sun. Indeed, when Judith now opened it to protect herself from the heat, three young Japanese women standing near the fountain burst into giggles. Judith tried not to explain their behaviour to herself; she knew she'd get it wrong. Laughter could be met with humour. Stares could be endured. Paranoia could be pushed down, out of reach.

But the old feeling was revived. The feeling that always depended upon where she and Tosh happened to be. At home, she'd forgotten. Or perhaps it hadn't mattered in the last place they'd lived. One afternoon in Toronto, she read from the window of the subway, *Death to mixed races*, but she told herself it didn't apply to them. How could anything so murderous make sense? There and here, when she and Tosh were together, they thought about it only if the rules, imposed from without, forced their participation. *Did you notice that time? Yes, I wondered if you did, too.*

From the guidebook, she now read the awkward, translated English. *The fountain is a monument dedicated to those who so craved the water. The mother and child statue in desperation fleeing from the ravage.*

The fountain had been erected in front of the museum, a long, glass building. The group had quickly dispersed. Perhaps the others were wandering the grounds or the streets, looking for air-conditioned tea-houses. Teruko had made it clear that the bus door would not be open again until five. Judith and Tosh began to climb the museum stairs.

The first room, though air-conditioned, contained rank, dead air. Two Japanese couples were moving off behind a partition. In the next room, displays were presented in realistic detail: twisted spoons, sections of bridges, chunks of concrete, mutilated buttons, fragments of clothing, flattened pots and pans, melted steel, indistinguishable char. Random objects that happened to be at or near the hypocentre that sixth day in August when citizens of wartime Hiroshima were going about the ordinary business of trying to stay alive.

Tosh walked on ahead, while Judith slowed to read every word. Most glass cases contained explanatory cards printed in English. As she zigzagged from one exhibit to another, a part of her was aware of people hurrying past, of a swelling of tension through the long series of rooms. Her feet were swollen; she could not have rushed if she'd wanted to. She looked through a window to the hills beyond, and thought of the slow shuffle into and out of the city. Before she'd left Canada, she had read about the death marchers fanning out in confusion, dragging sheets of skin, and dropping like charred bits of meat along the way.

She turned back to the display before her, a selection of photographs pinned to a black-and-white background depicting devastation. The faces in the photographs registered not horror, but bewilderment, numbness. These were the faces of the insensate. Victims of the human race peering out from inside skinless bodies into a camera eye. Whatever part of them was still living, was trapped inside bodies that decayed as they stood—bodies that gave off the blue flame and smelled of broiling sardines. Judith read from the scorched hollows of those faces what the Japanese themselves had written: *The chance of survival is the thickness of one sheet of paper.*

She was roused by a shout. Beside, behind. A Japanese man was shaking his fist in her face, frighteningly close. A short, muscular man, he wore a narrow band of cloth wrapped around his head and knotted at the temple. He'd been drinking—she could smell whisky—and he shouted in rapid Japanese. She backed away, but he circled and hemmed her to the glass. She looked for Tosh, but Tosh was nowhere to be seen.

She wanted to shout back, "I understand. It's horrible for me, too. But it's complicated. The world was at war . . . I had nothing to do with . . . it isn't my fault." Knowing that this would be ridiculous. She was trapped, pressed to the glass by a man whose anger was so immediate, he was aware only of its existence. He pounded the glass that protected the photographs, and the glass shook, and again he brought his fist close to her face. She braced herself, just as a guard rushed into the room and grabbed the man's arm, giving her a moment to flee.

She caught sight of Tosh relaxing against a windowsill near the exit. In his face, she saw their lives together. Love, normality; this was the man she knew. But other lives flashed before her. The man she'd left back there, consumed with hate; Teruko, waiting outside at the bus, no doubt in disapproval; the men and women in the photographs, caught during their last moments of survival—whether they were prepared to die or not. She looked towards Tosh again, and understood that, although he was here beside her, he could not help. As long as she remained in Hiroshima, as long as she was in Japan, she would be held accountable. For the shape of her eyes, and the colour of her skin.

What We Are Capable Of

When Sarah phones, Em has just torn every letter into fours, then eighths, sixteenths and, finally, fragments so tiny it would take years to put the *m*'s back together, or to match the dots with the *i*'s. No one will ever see these letters, though she can call any one of them into view at any time. Each word is stored in the memory part of her brain. She saw a map once, of the brain, its sections delineated like rivers: *knee, hip, abdomen, thorax*; and *neck, face, lips, tongue*. One rippled area was marked: *emotions*. Another—more than one, now that she thinks of it—was labelled *memory*. This is where Michael is stored: *emotions*; multiple caches called *memory*.

Perhaps, instead of tearing, she should have spent days and weeks dismantling the letters, character by character, with her sharp-as-a-knife sewing scissors. She could have created a spectacular alphabet of possibilities. She could have thrown the lot into her deep Scandinavian bowl, the one that sits on a low table beside her desk. She could have picked out fragments and put them together again like particles of an Icelandic saga that rearrange themselves with each telling. Recently, she'd opened a book about Isak Dinesen and read that all sorrows could be borne if they were put into a story, or if a story were told about them. She wondered if for Dinesen this had been true. Or if, after the telling, Dinesen had ended up with both story *and* sorrows. The weaving of words: to bear in mind, to bear tidings, to bear down, to be born.

"Mom," says Sarah, "are you there?"

Em hears the fullness in her daughter's voice, the portent, and thinks, *No, Sarah, I'm not. Not now.* But another part of her, a slumbering part, has been roused. She has been the parent of her child for twenty-two years—the last six without Owen—and though Sarah can surprise her, Em sometimes knows as much about the direction of Sarah's choices as she does about her own.

She imagines Sarah's face at this moment and matches expression to voice. *Tentative.* But there is something more; she senses and then sees the word *wound.* Open to attack. She cannot keep her mind from inventing this way—it is her peculiar relationship with words. If *she* knows uncountable truths about Sarah, then Sarah understands and puts up with this about her.

"I want to come home," says Sarah. "For the summer. I'll get a job waitressing until I go back to school. There's a flight to the island in the morning. I'm already packed."

"Fine. Wonderful. It's your home, too."

"Thanks, Mom."

"You want to tell me what happened?"

"Garry walked away," she says. She's crying softly. "I ignored the signs. He was seeing someone else for weeks while he was still living with me. You can say I told you so, go ahead."

"Not on your life," says Em. "Get yourself on a plane. Your room is ready."

After she hangs up, Em stands at the window and looks down over the narrow field that rolls to the edge of the sea. The blue of the sky is so startling it shocks her to be part of its brilliance, its glare. She thinks about the way she and Michael turned away from each other the last time they were together and she wills her mind: *Don't think about him. Don't.*

* *

How did it begin?

A way of speaking. They fell into it slowly. At first, neither she nor Michael allowed that it was happening. Had already happened. She remembers the word *risk*. They were excited by the riskiness of the language they began to use with each other. Perhaps she was supposed to know enough about herself that she could see what was coming and muster some counterforce to ward off the next thing. But she has never been good at predicting what will happen after the first mark is made. Not until every one of the signs has been followed to the end.

* *

In the early morning, Em leaves the house in the dark and drives the length of the island to the tiny airport, where she waits outside the fence. Night is turning to day. From here, she cannot see the ocean but she is surrounded by a circle of sea-sky. She is always aware, always renewed by it. Each of the island roads is drawn towards an expanse of milky blue as if, inevitably, the height of the next curve will lead off into the sky. She would not know how to live anywhere else, so much is she a part of this place. Even after Owen drowned she did not for a moment consider leaving. And though Sarah has left, in the way young people can and do, Em knows that her daughter is part of this place, and deeply connected, too.

Throughout Sarah's childhood, Em and Owen took turns telling stories—always stories, it seemed, that rose up from the sea. A gale, electricity out, the house rocking as if it might lift from its foundations and soar out over the Gulf—that was when Sarah begged to hear the tales: the phantom train that wailed through the night fog; ships that went down; women who raised their skirts and dragged themselves out of the Atlantic; men and women who survived the winters and the winds, who became builders of ships and settlers of land, who created what has become Sarah's ancestral past.

The plane taxis in and Em watches her only child shift her backpack and descend the steps to tarmac below. Sarah spots her mother and raises a hand in a wave. She has to go through the terminal first, and Em heads for the door to meet her.

Sarah is wearing her brave face and moves to her mother's arms. As Em draws her in and they lock together, she feels her daughter's body let go. Now she knows what Sarah is holding: real loss, real sadness. In a fleeting moment, she wonders if Sarah detects her mother's own comfortless shell.

During the drive home they face forward in silence as they recross the island and witness the opening of the day. The dark red of the earth spreads before them. Wisps of mares' tails curve in a row of feathers across the sky. The car crests the last hill and eases down the long sweep to the house. Em sees what Sarah must, returning: whitecaps sliding in from the northeast; gulls sailing low over the bottom field; tall hillocky dunes that block the view of the beach. At this time of year, spears of marram grass will be thrusting through the sand. Everything is fresh, starting anew. The sea beyond the surf is dark, almost black. Huge to a human eye. *Waters give, waters take away,* Em says to herself, thinking of Owen. Both she and Sarah draw a breath. Aloud, Em says, "The healing sea."

Sarah leaps out of the car with a whoop and runs down the slope towards shore.

* *

Though part of Em desires solitude, she is glad that Sarah is home. Even unhappy, Sarah has energy enough to fill the rooms. She says little except that the past month has been the worst of her entire life. For the first few days she goes to bed early and gets up late. She seems battered, slugged. This shows in her face, in the movement of her hands, in her walk, in her forced smile. Every morning after breakfast, she laces her boots, heads out the door, follows the path through the field and stomps over the dunes. Each time she goes out, she leaves something of herself behind. Em, accustomed to being alone, is aware of the extra presence in every shadow of the house. Sometimes Sarah does not return by the time Em leaves for the Centre, at noon. Em works four afternoons a week and is grateful that she's been able to switch from her former morning schedule. She has five new Vietnamese families in her care and at times she admits to feeling hopeless about the extremes of their neediness. But she has learned to set hopelessness aside. It is her job to provide the families with language.

I hav pasport. This issa potato. My babees namis Hang. Here is good country. This is what they tell her, as they learn. They write lists to show off their English: *boat, matchis, soljer, rats.* At one of the camps during the six-year journey that brought them here, they slept in hammocks high off the ground so rats would not crawl over them in the night. They had been robbed by pirates. Two of the women were raped. They speak with buried expression. On the surface, the information appears matter-of-fact. They want their new country; they want everything about it. They want to know everything about Em, too. In his notebook one young man drew a picture of her in long dress and high-heeled shoes, though she wears neither. Beneath the picture he wrote: *I think teecher pritty. Mikel say she has round eyes.*

Only once has Em bumped into Michael. The face-to-face encounter in the hall caught them both off guard. He could not, she remembers—though he would never admit this—he could not look her in the eye. What she saw in his face was discomfort, evasion. His classes were over and Em's were about to begin. But before she could enter the room where the families waited—mothers, children, uncles, aunties, babies; they brought their babies, who else would look after them?—she went to her office and closed the door and stood by her desk, shaking. Later, at the end of the two-hour session, Trinh, the old auntie of two young women in the group, reached over to pat her arm and said, "Teacher sad." Trinh tightened a cardigan about her shoulders and bent to pick up one of the babies who was playing on the floor. She tucked him to her hip and patted Em again, and made her way slowly out the door.

Taut, says Em, thinking of this. *Kindness, parting, grief.* Old Auntie Trinh had experienced countless partings before being forced to start a new life. "Hope," says Em aloud. This is one abstraction she will not have to teach.

* *

"We had a great time together," says Sarah. "He was funny. He had a way of joking about himself that made me love him like crazy. I can't figure out how things went wrong. What did I do? He didn't have the guts to look me in the eye and say, *This isn't working.* The worst part—are you ready for this?—is that *I* feel unworthy." She sinks to the rug in the living room and digs her hand into the bowl of popcorn she's carried in from the kitchen. "Why should I be the one to feel unworthy?"

Why, indeed? thinks Em, who's so familiar with the feeling she might have invented it. But she's supposed to know better. She's supposed to know more.

"Get angry," she says to Sarah. "Angry is better than unworthy." As soon as she says this, her memory releases an image so gentle, she doesn't know what to do with it: Michael, standing in the middle of her classroom, wags a five-dollar bill and grins as he invites her for coffee. And then, without warning, he takes her hand in his and raises it to his lips as if her fingers are at the end of the most delicate limb on Earth. Her body stills as his lips brush her skin.

* *

It's hopeless, they say to each other. *It's complicated.* Michael is married to a woman named Frieda whom Em has never met but whom she knows to be German. Michael tells her he has been with Frieda for thirteen years.

One Friday evening, Em is shopping in the pharmacy, in town. She looks out and sees the two of them across the street; they are speaking with a man she does not know. Frieda has beautifully shaped short blond hair and looks attractive and theatrical at Michael's side. She is the same height as Michael and, at one point in the conversation, she stretches an arm towards him in an angular way and encircles his neck. Her elbow points out sharply. It's easy to see that she doesn't think about this; she's accustomed to assuming the position. But he must be, too, because he moves neither away nor towards her. He keeps talking as if he hasn't noticed the choking stance, the bony armour placed around him.

The next day, a Saturday morning, Michael phones her at home. Em answers and for a few minutes they discuss their work. Then his voice says, "Did you receive my message?"

"Which one?" She hears a woman talking to someone in the background. She hardly dares to breathe.

"This one," he says.

"Yes. Did you receive mine?"

"Yes," says Michael softly, and they hang up.

How can we do this? she thinks. How can we? She is sorry she has ever seen Frieda. She can't pretend there is not another person, a real flesh-and-blood person, involved.

* *

Em looks at Sarah seated on the floor and is startled to see how small her daughter becomes when she pulls this far inside. Four years ago, Sarah strutted through the same room, showing off her new dress the day of her high school formal. She was wearing black velvet—long sleeves, low back, black stockings, new shoes. A part of her, as if this were a rite of passage, was awed and overwhelmed. A corsage had been dropped off in the afternoon, a ritual Em had mistakenly assumed to be a custom of the past. For hours Sarah drifted from room to room, detached in a way that had nothing to do with anyone but herself. Her behaviour was reminiscent of her child-self when she'd drifted in and out of rooms on her birthday, whispering, "Cake, cake, cake." Extreme pleasure spilled out of her then, as it did the afternoon of the dance. Em did not doubt that her daughter's more serious life was ahead of her, but when Sarah kissed her and thanked her for helping with preparations, Em was close to tears, so newly grown-up did Sarah appear to be.

Surprisingly, on that occasion, Sarah's expectations had been met. But Em remembers something else. When Sarah left the house and turned to say goodbye, a flash of uncertainty crossed her face. So quickly, Em might have missed it. Poised but vulnerable—Sarah, at the edge of the world.

"Mom," says Sarah, "how can someone love a person and then hurt them this badly? Did it ever happen to you? When you were younger, I mean. When a friendship fell apart? When nothing you did, no matter how you tried, could save it?"

"It happens to everyone," Em says. And then she adds, "But I don't think we try to wound intentionally." She speaks with the greatest of care.

* *

Always an early riser, Em wakes even earlier now that Sarah is home. She needs space, time alone. Her body agrees by taking up an amazingly accurate rhythm with the sun. Every morning her eyes open at the exact moment of sunrise. Each morning the time is slightly different, but she wakes with the change even if it's only three minutes or four. She slips into her robe, goes to the window, and watches the bulge of sun as it lifts itself out of the sea.

When she and Michael spent time together, they stood at this same upstairs window, watching the sun rise through the undersides of clouds as it spilled silver across the waves. Sometimes there was only greyness, or a thin line of navy separating earth from sky. Although the colours of the east were often like those of the west, she was aware of the subtle difference: in the east, there was a greater sense of light, of *becoming*.

One evening, Michael drove to the house unannounced. The two of them sat outside on the veranda and a great horned owl flew past with such grace they did not speak for several minutes. The owl had been as startled as they were. It hovered momentarily between house and shore and then abruptly changed direction, turning back with its wondrous undulating wings. Em didn't ask how Michael was able to get away. They both knew what they were doing. There was nothing to say.

* *

Everything is said in the letters. Michael goes to a tiny island in the South China Sea for fifteen days to receive applications from the camps.

The work is hopeful and hopeless at the same time, he writes. *Conditions worse than expected, worse than we've been told. Every day, thousands of faces at the high, barbed fence. When I enter the enclosure, I'm surrounded. People beg to be sponsored but this time we have only enough funds for two singles and an extended family of five or six. When I come back to my room in the evening, I try not to weep. I think of you, your* spirit, your voice. In this place, where humanity is crowded and shoved together, I imagine you alone on the shore, singing, walking into the wind. Or looking up at an indigo sky, convinced that every star is alive. The Big Dipper tipped upside down over your roof.

* *

Country big, the class writes. *The peeple big. They hav big hans. We laff and laff when we trying clothes they giv. I think Diep is cry from laffing hard. When autum comes we go with teacher to by boots. In winter our children play in snow like children here.*

* *

Do you remember when we drove to pick up the lemon pie at the bakery on the highway? he writes. *How you sang the Emperor Concerto all the way back? You're the only person I know who can sing the Emperor Concerto.*

The concerto had stayed in her head for days. The music forced her to acknowledge the wonder, the happiness, the sure knowledge that this had to end.

* *

Sarah finds summer work at Stan's, a seafood restaurant next to the wharf, two miles down the highway. Sometimes Em drops her off on her way to town; other days, Sarah walks. On Em's day off, Sarah takes the car. She works afternoons and evenings, alternating shifts with two local women.

Something about Sarah is changing, but Em is not sure what. A hard edge is creeping in. Sarah has phoned Garry, she tells her mother, but the call was not satisfactory. They discussed books and a sweater he'd left in her apartment; she'd given permission for him to contact the landlord so he'd be allowed in.

"It's all right," Sarah tells her. "Don't worry. He sees things one way; I see them another." To herself she mutters, "But there has to be an explanation I can understand."

Sarah is still stomping over the dunes, taking long walks by herself. She has made no effort to contact friends, though several former schoolmates have returned to the island for the summer. Em feels as if she can read Sarah's behaviour like a program that has been opened, bent back, frayed at the edges. First, you blame yourself. Occasionally, you get angry. Mostly, you're sad. There *is* no explanation that you can understand.

* *

Who tugs whom to the centre of this dark circle? She closes her eyes. After a late meeting at work, they stand together on the first floor, sinking, sinking. "I didn't know this was possible," he says. The streetlight outside illuminates the stairwell, but casts them in shadow. "Even if I wanted to stop," Michael says, "I don't see how I could."

* *

"The one place you can't get away from is inside your head," Sarah tells her, as if Em has never thought of this before. Sarah has been home four weeks now and though she's beginning to look rested, she hasn't let go. "Do you know what people say to me? *Time heals.* As if I have a chronic disease. It's the biggest cliché in the language and it isn't true. Still, it makes me furious that I feel like this. How could I have given up so much control?"

It happens, Em wants to say. *It slips away little by little, when it has nothing to do with control. When it is called connection, joy. It's only when you try to recover, pull back, that you become aware of how much you've given away.*

"Sometimes," she says to Sarah, "it's a miracle to believe

that even the smallest insight is possible." *And there's the practical matter*, she adds, but not aloud, *of what to do with so much pain.*

* *

Now that she works afternoons, Em takes her long walks in the morning. She watches the boats rocking side to side, offshore, while the lobster fishermen lower their traps. One early morning, there are two Cape Island boats, then a third. These turn, and turn again, while a stick figure leans over the side of each. The little boats circle like game players, as if the movement of one affects the movement of all. They change direction and begin to circle again. When the wind rises, the gulls make brave attempts to drift, land, settle on the waves. Sometimes the boats rock right off the horizon. Em climbs back over the dunes and sees how high the marram grass has grown in only a few weeks. She runs a finger up the smooth surface of a single blade, knowing that her skin will be cut if she slides it down in the opposite direction. The grasses grow in clumps, different shades of green, deep and dark at the base. Hidden underground is a vast network, spreading beneath the sand.

They shared laughter. Silliness. They couldn't have stopped playing if they'd tried. She sang for him when they were walking on shore, and when they were in the car. She sang every day. *Is it possible that I sang the Emperor Concerto?* she thinks.

It is.

I did.

* *

They see each other at work, except when Michael is travelling. When he is away, he writes to her. Frieda is not mentioned, though her unwritten name is always there.

It might be a long time, Michael's letters say. *We'll choose a*

252

place. We'll work it out. Neither Michael nor Em has any idea how *it* will be worked out, or where that place might be.

* *

Bed, pillow, room, write the students. *We hav the television, black and wite. We learn new words. Children are sick because cold at nite. When they grow big like children here they hav educasion. Good job. By house. We not own house. In our country, small house. Gone past. Old life.*

Em visits the family headed by Auntie Trinh. Seven people—she thinks they're related but she isn't sure—live in two rooms, one small, one large. A crib has been pushed near the door and two adult mattresses are spread end-to-end on the floor. Ignored by the adults, the babies crawl up and down the mattresses. One baby bangs a glass mug against the floor as he makes his way to Em on hands and knees. He bumps the mug in front of him and, miraculously, it does not shatter. There is an open purse on the floor and the second baby roots through this, but no one tries to stop her. The rooms are beside the elevator; the building is old. Em thinks that the walk through the odours of the corridor would be enough to cause hope to drop out the bottom.

But this is not the case at all. Auntie Trinh makes a pot of straw-coloured tea. The young women laugh and joke in Vietnamese. A man stands and smokes in the doorway between the kitchen and the main room. He does not join the laughter. It is only when Em is ready to leave that he speaks directly to her. His English is better than that of her students, she discovers. He is visiting from Ohio, a cousin they have searched for and found. He has been in America for three years. "We are trying to find the whole family," he says. "We want to be together."

Em wonders if the family will decide to stay here, on the east coast, after more and more family members make themselves known. This has happened before: the island becomes a way-station for a couple of years. Even if the sponsored families were to remain, the islanders would refer to them as *off-island*. Welcoming in their way, but an islander is an islander who waded out of the sea more than a century ago. Michael, unthinking, said one day, "She's off-island, isn't she?"—referring to a colleague who had lived on a farm outside town for twenty-seven years. Em's daughter, Sarah, on the other hand, will always be an islander, having been born *on-island*. Even though she lives *away*, whenever she returns, she is coming *home*.

* *

"Come on, Mom," she says. "We're going to the wharf. We'll buy fresh fish and get some roadside chips."

It's Saturday and they both have the day off. Em follows Sarah to the car. First stop is McCrae's Wharf. They push back the wooden door and slop across the wet cement floor where four men are cleaning cod. The men recognize Sarah because they take their breaks at Stan's, where she works next door. Em looks around and sees full bins of cod three feet high around the room. The fish have been cleaned, layered, salted.

"This morning's catch," says one of the men. He's locked into perfect and harmonious rhythm with three partners at a slab of metal—the gutting table. Each of the men, at the same split second, slashes a fish with his blade, removes the head, chops the tail, slits the body, tears out the guts and throws. If one of the men breaks the pattern, the guts collide in mid-air. The double-X of slop drops into two gutters.

Sarah stands and watches while one of the young men, about her age, interrupts the rhythm every four or five throws so he can aggravate his co-worker at the far end of the table—someone bearded and very fat.

"Cut it out," the fat man warns.

The young man grins, pretends he hasn't heard, slips back into rhythm. Each of the four wears high rubber boots and a heavy apron splattered with blood. One wall in the room is made of a sliding screen, ceiling to floor, leading outside to the wharf. The screen seems to be thick black mesh, but a closer look reveals that the mesh is a cloak of flies—tens of thousands of swarming flies, all on the outside, waiting their chance to get in.

The owner, a tall and bony man whom Em knows as Angus, wheezes in from the cannery side of the building. He seems to have shrunk into the physical frame of his former self. He is cleaner than his four employees—just.

"The boys went out, got two nice haddie in their nets today," he says, seeing Em. "We got plenty mackerel, too. Gen'rally, we keep the haddie for the restaurant." He nods towards Sarah. "If you want the haddie, it's all right with me." He calls over to the gutting table, "Ned, come fillet these for the ladies."

The young man at the end, without looking up, flips the guts of the fish he holds in his hand. The guts travel sideways the length of the table, past the two men in the centre, through the startled open hands of the fat man, and out again. The fat man curses, stops, and strikes for revenge. For one confused blurring moment, guts fly in all directions. The three at the table settle down again to slash, chop, slit, tear and throw. Ned grins, and hoses down his hands before he fillets the *haddie*.

"Ned's not full time," Angus says between wheezes. "Sort of apprentice, you might say. Home from school for the summer. He first showed up when the boats come in with the catch, twice a day. I tried runnin' him out the back, he come in at the side. I run him out the side, he come in at the back. So I let him stay. I even pay him for staying."

Ned has filleted and handed over the fish, winking at Sarah. Em and Sarah go out to the car, laughing.

"He comes to the restaurant every day," says Sarah. "He wants to take me out. Don't worry. He'll get the fish smell off. I can't believe I've never met him before. He was at a different school, that's probably why. He lives with his parents in the west part of the island."

She is still smiling.

* *

"You'd think I'd learn," Sarah says. "You'd think there'd be some way of getting it right. I feel as if I keep making the same mistakes. It's so hard to give up something when you think it's going well."

They've cooked the fish and warmed the chips and carried their plates to the veranda. Em can't take her eyes off the sea. Clusters of pink clouds drift sideways, creating an island in the sky, just above the horizon. She looks at Sarah's face and sees only a trace of sadness.

But Sarah is staring. "Mom? Have you heard one word I've said?"

"I've heard every word," says Em. "I'm thinking that you're pretty hard on yourself."

Sarah is silent, considering.

"Maybe all we're really looking for is someone to tell things to," Em continues. "Someone who won't be offended if we break out in tears, or hysterical giggles, or even hives."

But it's the energy of loving someone, she tells herself. It takes so long to let go because of the energy. Why would anyone want to give up the exhilaration of love?

They both laugh, but sharply. Sarah becomes serious again. "What about you, Mom?" she says. "I mean—you can tell me to mind my own business—but it has been six years."

Em looks away, feels her skin tighten around her. "I'm okay, Sarah," she says. "I'm okay."

* *

They surprise each other with their capacity to imagine, to love. It is that complicated. It is that simple.

Michael picks her up and they drive inland, for a picnic. They follow an overgrown trail, single file, until they reach the clear waters of a tiny river that empties into the sea. They slide down an embankment and comb the dirt and stones until they have space to stretch their legs. They sit in absolute quiet—aware of the ancient smell of river; allowing the warming sun. They don't move when the water ripples near their feet. A brown head, matted with water, lifts and stares. Unstartled, the head sinks and disappears. It's a muskrat, its den probably farther upriver where the banks are muddy. Late in the afternoon, Michael climbs the slope, reaches for Em's wrist and tugs her up the bank behind him. She feels as if she is being dragged. When they emerge from the trail and approach the car, a great blue heron lifts its wings and beats heavily away. *Remember this,* she tells herself. *Remember.*

* *

Michael is away when Em takes four of her students to the indoor market in town.

I buy chicken, says Diep, while she inspects and makes her choice. *The chicken used to be a egg.* The whole group is laughing while Diep counts out the money. Em looks up and into the face of Frieda, who is alone at the far edge of the market stall. There is a moment—not exactly of recognition—when Em sees the frown that crosses Frieda's face. Frieda's teeth press into her lower lip. She turns abruptly, and is gone.

Auntie Trinh has witnessed the exchange. *Finishee,* she says to Em, but Em does not ask what she means. *Finishee.* Em thinks of Frieda's face and remembers that, never once, has Michael mentioned his wife by name.

The previous fall, during a week's vacation from work, there had been a wild storm. Winds from the northwest blew day and night for four days. Michael, knowing she would not be able to get outside or go very far, arrived to see if she needed help. Wind battered the front window panes. The upstairs windows were coated with sand that splattered violently out of the air. Em had not felt locked in by the storm at all; instead, she'd experienced a sense of freedom, of space. She stood at the living-room window and watched the far-off breakers build at the horizon and crash to shore, spume flying high. It was difficult to recall that the sea had any other face.

Michael walked up silently behind her. "Come to the kitchen," he said. "I was outside and threw a bucket of water against the window. We can prop up our feet and look out and have tea."

Instead, when she turned to him, they had gone upstairs to her room. In the midst of the storm that battered the house from every corner, Michael was more gentle and loving than she had ever known him to be—more than she'd have thought possible.

Later, he stood in the kitchen doorway, his face turned away. She was clearing the mugs, dumping the remnants of their tea. *Over,* she said to herself at that moment. *We both know it's over.*

That night, though the storm subsided, she dreamed of waves rolling up through the field and crashing against the house. She dreamed an animal in the room, the blackest of profiles, its bleak closed jaws. She sat up and spoke to herself in the dark. "This," she said, "was once about joy."

* *

Em stops at the restaurant to pick up Sarah after work. She slides into a booth and asks for a cup of coffee. Sarah is joking while she works behind the counter. She's making her co-workers laugh.

She's better, Em realizes, watching her. Sarah has always been capable of humour, but now it's a tougher humour that will get her through. My adult-child, she thinks, smiling at the contradiction.

"Here's your coffee, Mom. I hope you don't mind waiting. There's still cleanup. I might be another half hour."

"I don't mind," says Em. "I'll start the student work here instead of at home."

She opens her briefcase and places the folder of loose papers on the table. She reads the first sheet, written by a student whom everyone calls Harry. Harry is not his real name but he's never told anyone what his real name is. Harry is twenty-three, but she thinks of him as an old old man.

We meet another peeple, he writes. *We leev our land. Sometim him leev her, her leev him. But that okay. That what we are capable. Sometim crying, sometim laffing.*

Em stretches out both hands and covers the words.

* *

What had taken her by surprise was the sensation that she was drowning. Michael returned from his last trip and walked away. He could not tell Frieda. That was all he could say. But Em had been cut adrift. She'd felt as if she were sinking into the sea.

She glances up now as a smiling Sarah comes towards her from the counter. There is nothing to be done but feel badly until you get to the end of it, she thinks. That is all. "Finishee," Auntie Trinh had said, that day in the market. A finite word. *Finishee.*

Sarah slips into the booth.

"You know Ned, from the wharf," she says. "He's coming over tonight." She grins. "I thought I was afflicted forever. Ruined." She stops. "Hey, have I interrupted a heavy moment here?"

Em looks at her daughter, sees the fierceness, the old capability as it moves into place. It has always been there but, until now, Sarah hasn't called it up for use.

"Yes, no, yes," she tells her daughter. She holds the edge of the table because it is solid. She thinks of Frieda's expression when they were face to face in the market, and admits what she has always known. *Frieda knew*. She slides her hand along the table. Looks through the windows in the direction of the wharf, the waves that slurp and lap over sandbars, the Gulf, the far-off river that reaches inside the continent for two thousand miles. In the distance, worn mountain ranges rise up like the slumbering backs of old whales.

She thinks of the open sea. How she strides into it every summer day, how she braces herself for the cold that pulls on her bare legs. Even on days when she doesn't swim, she leans forward to splash water up to her face so she can taste the sudden salt.

She leans into the back of the booth behind her and has a flash of memory again: Frieda's face at the market. *Sorrows to bear, sorrows to be borne.* She takes Sarah's hand in her own and feels it relax, let go.

Run, she should have told herself, long ago. *Run the other way.* Instead, she had chosen love—and deceit.

"Sorry I drifted," she says. "I was thinking about some of the things I've learned." *What we are capable. Meet another people. Sometim crying. Sometim laffing.*

Sarah gets up out of the booth. "Let's go," she says. "I'm moving on. No matter what has been left undone."

Poached Egg On Toast

∞

On the third day of December, he wrote in pencil on the kitchen calendar: *Robin in front yard.* The robins had migrated before the middle of October, and he wondered what this stray would find to eat. It was gone by the end of the day.

December 24, he was shovelling snow from the path that led to the sheds and he looked up to the sky to see Jesus Christ reclining in the clouds. Details were vivid and clear. Christ was wearing a loose robe, and his eyes were kindly as he looked benevolently and sorrowfully towards Earth.

Arthur banged the snow from his boots and went into the warm kitchen. He stood awkwardly, pencil in hand, wondering how to mark this on the calendar, knowing it for the momentous event it was. He decided on the abbrieviation *CHR*. If Ada were to ask, he'd say Christmas, one day until. Something like that.

January 31 was the coldest day Arthur had ever lived through, all the years of his life. He walked as far as the clump of trees in the middle of the field and stumbled back to write in his black diary: *I thought the sky above the planet would crack. I understand now, what the medievals saw when they described the dome cupped over the flat earth.*

Ada only raised an eyebrow when she came across notations on the calendar. Ada had her three meals to cook every day, which she liked to do, and she had her friend, Elizabeth, who lived on the opposite side of the field. Every Thursday night, she and Elizabeth went to town to see a movie. Ada did not feel the need to write any of this down.

April 16, Arthur wrote on the calendar, *The blooming of the lily*, though he hated lilies; they reminded him of death. Ada had brought this one home on the bus from town, and carried it in her two hands across the field as she walked from the bus stop.

These were the weeks when Arthur worked furiously in the garden, keeping an eye on grackles that strutted like executioners in their blue hoods. He had to put up with them at his feeders if he wanted to keep the jays.

May 26, he entered in the diary: *Mewling and caterwauling in the trees. The orioles took the string I chopped for them, and disappeared.*

That was the same morning he and Ada had the fight over what she'd given him for his breakfast, though he made no entry to mark it.

He'd only mentioned, albeit complainingly, that he was tired of eating poached egg on toast; he'd had it three times in the past ten days.

"I wouldn't be fussy if I were you," said Ada. "There are only so many breakfasts I can think of to make."

That's when Arthur should have kept his mouth shut, but instead he shot back, "Why I could think of a hundred breakfasts, each one different from the last."

"I'd like to see the day you'd come up with a hundred breakfasts," said Ada, "even in your imagination. Especially when you've never cooked so much as one for yourself."

They sat to a meal together later the same day, but the next morning Ada did not get up.

Arthur posed upright in his chair in the living room and waited, and then he went to the kitchen to put the water on for his tea. He returned to the chair and waited again. Ada did not get up.

He tore a piece of paper from a pad of yellow foolscap.

Corn fritters, he wrote. His stomach contracted in hunger, from the writing of it.

Corn flakes, he added. These were pretty harmless.

muffets

shredded wheat

He paused and inserted as a heading, Occasional, which he underlined.

Ada had to be pretending to be asleep, he knew for a fact that she'd never in her life stayed in bed so long.

kipper snacks

sardines, plain

sardines with tomato sauce

sliced tomato with black pepper, on toast

fish

He changed his mind about fish, and turned it into a heading of its own.

Fish

bass

trout

pickerel

salmon (canned)

sole

finnan haddie

He heard Ada stir and he hid the list inside the dictionary. He got up and put on his jacket and went outside. He walked as far as the trees in the middle of the field. There was a small rise there, and he could see all the way around in a broad circle. He placed each foot deliberately, rotating one hundred and eighty degrees. He thought of the word *view*, and remembered discovering in the dictionary that one of its meanings was "footprints of the fallow deer."

When he'd been a young man and had taken his rifle to the

woods, he'd been excited by the stillness, the sudden startle of the deer. But there were no footprints this day. There'd been none to notice even before he'd marked on the calendar six weeks earlier: *The last melting of the snow*. It had been twenty-three years since Arthur had hunted. His rifle had been resting in the gun rack all of that time.

He stayed outside the rest of the morning, and tried to expand the breakfasts in his mind. Without enthusiasm, he could get no further than *finnan haddie*.

* *

Lunch was ready when he went inside, and he was glad to get some food into him. As soon as Ada turned to the dishes, he sat in the living room and went back to his list.

cottage cheese
apple fritters
jello – orange
    – cherry
    – blackcurrant
    – lime

He included only the flavours he would eat, and he counted each as a separate breakfast. He created another category.

Cold Meats
chicken loaf
Delicia loaf
mac & cheese
head cheese
bologna, fried

He thought with pleasure of the bubbles that pushed up through the rubbery red circles as they sizzled in the cast-iron pan. The slices had to be exactly the right thickness.

The rest of the day, Arthur turned the earth in his garden and put in seed and, while he worked, he considered going to town.

He had only vague thoughts about what he might do there, and put the trip off to another day. Before he went to bed that night, he lifted the blind and stared out. There was the moon, a slice of lemon, tilted in the sky.

* *

Neither he nor Ada brought up the matter between them. Ada stayed in bed every morning, and Arthur rattled from one room to another, listening for any sound at all. They'd been sleeping on the edges of the bed, careful not to touch. He hated that. He was used to Ada's warmth seeping into him.

Warmed up, he wrote.

giblets
potatoes & cabbage mixed
hamburger boiled, with gravy
meatballs
macaroni
homemade spaghetti with toast
Irish stew
meat pie with crust
turkey and dressing (seasonal)
chicken pot pie

A good run. He had thirty-six, but he'd hit a block. He went outside and watched the changing light as the wind cleared the clouds. The first green shoots were lined up unevenly in his garden and he made a note in his head to mark on the calendar: *Life pushed through earth.*

He felt something like sorrow as he stood there. It was too late in his life to start cooking on his own, pushing pots and pans around the kitchen. He knew Ada would be lying in bed listening. She'd dug in her heels before and, when she was like this, there was no telling if she'd give in first, or give in at all. She was still cooking his lunch and his supper, but even though she knew he had to have a good solid meal in the morning, she was behaving as if the idea of breakfast had never been thought of at all.

After lunch, Ada said she was going to visit Elizabeth for the afternoon. Arthur waited until she left and he took the bus to town. He paced Main Street and wished he'd never complained. The tension in the house had clamped over the two of them like the steel trap that hung from a long spike in the shed.

Ada was spending more and more of her time with Elizabeth, and Arthur was no longer privy to the bits of gossip and fun she was used to bringing home.

Arthur watched a man speak rudely to his wife outside the A & P. For a moment he thought that he himself would burst into tears in the street. He went to the next block and walked past the florist twice before he entered the shop. With his head down, he ordered twelve roses for Ada and gave his address to the woman at the counter. She handed him a tiny blank card to fill out, and he stared at it in his large palm. He had not considered this, having to include a message. He gave the card back to the woman and cancelled the roses.

He slipped into the diner by the bus depot and sat in a booth and asked for the breakfast menu, though it was afternoon. He ordered only coffee, but began to write on a shred of paper from his wallet.

omelette, plain

cheese and mushroom omelette

Hawaiian omelette with pineapple

He did not fancy what the Hawaiians mixed with their eggs in the morning.

pancakes with syrup

pancakes with blueberry sauce

Without ceremony, the waitress appeared beside the booth and took the menu away from him. She lifted it right out of his hands.

Ada was still away when Arthur returned. He started a new column and wrote out the breakfasts he'd borrowed from the diner. After that, he kept on writing.

corn syrup with toast

bacon (not cooked hard)—He had let Ada know that sometimes she left it too long in the pan.

lasagna (leftovers)

ravioli (leftovers)

cheese chops

He heard Ada coming, and he stashed the list.

* *

Arthur began to dream about plums served on doilied trays, about grapefruit slit with a delicate silver knife. He woke one morning and thought: *Maybe Ada has forgotten the fight.* And then: *Maybe she's told Elizabeth.*

He imagined the two women laughing over a fight that now seemed to have taken place a long time ago. A fight that was nobody's business but his own. His and Ada's, though it was never discussed. Breakfast had simply ceased.

He sat in the chair in the living room while Ada pretended to sleep, and he pressed heavily with a pen into his black diary: *I'm not a useless old fool. I come from a long line of men that were not required to do their own cooking. It's the way things have always been, though once a year at Christmas my father made his four-meat pâté. Rabbit was the fourth meat because it was in the family tradition. I never saw him cook anything else.*

How would he give her the list, even if he did get it done? Somewhere in his mind, he knew he'd attached an unlikely outcome to the hundredth breakfast. Ada would rise early and come to the kitchen in her faded maroon robe and her soft slippers, and she would stir quietly about the room while he sat at the table and waited.

There must have been something else, something besides him complaining about his poached egg on toast. Something deeper, darker, something further back. He couldn't for the life of him think what it might be.

Black pudding, he wrote.

sausage regular

sausage *Oktoberfest*

bananas, flecked with brown

Fifty.

* *

Thursday morning the following week, Arthur put the kettle on and boiled the water and made a large pot of tea, two teabags. He let it steep four minutes, and poured the tea into Ada's cup and added a drop of milk. He carried it to their room and stood at the end of the bed.

Ada did not stir; her breathing did not alter. He set the cup on her bedside table and, on his way out of the room, he thumped the end of the mattress with his foot.

Before he went outside to work in the garden, he put on his cap and tied a bandanna around his neck. As he passed the mirror, he glanced back quickly, thinking he'd seen a bandit.

All morning, he watered and weeded until his back ached from bending. He scanned the sky, looking for cloud formations, and he listened to the birds raise their young. The baby jays were learning to fly. Every once in a while, a blue ball of fluff drifted past, slow-landing on the earth.

Everything had its life. He'd read in the paper that trees knew when someone was going to chop them down. Their terrible cries could be measured electronically as the axe hit. Arthur believed this. What was being discovered every day was wondrous.

What he did not like was the way things were reported on radio and TV. Instant this and instant that, everything was instant. War inside your own house the same moment it was happening around the other side of the world. He could do without that. The whole business made him weary.

When he went inside, he could not tell if Ada had drunk the tea he'd made. The cup was washed and dried and back on the kitchen shelf. Ada was nowhere to be seen. Though Arthur was tired, he pulled out the list.

ham, fried
side pork
applesauce (cold)
Spanish rice (warmed)
peanut butter on toast
liver and onions

His favourite. He hadn't eaten liver and onions for a long time. He began to think the list was foolish, but he had fifty-six; he was past any point, now, where he could do a back turn.

toasted cheese sandwich
hot scones with raisins
bread pudding, crisped under grill
cheese biscuits
waffles with syrup
bran muffins
home fries
fruit salad
pigs-in-blankets

He went to his room and hauled down the covers, and in the middle of the day, Arthur went back to bed.

* *

When he woke, he realized he'd eaten neither breakfast nor lunch. It was Ada's night to go to the movies. Before all this had started, he used to mark the films she went to on the calendar.

He never wanted to go himself but, every Thursday when Ada came home, he was used to hearing about the story and the movie stars. He especially liked to hear about the reruns, the old movies done up again, readied for the big screen, like old tarts. Bogart and Bacall. Cagney. Rosalind Russell, now there was someone who could act.

He saw that his supper was in the oven. He'd slept a long time. When he looked out across the field, he realized it was the first time he'd missed standing at the door on a Thursday evening, watching Ada's back as she crossed the field. She always called on Elizabeth first, before the two of them took the bus to town.

He ate his supper in silence, listening to marauding bands of starlings as they roved from tree to tree across the field. He brought the list to the kitchen.

Salmon patties, he wrote.

dish of prunes

He put down the pencil and picked it up again. He felt his face flush as he wrote and underlined:

Eggs

scrambled

once over

sunnyside

He went outside and stood on the step. The sun was being pulled under the hills and there were streaks of charcoal above the horizon. Since last winter, he'd checked the sky frequently for signs of Jesus in his robe, but he'd never seen such a vision again. He remembered the date of it, December 24. His mother used to tell him when he was a small child that, at the stroke of midnight Christmas Eve, all the animals in the barn spoke to one another. Now, the seasons seemed to glide past; fall would be here and then winter would cover his roof, his garden, his shed.

He returned to the kitchen table.

boiled egg, 3 minutes sharp

eggs Benedict—these, he'd only heard about. Ada had never made them.

Western sandwich

egg-in-the-hole

He went to the gun rack and took down his rifle. As he passed the mirror, he saw that he was still wearing the bandanna. He loaded the rifle in the kitchen.

poached egg on toast

He left the house and walked to the clump of trees in the middle of the field. He sat on the earth, sheltered by trees. He thought he might catch the first star, but three blinked together as if they'd been visible all along and he hadn't been alert enough to notice. He closed his eyes and thought about the list. It had been easy enough at first, but he was beginning to run down. He did not know why he'd loaded the rifle, why he'd brought it here, to the rise in the field. He sat holding it, pointing the barrel towards the sky. In an hour or so, Ada would be returning. She and Elizabeth would step down from the bus in the dark and Elizabeth would arrive home first and wait while Ada crossed the field. Ada sometimes called back when she reached the step, to let her friend know that she was safe. Not that there was anyone around. They just did that; they were in the habit of calling back and forth through the dark.

He began to feel the coolness of the night as he waited. Birds were settling around him, a soft shudder of wings. Far off, he heard the bus pause to drop its passengers, and it threw out cones of light as it turned to go back to town. Arthur sat upright, his fingers swollen against the rifle.

A few minutes later, the voices of the two women rose and fell through the dark. There was a murmur as they stopped at Elizabeth's doorstep and then, silence, when Ada set out alone across the field. She had to pass in front of him; the path was below the

clump of trees where he sat stiffly, on the ground. It was too late
to go back to the house; she would hear him, if he moved.

The argument was of no importance, he saw that, now. He
and Ada had drifted to this place together. They'd been living
their lives, and anger had erupted and settled in a still, dark
pool. He could scarcely imagine why he'd been so stubborn. But
she, she was as stubborn a woman as he'd ever known.

She was passing now, below the trees. The curve of her shoulder, her silhouette, was as familiar to him as his own unspoken
voice. He cocked the rifle, and was startled to hear the *snick*. He
aimed at the sky and pulled the trigger, and the roar nearly
knocked him onto his back. The throb and flutter in the trees
fell silent.

Ada's pace did not alter one bit; she did not even look his way.
She reached the house and went in, and again he saw the curve
of her in the light as she removed her jacket and walked
through the living room to close the curtains. He tried to get
up, but his knees would not hold him. He had to rub his legs
and feet to get them to move.

From where he stood in the field, he might have been underwater. The lighted house seemed to recede as he waded above
the path, his thighs thickening with the chill.

If there was a way of surfacing, he'd never learned it. The list
was three-quarters done; Ada would probably never see it. She
might not even speak to him when he went inside. He felt foolish holding the rifle, firing it into the air. He did not know how
other men and women faced their differences, whether it was
all a matter of blunder and chance. He knew only that he'd had
to let Ada know he was serious about wanting his breakfast. He
only wanted her to understand.